THE BUZZ ON
TEETH

The critically-acclaimed novel by
HUGH GALLAGHER

"THIS SHOULD BE ON TOP OF THE MTV GENERA-TION'S READING LIST. . . . Comparable to the novels of Jay McInerney and Bret Easton Ellis, Gallagher's story of a young man's love/hate relationship with our pervasive youth culture and rock 'n' roll celebrity as he tries to get a foothold in the adult world is funny, insightful, sensitive, and bold. . . ."

—*Library Journal*

"In a tone reminiscent of Jack Kerouac's *On the Road* . . . Gallagher gives a voice to a generation that yearns for more than the MTV and pop magazines its seemingly shallow culture offers as a means of definition."

—*The Austin Chronicle* (TX)

t e e t h

HUGH GALLAGHER

WASHINGTON SQUARE PRESS
PUBLISHED BY POCKET BOOKS

New York   London   Toronto   Sydney   Tokyo   Singapore

My deep thanks to Owen Laster,
without whose generous support
these words would not be

WSP

A Washington Square Press Publication of
POCKET BOOKS, a division of Simon & Schuster Inc.
1230 Avenue of the Americas, New York, NY 10020

ISBN: 0-671-55167-1

First Washington Square Press trade paperback
printing February 1999

10 9 8 7 6 5 4 3 2 1

WASHINGTON SQUARE PRESS and colophon are
registered trademarks of Simon & Schuster Inc.

Cover design by Jeanne M. Lee
Front cover photo credits:
 X-ray photo by Javier Domingo/Phototake/PNI;
 goldfish by Herb Olsen/River Wood Gallery/PNI

Printed in the U.S.A.

The teeth are hard and fall out;
the tongue is soft and remains.

—Chinese proverb

New York

I. dusted

My dentist's calm, bearded face appeared above me. For a fleeting instant, I caught a reflection of myself in his polished glasses: trapped in the chair, wrapped in a bib, bathed in the hot white light of the angled work lamp. Then his hands were up, steady and balanced, gripping the glinting metal tools.

"OK, let's see what's going on in there," he said.

I opened wide, watching Dr. Deal wince as my jaw cracked with a loud pop in the examination room.

"That's going to catch up with you, Neil," my dentist said with a sigh. "In a few years, you keep doing that, the cartilage is going to be gone."

"Anybody can crack their knuckles," I explained as the metal tools moved toward my mouth. "But only a select few can crack their articular eminence."

"Only knuckleheads like you," he said, shaking his head in mild disgust.

Dr. Deal and I had racked up a lot of time together

3

over the years. Aside from the sweat-and-blood days of filing, scraping, and drilling, we had shared many relatively benign hours of waiting. Waiting for the casts to set, waiting for the X-rays to develop, and back in the early days, waiting for my jaw, contused and tight with pain, to ease open enough so my broken teeth could be reached.

"Well, there's not much to say, Neil," my dentist told me. "Your mouth is a wreck and you need to fix it."

It had been five years since I had met Dr. Deal, and over our endless stretch of appointments, we had achieved a unique bond for a dentist and his patient. Dr. Deal shared with me the strange, terrible beauty of his chosen profession: the drama of the root canal, the pinpoint precision of a post and buildup, the grim undertaking of a subgingival curettage. In turn, I recounted my wildest escapades as a struggling downtown writer, embellishing my favorite big city nights through mouthfuls of settling cement.

"Little buildup here," he noted, scraping near the gum line. "I know they're broken, but you still gotta brush 'em."

"I nrrrhgn," I managed to respond as he rooted around in my fourth quadrant.

Dr. Deal scraped away at my incisor, shaking his head and frowning. "Don't know how you've gotten by so long like this. You're just lucky all the damage is inside; wouldn't be getting many dates if the girls could see this mess."

Holly, Dr. Deal's cheery, rotund assistant, poked her head in the door and gave me a wink. "How's it going there, Neil?"

Over my frequent visits to Dr. Deal, I had become

somewhat of an object of affection for Holly. She was sympathetic to my plight, knowing that dental insurance was beyond me and my income was minimal.

"Dr. Deal's lecturing me again," I told her, working my tongue around a long steel pick to speak.

"I'm not lecturing you," he protested wearily, gazing into my mouth. "And you're not a seventeen year old kid anymore, like when I first met you." He pushed at my gum line. "How old are you again?"

"Twenty-two."

"Well, that's the time to start taking care of business like this."

"But they don't hurt."

He tapped lightly on my last right molar.

"OWW!" I winced. "Except for that one."

He clicked a switch on the foot of the chair, and I was raised to a sitting position. Reaching round my neck, I unlatched my bib, then took the paper cup of minty green liquid off the tray beside me.

"That tooth needs a root canal, and one of these days you're going to wake up screaming. Why don't you just take care of it?"

I spit out a stream of green into the copper-colored sink. "The last thing I want to do with a thousand dollars is put it in my mouth."

"Just think, Neil. If you had taken on the Great Work when I first offered it, you'd have a near perfect set of teeth by now."

The Great Work was Dr. Deal's noble and awesomely expensive plan to rebuild my mouth. Knowing of my slim financial means, he had taken it upon himself to chart out a gradual building and billing procedure that would have, slowly and painfully, righted the wrong of my dental disaster over the course of a couple years. I appreciated his concern and had even been tempted to embark on the Great Work a few times, but had always backed down. Aside from the astronomical sum it would cost, the idea of committing to anything that took longer than a few months was beyond my current conception of time.

"We could start today . . ." he pushed.

I gazed longingly outside the window, to the people passing on the sunny spring streets, their bodies flashes of color through the horizontal slats of the blinds.

"Can I go now?"

Dr. Deal sighed and got up from his wheelie stool. "Yes, you can go." I picked up my backpack and headed for the door.

"But Neil?"

I turned to face my dentist.

"I don't know how far you're going to get with teeth like that."

Because of the teeth, I was late for school, but it wasn't as if anyone would notice. The guards never checked IDs at the main building of Washington Square University, and over the years since I had moved to New York, I had been secretly scamming myself a college education. I would peruse posted schedules at the beginning of each semester, track down what I wanted to learn, then discreetly mix myself into the academic flow.

I wondered, sometimes, what my father would have made of my hustled curriculum, but conversation between us was minimal since I had escaped home, and when we did chat, the subject of college was acutely avoided. Since we were kids, my dad had picked out a state school and started saving for my older brother, James, and me to get an education, which had been his dream ever since he had scraped his way through night school. James had duly gone, but in the few high school visits I made to the leafy, bland campus of brick buildings, beer kegs, and dopey suburban kids stuck in the thick of nowhere, I decided that State School would make me the campus drug dealer, like my brother, or a suicide case. So I left high school and went straight to New York City, to get educated in my own style, and my dad had never forgiven me.

I never did get the diploma he had wanted, but by sneaking into Washington Square University, I assembled my own customized undergraduate smattering, from *Medieval Japanese Lit* to *Post Human Theory*, and met a gang of girls who would never have crossed my path at State School. Nadia, who I had met in a cinema studies class on the French New Wave, was the latest of the bunch. A sexy foreigner who strolled into class under a signature fragrance of perfume and marijuana, she had me intrigued from day one. I had overheard her speaking French with the professor, so after a screening one afternoon I asked her if the translations during the sex scenes were accurate. She laughed at my dumb joke, and from then on we were sitting side by side in the flickering darkness, taking in the mise-en-scène together.

Nadia's ridiculously loaded parents were relentless matchmakers, and from overseas, they engineered a never-ending parade of Euro bores to wine and dine their daughter. Of course, they didn't care at all about

7

what *she* wanted, so when Nadia and I began sleeping together, I knew at least part of her passion was an avenging lust. I didn't mind, though. She was pretty hot, lived in a sweet space with a gorgeous view, and took me every so often to glitzed-out uptown affairs with her junior ambassador friends. She spent most of her time getting stoned, and most of her father's money on whatever she felt like.

"Mr. Neil, you missed school today. I hope you can tell me where you've been?" she teased me that night, greeting me at her apartment door with her big Belgian boobs shifting aimlessly in a dark blue designer silk shirt.

"Chilling in the tooth chair," I answered, leaning close for a kiss.

She scolded her fluffy white cat, who had jumped up on the counter, then wrapped her arms loosely around me.

"Why don't you get dentures?" she said, lightly tapping my front teeth with her finger, gazing up at me with a light smile. "Things would be so much simpler, no?"

Our lips met, and I felt her warm tongue slide inside my mouth, soothing in comparison to the cold metal my dentist had plied me with earlier. I kissed the young heiress, subtly and expertly fending her explorations off from the broken back side of my bite, as I breathed in the musky scent of her boutique shampoo and slowly ran my hands over her body.

"Since you missed the movie today, we'll have to watch one now," the young Belgian beauty said to me, breaking our kiss and walking to the TV. I followed her down the carpeted stairs, knowing what was cued up, and wondering if I could sit through yet another screening.

Nadia was obsessed with *Heavy Metal Thunder*, a classic sixties movie about two hippies with a broken sitar who crisscross America on motorcycles, in a quest for the ultimate hit of acid. Actually, the word "obsessed" would imply some sort of energetic enthusiasm on Nadia's part, of which there wasn't much; it was more like she had merely ingrained this film into her idle life. We watched it every time I came by; I supposed she got stoned and watched it every night.

We sat down on the floor of the main room, leaning against a soft leather couch that probably cost more than my rent for the entire summer. There was a thick scatter of pot on the glass table in front of us, and Nadia started in, slowly rolling a thick, blunt instrument with which to deaden the night. Flicking the remote, she filled the room with familiar freedom-rock chords, as the grinning hippies speeded through a bygone era in a sun-dazzled high.

"It's so sad about your Nile Rivers," Nadia said, after slowly licking down the side of her freshly rolled joint.

I leaned back into the couch, settling in for one of Nadia's bored, but surprisingly insightful wanderings through "my" culture.

"*My* Nile Rivers?"

"With so many people there, you think someone could have helped him, or done something."

My face quizzed up as Nadia pulled down a drag of smoke, brow furrowed in that stoner look of deep concern.

"What are you talking about?"

"Here."

As always, she offered me the joint, and as always, I turned it down. I hadn't smoked much since fifth grade, when my older brother would wake me up at seven in the morning, before he went to school, for bong hits out the window. James hated getting high alone, and as a consequence, I spent the end of elementary school in a haze of surreal dodgeball games and psychedelic recorder recitals. I hadn't been much for drugs since.

"What's happened to Nile?"

"You didn't know?" she said after a moment, speaking like a dying old lady as she held in her smoke. "Nile Rivers died this morning. Or last night . . . whatever you want to call it." She blew out a thick rush of heavy smoke. "Where have you been, Mr. Neil?"

In a split second, I had the remote, flicking off the movie in the middle of the Las Vegas acid freak-out.

"But this is my favorite part," Nadia said dully.

My thumb pressed down on a triangle button, and a blur of Friday night images flew by on the glass screen: prowling leopards, exploding buses, shuddering antiaircraft artillery, orgasmic moans, congressional speeches . . . I swathed through them all until I found The Channel. Within two music videos, the news I needed was on.

The reporter, a sober-faced rock critic in a mod black suit, spoke coolly into the camera as a picture of Nile Rivers hung in the air above his left shoulder.

"And the death of Nile Rivers, early this morning in front of Los Angeles' Black Adder Club, continues to shock the young Hollywood community. The twenty-five-year-old actor, a devoted vegan, Buddhist, yoga practitioner and ani-

mal rights activist, died of a heroin overdose on Sunset Boulevard."

Without explaining much more, the news fragment ended, overtaken by the frantic massacre of a hyperkinetic cola commercial. Numbly, I depressed a series of buttons on the remote, bringing back the hippies.

"See, I told you so. Isn't it sad?" Nadia said, puffing leisurely on the joint.

"Yeah," I answered, not able to come up with much more. I leaned back against the couch, waving away another offer of the sweet smoke.

Nadia got high and then we messed around for a while; by the time the celluloid bikers were freaking out in the New Orleans voodoo ceremony, we had consummated the evening. The rest of the movie ran as Nadia and I idled on either side of the couch, and when the credits rolled, I was up and on my way out.

"I suppose now you'll have to write something about it," Nadia said to me, raising her hands up into the air and pulling down a deep stretch.

"An exposé of our torrid affair?"

"No," she said with a slight laugh. "I don't think that would make for very stimulating reading. I mean Nile Rivers. For your magazine. What do you call it?"

"Dusted." I pulled on my black V-neck sweater, then ran a hand through my tight buzz of hair, even though there wasn't much to smooth back in place. "But I'm not writing for them anymore, remember? It folded."

She gathered her hair into a ponytail. "Of course it folded, silly: it's a magazine, it has to open and close."

I was about to explain to her another trick in the American lexicon when she fell back on the couch and giggled.

"I'm sorry—I'm being stupid now that I am so stoned. I know what you mean. *Dusted* is *fini.*"

"*Oui, mademoiselle, très fini.*" I laced up my boots, and Nadia slid down to the floor, back against the couch, deep blue blouse half-unbuttoned. She took another deep hit from her joint, then turned and exhaled the stream of smoke directly into her cat's ear, which sent the pet flying into the bedroom.

"That's how you get a cat stoned, you know," she said.

As I left Nadia's and weaved through the Friday night stream of downtowners, past haircuts and addicts, bars blasting music, and gleaming mini-jeeps roaring over glass-glittered streets, the news about Nile Rivers commanded my mind. I tried to feel sad, but couldn't come up with much more than a dull emptiness; deciding it was no mood to make the scene on, I cut cross Second Avenue and turned down the leafy shades of Fifth Street. Past the precinct, past the park, I made my way home in quick strides, dodging a cooled-out duo of skateboard punks who darted past, laughing in the darkness, baggy clothes rippling in the balmy spring night.

Scaling the dimly lit stairs to my sixth-floor walk-up compartment, I keyed the lock, kicked shut the brown metal door behind me and collapsed, heart pounding, in the mushy cushions of a street-scavenged red velvet couch. After I had caught my breath from the climb, I flicked on the overhead light and edged past the cluttered kitchen table to the closet in the corner.

When I had shared the minuscule pad with Flash,

the cofounder and New York chief of our now defunct mag, the closet had housed his pet lizard, Pablo, but my friend had taken the bug-eyed roach killer with him back to Hollywood in the wake of *Dusted*'s demise. Since then, I had converted the tiny, still-stinky space into the *Dusted* archives, shoving in the leaning stacks of milk crates filled high with back issues, readers' letters, micro cassette interviews, editor's notes and compatriot 'zines.

In the three months since my magazine folded, I had made it a point to avoid the archive closet. I still hadn't quite pulled my life together from the loss of my cash flow and adopted family, and limping down memory lane didn't seem like a step toward health. Aside from that, there was the overwhelming chaos of it all, thanks to my ordering system of shoving and stuffing. Tonight, though, I needed to find something, and as each plastic crate came out in turn, I realized it was my payoff for years of filing folly. Alone in my compartment, the hours slowly melded together, as my hands sifted slowly through the collected mess of memories, searching for one in specific.

Stu, Terrance, and Flash, three ex-skateboarders from L.A., founded *Dusted*, the seminal underground mag of the early nineties, without a day's printing experience between them. It was the money from the Mack that made it happen; as an owner of three skateboard teams, a bike company, and the biggest skate park in southern California, the Mack was clocking more dollars than he could count. On a whim, he decided he wanted a magazine. Flash, Stu, and Terrance skated on his team; Flash was funny, Stu was smart, and Terrance was something of an artist. So he bought them a warehouse in Long Beach, told them to dream up a name and write whatever they wanted, then threw money at them until it started to work.

I still remembered the early issues of *Dusted*, which I had collected like a fiend back in suburbia. Compared to the tedious anger of my parents' home, the bright splash of half-written articles, punked-out photo collages, and underground skate star interviews seemed like transmissions from some radical, alien planet. No one in town or the world at large was down with *Dusted*, and for a brief beautiful while, I felt clued into a sly, secret scene that was somehow eluding the bloated fish of the mainstream.

I had discovered *Dusted* on one of my forays into what passed for "downtown" in the lame little city near my high school, and began an immediate postal crusade. Sliding with ease into the voice their pages maintained, I sent them letter after letter during my high school senior year, trying to get hired. At first, I merely detailed my acute case of high school boredom, but when the details ran dry, I began with the lies. There were the daily kung fu brawls with the postman, my frustrated experiments with antigravity sex toys, a brief battle with CFDD (Compulsive Furniture-Dismantling Disorder), and the ongoing mercy missions to a troubled parallel dimension, built entirely of cheese and peopled with canceled sitom stars of the eighties.

In sweet synchronicity, *Dusted* moved Flash out to New York City, to start the East Coast wing just as I was set to graduate high school. By that time, the magazine was becoming well-known, and Stu and I had written back and forth several times. He suggested I head to New York; they couldn't promise anything in terms of work, but the crew liked my writing, and they needed people in the city. So after breaking it to my father that I wasn't going to State School, and tracking down the friend of a friend's brother who had a spare couch in Brooklyn, I announced to my family, my teachers, and anybody who cared to listen that I was heading to New York to be a writer.

And then, I broke my teeth.

My knees creaked on the apartment floor as I shifted my weight, leaning back against the wall. My tongue wound around to the back of my mouth, past the snapped incisor, through the gaping hole that had once been an upper tooth, over the rough, chipped surface of my bite, back to the three molars that had been cracked clean in half five years ago. The pieces remained loosely anchored in my gums, and over time, I had taken to pushing them apart and together, apart and together, in a nervous habit no one would ever knew I had.

I felt the imagery coming back in my mind: the laughing, drunken high school party, the storm of police, screaming panic, a tiny open window, my body sailing through it, and the sickening crunch as I fell, chin impacting on the cement. Staggering to my feet, I had seen the cursing faces trapped in the window frame behind me, then felt the taste of cracked teeth spreading over my benumbed tongue as I turned and ran, crashing through a dark woods washed in the bleeding red of spinning siren lights. . . .

Violently, I shook the pictures out of my head. Over the years, I had become adept at crushing the memories, squeezing them from my mind before the horrible recollections could fully form. My teeth, with all the expense and misery they had wreaked upon me, hadn't stopped me from coming to New York. They hadn't stopped me from earning my spot as New Jack Poet Warrior for *Dusted*, and they wouldn't stop me tonight. Pushing the past away, I edged back onto my feet and walked into the archives, pulling down yet another paper-heavy crate.

It was in the pink shades of dawn, with twelve milk crates' worth of memories spread over my apartment floor, that I salvaged the object of my intent. Sinking back into the old couch, I held the microcassette up in the morning light, marveling at the careful precision of the label. Two years back, my handwriting on each interview tape had been neat to the point of reverent; rock gods and movie stars had been glamorous ambassadors from a glittering universe then, instead of just another part of the job. With a sigh, I slid the tiny cassette into my old battered player, pressed a button, and listened to the smooth whir of rewind.

Nile Rivers had been my first feature profile for *Dusted*, and even though I had never met him before, or spent time with him since, it felt like I had lost a soul brother. Everyone my age had grown up with Nile as the superstar in every kid movie of the eighties. Nile Rivers as the orphan who learns telepathy from the crotchety old sorcerer on Venice Beach; Nile Rivers as the isolated, boy-genius geologist who thaws out a frozen cave girl in the arctic; Nile Rivers as the bashful, neglected child who salvages a magical talking convertible from the thugs at the local scrap yard . . .

He was something of an exotic legend, having been

raised by hippie parents as they traveled round the world in the seventies, then hitting Hollywood at age twelve to become an instant star. He had made the transition from teenybopper idol to young heartthrob with smooth ease, disappearing for a few years before being reborn as an edgy leading man in a few gritty, low-budget indie flicks.

Nile was loved by even the cruelest of cynics and, from his hippie roots, had grown into a kind of spiritual consciousness for young Hollywood. Hardly did the long-haired actor appear in the media without a word on Buddhism, yoga, love, or the plight of the rain forests; and for this, his dark, heroin-addled death was a brutal shock.

The recorder in my hand stopped whirring, then clicked off. Closing my eyes, I pressed play and went back two years in time, across the table from a movie star in an East Village café.

So what's your new movie about?

—Oh you know, life and stuff. Some love. Mostly a lot of guns. Hollywood is so into doom. Makes me sad sometimes. But we shot it in Brazil, so it was good to be in the jungle. Ever been to Brazil?

Nah, I haven't done much traveling.

—Bro, you got to travel. That's like, the most important thing in life.

What's your favorite place?

—That's tough. My parents took me all over.

The Middle East, maybe? That's where you got your name, right?

—Word. Conceived on the banks of the Nile River; you know, hippie stuff with my parents and all. Yeah, Egypt is deep—the whole Middle East is wild, but I guess in terms of total cosmic depth, there's nothing like Southeast Asia. Ever been?

No.

—Amazing place. Anywhere: Thailand, the Nam, Indonesia. Just hop on a plane and go, bro. It'll blow your mind. . . . Say, where did you grow up?

Snnnrrbbng.

—What? I can't hear you.

Suburbs.

—That's weird. You look like a traveler.

I do?

—Yeah, you got that seeker kind of vibe to you. I knew it when you sat down. So you got to go out there, explore yourself.

You mean the world?

—I mean yourself, the world, it's the same thing. Every part of the world is a part of you. And traveling the world is like traveling your Self. It's important, you know, to like, get out there, so you can really walk through your Self, be inside your Self. And you're a writer, right?

Yeah.

—That's magic. Movies are OK, but you need all those machines: cameras, lights, microphones . . . and all those people, too. And the money, yo, it's crazy. Distorts people spiritually, you know? But writing . . . that's just like you and God. You're blessed. If I were you, I'd just travel all over the world and write.

Yeah, I probably should. But . . .

—There's a kooky story I heard in the Middle East when I was little. This ant, like, he decides to go on the holy journey to Mecca. All his friends say, "You're crazy. You're just an ant, you can't make it to Mecca." And this little ant just shrugs and says, "Big deal, so I die on the way."

I didn't know ants could shrug.

—I love that story. That's like, what it's all about for me.

I stopped the tape and leaned my head back against the brick wall, feeling eerie at hearing the voice of the dead actor. But it wasn't just Nile Rivers who was gone; the Neil that had been trapped in the magnetic tape along with him was gone, too. Time in the city and my series of celebrity profiles for *Dusted* had worn down the dazzle I had earlier seen the world through. Slumped against the wall beneath the window, I depressed my thumb on the rewind button over and over, repeating fragments of the dead actor's voice:

Just hop on a plane and go, bro. It'll blow your mind . . .
bdddddddtp!
blow your mind . . .
bdddddddtp!
blow your mind . . .
bddddddddddddddtttttp!

Finally, it hit me: it was all over. Nile Rivers was dead, my teeth were still broken, and *Dusted* was truly *finis*.

Nadia could tee-hee and blow pot in her cat's ear, but my life plans would have to be a bit more substantial. The check for three grand I had received for the last installment of *Neil Before God*, my manifesto-in-progress that had been serialized in *Dusted*, was just about gone. I hadn't done much since the magazine folded but avoid the archive closet, and it was getting about time to bust a move.

I stood up and stretched in the early light, then walked to the phone. Gazing at the single red wink from my answering machine, I found myself hoping against reason that it might be Milena, even though my Italian dream woman still didn't have a phone, as far as I knew. I closed my eyes and saw her olive skin, her black hair, her brown eyes, heard her foreign whispers in my ear . . . and then I pressed the button.

It wasn't Milena. It was Stu: big-ol'-butted, hairy-legged Stu. I should have guessed. He was the type who would call to talk about Nile Rivers, and plus, I still hadn't given him a definite answer on watching his West Hollywood pad. Stu had answered *Dusted*'s demise by finally getting married and was leaving for Europe on his honeymoon in just a few weeks. The tape began, and my old editor's voice filled the room:

"Calling the Irish Samurai . . . are you in, Samurai? Hmm, guess not. Nile Rivers . . . crazy huh? But where one life ends, another begins . . . like maybe a new life for you in L.A. Have you decided whether you're gonna come out here and guard my abode? Sylvia wants to know, because if we're going to have to get the New Guy, she wants to put the TV and stereo in storage. You're our first choice for relative responsibility, so call back. Soon. Okay, late."

An early sun was beginning to scarlet the city. I pulled my chair to the window and sat in silent contemplation, gazing in turn at the rosy-hued skyscrapers and the quiet mess of my history spread along the floor. My tongue wound absently around to my three lower molars, and I shifted the loose pieces apart and together, apart and together again in my mouth. It was something I did a lot when I was thinking.

Hollywood

2. the wedding

Flash eased into ninety and we overtook a mobile home. I watched as two senior citizens turned their pale faces in slow unison, tracking our vehicle as we passed their air-conditioned vacation sarcophagus. Vague, blurred images of their fading lives collaged through my mind in milky black and white.

"So how are your teeth?"

I looked over at my old friend, at the bright green hair, the shining blue eyes, and the color-flushed tattoo of his pet lizard, Pablo, crawling up his right arm. It had been months since I had seen Flash, and only hours since he had picked me up at LAX. Beyond him, I saw the winding California coast speed past: grey sea rolling up against a cool, indifferent beach of black rock.

"Shattered, battered, and in need of repair," I answered.

"What'd Dr. Deal say when you skipped town? Is he still hot for your virgin bicuspid?"

I reached around with my tongue, instinctively feeling the long, solid tooth on my right side. It was the only upper that hadn't been root-canaled, and Dr. Deal had dubbed it my "virgin bicuspid," becoming excited at its mere mention, describing how he would use it as an anchor for the entire reparation process "He was bummed, kinda. Said he coulda fixed my whole mouth if I only gave him the time."

"And you said *no way* because you're PUNK!"

"Or maybe just dumb," I said, playing with the electric window.

"You hopped a bird to Hollywood!" Flash shouted, grabbing my shoulder. "Because there's teeth for the taking in this town! Gold ones, silver ones . . . I tell you, the streets are paved with teeth. You're gonna make a mouth for yourself here, kid, I just know it!"

My natural instinct would be to artfully dodge anyone with a name like Flash, but in actuality, the grinning green haired kid was my closest friend. I had lived with him for a wild, laugh-riddled two years in New York before the magazine he had cofounded went under, and watched with no small sadness as he returned to his native California.

"So there must be a plan; you're always on the make," my friend said, ripping open a bag of peanuts with his teeth, then crunching through a handful of them. He shot me a sly grin. "You gonna Bop the Cheese?"

I groaned at his mere mention of *Bop Cheese:* the cultural steamroller of a teen magazine headed by the notorious Mandy, a schitzed, flipped, estrogen-amped blond lady who said "babe" all the time and laughed on her inhalations. Backed by mad corporate loot,

Mandy was on a slash-and-burn mission to corner the entire youth market of the world into the pages of *Bop Cheese* and had been after me for years to ditch *Dusted* and join ranks. She even flew me out to L.A. on the eve of our collapse to offer me a full time job. But even though rumors of *Dusted*'s demise were in the air, I had turned her down as a matter of honor. *Bop Cheese*, with its glossy pages of acne-medication ads, ecstatic celebrity blurbs, and violent, near demented barrage of exclamation points stood for everything I was against in this world.

"Can you believe that Mandy still calls me after how hard I dissed her?" I said to Flash, shaking my head.

"So if you're not going to Bop the Cheese, what's your angle, kid?

"Neil before God."

"THE MANIFESTO!" Flash yahooed and slammed on the horn. "You're going to finish your manifesto and rock the world! I knew this day would come! And to think, I was there at the birth of it all." He swerved the wheel and we passed a school bus full of kids. "But I thought you were only going to write in East Jabip . . ."

Once *Neil Before God* had began in *Dusted*, readers and fans had started pressuring me for further installments. Of course there weren't any, but to cover my rep and get readers off my back, I produced the Theory of East Jabip. My theory, printed full page in a special script font Terrance had designed, maintained that the only manifestos worth reading had been scribed in some exotic, foreign locale, like Paris or Mexico City. But as both these geographic areas had been sapped of their exotica status by previous writers, I claimed that

27

Neil Before God could only be honestly realized in a place like East Jabip. Where this imaginary, expatriate lit haven was, I had no idea, but it served to take the pressure off until I actually started writing.

"Yeah, when I get serious, I'm Jabip bound," I answered Flash. "But I'll get a start in L.A. Stu offered me his place for May and June, and I've got some investigations to make in Image City. My manifesto's gonna start with the death of Nile Rivers."

"Damn . . ." Flash shook his head slowly. "That was so sad. What are you going to say about it?"

"Don't know, really. Got to get flowing first."

"That was one of the worst parts about *Dusted* going down . . . everyone loved *Neil Before God.*"

We passed a few cars.

"I miss it," I said to Flash. "I mean, working with you guys."

"Yeah, me too."

A while went by, tires humming smooth over the highway.

"So, how's the show?" I asked.

He pushed harder on the gas, and the needle trebled at 95. Flash was driving, so of course we were speeding. And of course, we would never get a ticket. Flash didn't get tickets, ever. Flash didn't get anything but green lights and checkered flags the whole way around the course. Out of all of us, he had survived the *Dusted* demise in finest fashion: it was two weeks back in Hollywood before he had parlayed his underground cult status into his own development project for The Channel.

"I'm a little nervous, but it's good. Real good. Guess who I'm interviewing first?"

"Pablo?"

"Better."

He pushed a tape into the deck, and a ridiculously fat drum fill rolled through the car, triggering a montage of memories: forty-ounce nights, acid dawns, broken skateboards, hip-hop, stage dives, and a scattered string of punked-out articles. The number of times Flash and I had listened to this track together could never be calculated.

"Damn, Flash, you're already working with the Pepper?"

"Yeah, isn't that fresh? We've been hanging out, figuring out some crazy stuff to do for the show."

Rage Against the Chili Pepper were the founders of white boy hip-hop and were the only sound group in an otherwise doomed genre. Their multiplatinum, bumping anthems had been spinning somewhere all through the *Dusted* days, but the four Brooklyn boys had always remained untouchable voices, set deeply back in the speaker system. Now I felt a wave of my envy mixing with the bass line, knowing that Flash, my friend, was in on their million-dollar house party without me.

"If you need any writers for your show while I'm out here, you know, I could probably take some time off my manifesto."

Flash scratched at his tattoo. "Thanks, that's really cool. But, uh, The Channel pretty much has it under control."

"Oh."

We were quiet for a while, and Flash flipped a tape of old lounge music in the deck. A white convertible filled with laughing young girls somehow passed us,

29

their hair whipping wildly in the wind. Suddenly, Flash reached into the backseat, grabbed a cheap toy guitar, and threw it at me.

"I've got to sing! COVER ME!" he shouted.

I fingered the tiny instrument and pulled a series of twangy, synthetic chords out of its plastic body, as Flash began another of his trademark stupid songs.

> La la! Yeah yay
> . . . it's day
> And I'm driving with Neil,
> I'm at the wheel, and
> we're going to a wedding
> where we will . . . will . . .

". . . start beheading . . ." I filled in from the next seat.

"All the bitches and glitches," he sang back.

". . . who don't comply with our wishes . . ."

He stepped on the gas. "Take it, Neil! Ishes! Ishes!"

But I lost the tune. "Uhhh, and we'll break all their dishes. Um, 'cause our flavor's delicious. And . . . we eat knishes?"

"NEIL AND FLAAASH!" my friend howled, reaching over the gearshift and strumming a furious crescendo finale. "Damn Neil," he said, throwing the guitar in back, "you're the best person to do songs with; you can always rhyme. Why don't we do them more often?"

" 'Cause I live in New York."

"We should do it by fax then. YAHOOO!"

I looked over at my friend with a half smile and saw his bright blue eyes flicker in the rearview mirror. We rapidly decelerated, and a cop car blazed past on our right; a minute later, we overtook the white convertible of girls on the side of the road, pleading desperately with the implacable, mirror-shade officers.

"Girls, girls, girls," Flash said, shaking his head. "Better to be five minutes late to the party than fifty years early to the grave."

My friend popped another peanut in his mouth and crunched down on it, stepping on the gas and bringing us up to speed.

Three hours later, Stu was a husband. As we filed out of the small stone church, I looked around and assessed the crowd gathered in the afternoon sunlight. There were a handful of relatives that I didn't know, a few writers from other magazines, a couple editors, their girlfriends, and a bunch of stoned skateboarders and unemployed BMX riders who held the link to *Dusted*'s origin.

Stu had been my editor; more of a title than a position, actually, 'cause he didn't really mess with my prose. His fiancée I didn't know too much about, other than that she had two tiny, mushy-faced dogs that peed all over the place and yipped at strangers. This ugly little canine duo would be part of my responsibility over the next two months, and part of Stu's responsibility for the rest of his life.

I watched as Flash moved through the crowd with an instant camera, snapping shots and clapping people on the back. He left laughter in his wake and never stayed in one place too long, almost on the run, it seemed, from conversation. For the fifth time in as many minutes, I watched as he blocked the hired photographer's angle and saw anger brewing on the face of the dumpy, sweaty guy, weighed down by a string of cameras slung round his neck. The green haired TV-star-to-be didn't seem to notice, though, and I watched as he jumped up on top of a car, camera in hand, catching a BMX rider sparking up a joint behind his rundown van.

Moving away from the chatting crowd, I found Terrance under the shade of a leaning pine tree, near the side of the old stone church. A tall, gentle guy with a smoothly bald head, he was the designer and cofounder of *Dusted.* Although eight years my senior and married, I was as close to Terrance as anyone in the crew. He had made a slew of jazz tapes for me over the years, always laughed at my jokes, and was the one I went to when looking for advice. In many ways, Terrance had become the older brother I needed, after James had gotten hit by a bong.

"How come the photo session is taking twice as long as the ceremony?" I asked him.

"It's always like that . . . same thing at my wedding."

"There's something wrong with this camera situation," I decided. "Everyone's too uptight about their pictures. I don't think I'm going to allow photos at my wedding."

"You think your Italian woman will agree to that?" he laughed.

"Of course she will. Europeans go for that kind of thing."

"When's the last time you guys hooked up, anyway?"

"Since she came out in the fall, we haven't."

"She still doesn't have a phone?"

I kicked at the dust. "Nah, crazy, isn't it?"

"For you, no. Only Neil would fall in love with some Italian lady in London who doesn't have a phone."

It had been a year since I had met Milena, on my first trip abroad. Taking Nile Rivers's advice, I had conned Stu into sending me overseas for a European installment of *Neil Before God.* And I wasn't a week in London, high on the thrill of leaving the States for the first time in my life, that I met a gorgeous Italian woman in the park.

Sitting on a deep green London park bench in the midday sun, I had been slicing into an apple with my pocketknife when a curiously accented voice had spoken up.

"Don't you like to bite your *happle?*"

I had looked up to the bench across the path and saw a lean, black-haired woman looking at me, a puzzled smile on her full, red lips.

"My apple?" I asked, smiling at her foreign phrasing.

"Yes, your *happle.*" With a slender finger she pointed to the fruit in my hands. "The best part of eating an *happle* is the biting, you know."

"Yeah, well, my teeth aren't so good," I said, slicing out a section with my knife. "But you're welcome to a bite, if you like. It's a tasty *happle.*"

She had laughed at my imitation Italian accent, then came closer, sharing with me the fresh fruit on the sunshining summer afternoon. From there, we had struck it off, laughing our way through a few days, kissing away the next, and finally making love in her Camden Town flat for two weeks straight as my vacation time ticked away.

I remembered how the sun had shone through the window in her flat, softly illuminating her olive-skinned body, as I landed whisper kisses all along the lines of her face.

"I can't leave you," I had whispered. "You're amazing."

Milena had smiled slowly, from the corner of her mouth. "I'm just the first girl you met in Europe," she said, "Really, it's true." She had stood up then, naked in the sunlight, and began to get dressed for her day's work at the record store. "You're going to have a brilliant holiday, just wait. You'll come back and tell me I was right."

And she was. For two months, I rode trains, hopped buses, and caught boats across Europe, down through Italy, amidst the islands of Greece, even making it as far down as Turkey, where Nile Rivers had traveled as a child. Foreign voices and scenery flowed through my mind, and for the whole trip I had been surging with pride at being the family's first to leave the States. I picked up presents for Milena as I went along—an Italian espresso blend she couldn't find in London, her favorite cigarettes, sold only in Paris—and all the while imagined a future as some expatriate punk lit phenomenon, with Milena as my *happle*-munching muse.

But after returning to London and living with her for a month, funds funneled away, and I had to make a rough decision. Even though I had never met a woman who thrilled me like Milena did, my hard-earned spot as New Jack Poet Warrior at *Dusted* was at stake, as well as my room at Flash's. My Hollywood friend had played a big part in luring me home in the end, holding his lizard up to the phone so I could hear its lonely hisses, and detailing all the wild escapades he needed my help to execute. So with my job in mind, I had kissed Milena good-bye; had I known the Mack would go bust within the year's end, I would have played a different hand.

"Do you write any letters?" Terrance asked, interrupting my thoughts.

"Yeah, but she doesn't read English so well, and she's not much for mail. She sends me some love notes once in a while, but they're pretty short. She's got sexy handwriting, though."

"What the hell is sexy handwriting?" he said, laughing.

"I don't know—these big fat loops on her *L*'s . . . and she's got killer *S* curves."

"A women like this would only find you, Neil," Terrance repeated, shaking his head. "Sexy handwriting and no phone."

"How rad is that, though?" I pointed out. "You got to be pretty goddamn cool to not have a phone. I mean, you don't even *care* if anyone can reach you or not."

"Maybe she's a secret agent."

"Maybe Sylvia's a secret agent," I said, nodding toward the beaming bride bedecked in white. "She's getting Stu to quit the magazine racket. Quite a coup."

"Yeah, Sylvia's a deep-cover *Bop Cheese* decoy, eliminating the competition by whining about security and health care."

I watched Flash dash before the young newlyweds, snapping pictures and acting like the press, making them both break into laughs. "And what about Flash? Think he's safe?" I said to my older friend.

"I don't think you'll ever have to worry about Flash.

I heard his show's got the biggest budget on The Channel. They're even considering sending him out on the Chockapolacka tour."

My eyebrows raised in surprise. "Damn. Round the States, with the Alternaverse stars and everything?"

"Round the world, kid. Chocka's going global this year." Terrance picked up a wood chip, tossing it at a squirrel and missing wide. "And what about you? What's the Irish Samurai going to dig up in Hollywood?"

"Neil Before God, kid."

"East Jabip," Terrance said softly with a smile. "Never figured it was in Hollywood."

"Yeah, well, I figure trying to write a manifesto in the screenplay capital of the universe is pretty *avant-garde.*"

Over his shoulder I saw the photographer leading Stu and his wife through the graveyard and out into the forest, for their portraits with the wedding party.

"Terrance, I've decided something else."

"What's that?"

"At my wedding, all the best men will be dressed as ninjas."

He laughed. "Your wife will never go for it."

"Then she wouldn't be my wife."

"You don't know much about women, do you, Neil?"

By the time evening descended, the party was already fading. Dark beer had been flowing free in the cool, Northern California night, but there weren't many revelers remaining as I sat before a crackling fire in the pinewood bar by myself. I pulled at the suit I had borrowed from Terrance, which didn't quite fit, then lost myself in the amber liquid of my mug, watching the foam create swirling, abstract patterns under my eyes. Somewhere deep inside, a slight fear stirred, and I was just about to drink it away when a voice pulled me out of the glass.

"So, Neil."

I looked up from my beer to see the New Guy sitting down next to me. A goofy, Midwestern college graduate, he was a *Dusted* groupie who had bombarded the L.A. office with letters and phone calls, until Stu had no choice but to offer him a vague invitation for an internship, just to cool his jets. Even though the New Guy's timing was off, landing him in town just as the show collapsed, Stu and Terrance had hooked him into a job over at *Buddha Smoke*, an underground, anarchist, pro-drug, pro-decadence, anti-everything-else skateboard mag whose mission statement was to piss off as many Christians as possible. For the next few months, the New Guy would be honing his *stylo* in their sketchy, edgy world, and I did not envy his position. Most of the skaters I knew were either constantly blunted, mentally stunted, or too cool to even say "hello," let alone get an article out of. At fifty cents a word, that action just didn't cut it.

"Yeah?" I answered.

"Terrance told me you're in Hollywood to write *Neil Before God*. Is it true? Is it finally happening?"

"Yeah, I've got my boys working on it as we speak."

"I can't wait to read it. I loved your last chapter . . . about those German tourists in the East Village looking for fast American girls, and Pablo's escape to the roof, and that guy who played harmonica in your hallway for a week, and that time when you were four and got stung by a bee, and the . . ."

The New Guy went on, reciting almost by heart all the string of memories, ideas, half-formed notions, invented characters and real-life reporting I had twisted together over the past year. I had three chapters of *Neil Before God* printed in *Dusted* before we folded and had no idea what it was about, or even why I called it a manifesto, aside from the fact that it sounded bigger and badder than "book."

To deceive people like the New Guy into thinking I knew what I was writing about, I had titled my random installments Chapter 15, Chapter 3, and Chapter 26, referring to them as pieces of a greater work in progress. It was all a bluff, though, and ultimately, *Neil Before God* didn't represent much more than my driving ambition to get laid. Even at that, it hadn't been much of a success, and I didn't like talking about my manifesto, except in broad, nebulous terms that would disguise my lack of direction. Suddenly, I found myself annoyed and slightly threatened by the New Guy's rampant interest.

"Yeah, well relax," I told him, cutting off a quote. "It won't be done for a while." I felt a little bad for being cold, but everybody got away with treating the New Guy like their little brother; it wasn't that we didn't like him, it was just that he was the New Guy.

"Sorry, Neil," he said as I stood up.

"Nah, it's chill. Come on, I'll buy you a beer."

"They're free."

"Well, I'll pour one for you then," I said, heading toward the bar. "And let's find Flash."

"He left."

"*What?*"

"Yeah, he was looking around to say later, but couldn't find you. Had some taping to do back in Hollywood."

"Oh, right," I said dumbly. I hoped the New Guy wasn't picking up on the shock that hit me, knowing that I had been ditched without so much as a "late." If it had been a year ago, Flash and I would have been off together on some adventure by now, breaking into the hotel whirlpool or driving out to the beach looking for elephant seals. Anger flared through me that he hadn't told me his plans, and I wished that I was in the car with him, headed back to L.A.

But then again, Stu's wedding was my first, so it made sense to get the most of it. I'd been to more than my share of Irish wakes, as my dad's brothers and sisters died off of cigarette smoke, booze, and fried eggs, but I had never before witnessed the joining of two young lovers. From all the hype I had heard on the ceremony, I had expected a wild night of bubbling champagne and saucy bridesmaids, but I was instead left with a babbling, drunken New Guy, and a yawning cadre of older couples.

Without appearing too desperate, or at least trying not to, I attempted to keep everyone up and excited about staying out late, drinking too much, and doing something excessive. The fears that had been swirling earlier were coming back, and as the implications of my move started to sink in, the last thing I wanted to be was alone. I had left New York, broken my lease, and taken a dive into the Hollywood void with nothing but a tattered manifesto and a mouth full of broken teeth. No one, though, seemed to pick up on my need, and two by two the wedding party had disappeared into their bungalows, with Terrance and his wife being the last.

"Don't leave any stains," he said, tossing me the keys to his family truckster.

Everyone else had reserved a pine bungalow for the night, but being of limited funds, I had opted to forgo the hundred-dollar expense and sleep in Terrance's van. Slinking through the grounds on my way to the parking lot, I came across the porch of some trustworthy soul who had left a cooler of cheap beer out. (*"Hell, hon, we're in the middle of nowhere, who would steal our brew?"*) Grabbing one, I popped the top and walked back to the van to spend the night. I tried to fold out the seats, but had about three beers too many to master the mechanism, and ended up just sitting dumbly in the passenger seat.

Looking at the snoozing, cozy bungalows nearby, I realized that I was once again chickless in the thick of night. I usually dealt with this seemingly constant situation in my life by repeating the mantra: *Simple, common people have simple, common relationships; exceedingly rare and legendary people have exceedingly rare and legendary relationships.* This little word game, along with a tug and a bottle of beer, had gotten me through most of my lonely nights, but tonight, it didn't seem to soothe me.

As I sipped my beer, I remembered how I was always the last kid to kick in at the pajama parties when I was little. In an attempt to keep someone up with me, I would reel through stories all night long, stretching into increasingly desperate elementary-school existentialism to fight off the solitude of sleep. But eventually, dawn would come, grey and dull, to slowly illuminate my situation: stranded in my pajamas, surrounded on all sides by the soft, peaceful sounds of young boys deep in sleep.

It was fifteen years later, but not much had changed; all the kids were asleep except me. I was twenty-two years old in an empty car, sipping stolen beer in a borrowed suit, and feeling very, terribly alone.

3. stu's place

"Here, let me show you how to work the security system," Stu said, picking the remote off an amoeba-shaped end table and flicking on the TV set.

I looked around at his West Hollywood pad, where my life would be unfolding for the next two months. A heinous, wraparound pea green sofa dominated the main room (which Sylvia, I was sure, would haul to the curb within seconds of their return), along with a tangle of video game controllers, cables, and cartridges that lay before the massive television. To the left, a sunlit blue kitchen was cluttered with wedding gifts, and a short walk down a dark, uneven hallway led to the cavernous back room known among the *Dusted* gang as the L.A. Harbor.

The discarded information from the lives of strangers—used records, old photo albums, letters, magazines, books—that lie tossed on the sod-cut corners of West Hollywood served Stu with a life purpose. Col-

teeth

lected and stored in the Harbor, the stacks, shelves, piles and boxes helped fill a void in his life that I supposed would never be fully satisfied.

My host flipped through the TV and skidded through twenty stations, finally landing on The Channel. A skinny white kid in an oversize T-shirt thrashed a guitar while thick, writhing snakes fell from holes in the ceiling.

"Just think, Flash will be on there next season," I said flatly. "And we can say we knew him when."

"Whenever you leave the house, make sure the TV is on. Turn up the volume so you can hear it in the hallway, then pull the drapes closed on all the windows."

"That's the security system?"

"It's the best we can do right now. There's been like, eight robberies in our building in the past month. If anyone breaks in while you're here, I'll kill you."

"I'm sure the security system will keep them at bay."

"Right. We've evacuated all the plants and the mushy-face dogs over to Sylvia's mom's, so there's absolutely nothing here that you could kill."

"Except the Beast," Sylvia said, jamming one last item into her backpack.

Stu went over to help with the zipper. "Yes, slay the Beast and you will be rewarded handsomely."

"*Qué?*"

"The Beast is a roach the size of a small, malnourished cat that lives in our bathroom. Sylvia and I have been waging war against him since we moved in, but the creature seems to be indestructible."

"That's what the brick in the shower's for," Sylvia added.

"Great."

"C'mon, I'll take you back to the Harbor," Stu said, and I followed him down the dim hallway.

"Check it out," he said as we entered his cool, shady temple. "I scored an entire collection of early-eighties New Wave yesterday." He flipped through a crate of records, presenting a pale parade of mascara-massacred Brit synth stars. Trapped in the hit covers of a past decade, their heavily made-up faces held a grim warning, which I spoke aloud:

"The harder in fashion you are, the harder out of fashion you go."

"Not something you'll have to worry about, Neil," Stu said, gazing in slight disgust at my *Karate!* tank top, tan golf pants, and black boots.

Aside from the booty he collected on the streets, Stu was a compulsive letter writer and 'zine trader. A good portion of the L.A. Harbor was devoted to these independently produced mags, manufactured on borrowed time and hijacked office equipment in the fluorescent hell of corporate America. I realized now, standing in the density of the L.A. Harbor, that I would be living in the midst of a unique archive. In the thousands of pages of letters and 'zines, Stu had surrounded himself with the disjointed narrative of a loosely bound generational tribe.

Alongside his extensive back catalog of abandoned records, my old editor had just about every single pop music recording of the past three years. One of the beautiful benefits of *Dusted* had been the flood of tapes, videos, and CDs that every label, both indie and major, unleashed on our office in hopes of pulling positive press. The sheer volume of middling pop music being produced every day in America I found astounding, and the teetering towers of CDs and promo-only cassettes seemed nothing to me but a testament to late twentieth-century cultural entropy. As we walked out of the Harbor, I wondered if Stu feared earthquakes, and the prospect of being crushed in an avalanche of mediocrity.

"Look, Neil. There's one more thing . . . about the car."

I didn't like the tone in his voice.

Stu scratched at his baseball cap. "Um, it kicked on us just before the wedding."

"What are you saying?"

"I'm saying my bitchin' T-roof is out of commission. Something's wrong with the transmission, and we didn't have time to deal with it, so . . ."

I pondered this new development in silence. No car. L.A. on a bike . . . This was Sylvia's doing, I could tell. I looked over at her smug smile as she pushed a white tennis shoe into her pack. She had probably convinced Stu to make up some story so I wouldn't be driving "their" car. In the short time I had been there, she had already twice emphasized her stake in Stu's claim.

"*Ours* . . . honey, remember, it's ours now," she would say, tagged with a sickening sweet smile whenever Stu made the mistake of claiming anything as "his." So it wasn't Stu's bitchin' T-roof I couldn't drive, but "theirs." Two weeks ago she had been working retail in a clothing outlet and living with her parents, now she had a car, a roomful of presents and was jetting off to Europe. Not a bad scam.

"So you're saying I'm stuck in L.A. without a car?"

"Well, at least, not that one."

Nearly dumbstruck at the prospect of two months immobile in the exhaust capital of the world, I stared at Stu. "Why the hell didn't you tell me this before I came?"

"Look, I didn't know! You think my car warned me that it was going to freeze up a day before the wedding? We had to borrow the in-laws' bucket just to make it to the church."

"How am I supposed to live in Hollywood without wheels?"

"You can use my BMX bike for essential movement, like the store," Stu said, pointing to his Blue Line in the corner.

"Man *cannot* get laid on a bicycle. That's God's law, and you know it, Stu. What are you doing to me?"

"What can I say . . . pop a wheelie, maybe you'll impress some of the girls at summer school. There's Flash, too; you guys will be hanging out a lot. And besides, instead of aimlessly driving around, wasting precious fossil fuels, you can stay here and work on your screenplay."

"I don't have a screenplay."

"What kind of brash young upstart comes to Hollywood without a screenplay?"

"The kind of brash young upstart who's writing a manifesto."

"I thought you gave that up with *Dusted*," Stu said, adjusting the backpack straps.

"Excuse me, my manifesto is not something that is given up because a mere magazine crumbles. I'm making literary history this summer . . . on your computer, even."

Stu had always acted strangely when it came to my

manifesto. He hardly mentioned it, except for a "good job" or "nice going" each time I pounded out an installment; low-key responses that clashed heavily with my flood of reader mail. It bugged me more than a bit, and sometimes around my old editor, I felt like a little kid begging to be noticed.

"This building will be a pilgrimage site for the faithful after the worldwide cultural impact of *Neil Before God*," I went on as the newlyweds gathered up their bags. "There's gonna be disenfranchised kids camping out on your doorstep in a few years, selling stickers of me."

Stu slipped his sunglasses on and checked his watch. "Great, leave a dirty pair of underwear that I can sell as a souvenir."

I watched in the dim apartment as he and Sylvia moved toward the door, past the pile of wedding presents, weighed down by their brand-new backpacks.

"Farewell, guardian," Stu said. "Protect our humble home."

Sylvia squeaked past Stu out the door. "Bye Neil," she said, with a smile that made me want to break her pinkie.

"It's gonna be massive Stu; my manifesto. I know it," I said, trying to convince myself.

He smiled and nodded his head. "May your ink flow true, Irish Samurai." And then my old editor closed the door on me and walked out the door, into his honeymoon.

Later that evening, I paged Flash and waited around for him to call back. An hour passed in the empty apartment, and with still no word, I finished up my last microwave burrito and decided it was a *Neil Before God* night. Setting the security system to a Japanese cooking channel, I slid a notepad into my back pocket, wired myself into my cassette player, and rode out into the Hollywood night.

I glided smooth through a few empty intersections and soon hit Beverly Hills. Reaching to my hip, I edged up my music and then pressed hard on my pedals, weaving patterns of scattered energy through the Hispanically manicured blocks. There had been a short span in my history when a possible pathway to one of these homes had been made open to me, but I had turned it down. Bunny hopping over a curb, I ran my tongue over my ruined teeth and wondered if I had maybe made a mistake.

It was in *Dusted*'s final, glorious year that a "buzz" began about me in the industry as a hot young writer with favorable flavor factors. Of course, I was always convinced that I was the best, but when the rest of the world suddenly agreed, I wasn't really ready. In a violently opportune month, my tiny East Fifth Street compartment was laid siege by a bombardment of phone calls from agents, publicists, editors, film people—even a choreographer called at one point—in a rabid attempt to get a piece of the buzz. The peak of this experience was reached in my encounter with Mandy and *Bop Cheese*. Sweat breaking on my brow from the effort of cycling, I went back in time to remember the night she called.

"Hey, this is Mandy, I want to talk to Neil," an unknown woman had said to me the instant I picked up the phone. She spoke in a friendly, *hey there!* way that made me think we had just been playing canasta the weekend before, even though I had no idea who she was.

"OK, hold on," I had said, waiting a second before I started speaking again. "Hello?"

"Neil?! *Dusted* Neil?" But Mandy didn't even give me a chance to confirm her statement. "Babe. *We! Love! You!* I have been reading your stuff for years and think you are terrific and want you writing for me NOW and FOREVER babe. L.A. is dying for you!"

"Who is we?"

"I'm starting a new magazine called *Bop Cheese*. We're backed by the Eternity Corporation, and we're talking big operation here, babe. We've got everyone writing for us, anyone who's anyone and even a few somebodies. It's going to be fantabulous, Neil, and Mandy wants you in on the ground floor. So what's it gonna take, babe?"

"Well, I'm always in need of a few teeth . . ."

"PHAA! That's right, Neil, you and your TEETH! Oh you're classic, kid, too much. Listen, babe, you write a *paragraph* for me and you'll have enough for a whole new mouth." Her voice dropped a level and she slid closer into my ear. "By the by, babe, what are they paying you at *Dusted?*"

"Mandy, please, I'm not at liberty to discuss such issues over the phone," I said, copying a line from a movie I'd seen the night before.

She had laughed, or kind of brayed. "*PHHAHHA!* Too much, kid. You're too much. OK then, how about you come out to L.A. to talk?"

"Well, you sound nice and all, but I don't think I can write for you. I'm pretty bound to my friends here."

"Just come out and *talk*, babe. Listen to everyone before you decide anything . . . what are you, twenty? Nineteen? You got a lot to learn about things. And you need a vacation; I can hear it in your voice. I'm booking a flight for next week."

And before I could squeeze in another syllable, Mandy exited in a flurry of *ciaos* and *babes*, leaving me sitting by the window with a dead phone in my hand.

I gave the *Dusted* boys full knowledge of Mandy's move on their scribe, as I didn't want them to think I was slinking around behind their backs. Flash encouraged me to follow through with her as a joke, maybe making a manifesto installment of it, so I decided to pack a bag and ready myself to meet Mandy.

I touched into the city of Angeles a week later and was met at the airport by a slouching, bug-eyed guy with a handlebar mustache, holding a Neil sign in front of a long, dark limo. My bag was stashed in back, and I sat behind the smoked windows as we moved across the arcing overpasses, toying with the radio and gazing down the electric avenues. Finding a bottle of expensive vodka in the fridge, I had poured the smooth liquor over ice into a glass, stretching out on the maroon velvet seats. Then a fear suddenly hit me as I rode along in the dim interior lighting, alone, without my laughing friends; for a second I felt as if I were in a hearse, being delivered to my own funeral.

The limo dropped me off at an ultramodern hotel near Studio City. I checked in and was led to a room where everything seemed to be made of glass, and three free porno channels were served up in stereo on an adamantine television set. After angling the screen toward the bathroom, I hit the lights, ran water in the tub, and mixed myself a thick Black Russian from my complimentary bar. Sliding into the warm water in the flickering blue porno light, I reminded myself that it was all just a joke to laugh about with Flash back in New York.

The limo picked me up in the morning and brought me to a corporate tower on Wilshire that served as *Bop Cheese* HQ. And after a silent, smooth elevator ride direct to the fortieth floor, I found myself in the heart of the *Bop*, for a man-to-Mandy match.

"BABE! WE MEET!"

She had shot toward me in a jingle of bracelets and a bum rush of perfume, all blond hair, giant white teeth, and gym-perfect body, taking me by the hand and leading me into her office.

"Come on, sit down. We've got some business to discuss."

"What's that?" I had asked, easing into a black leather sofa as she sat down across the table.

"The business of you leaving *Dusted* and coming to write for me," she said, crossing her legs and lighting a cigarette. "I smoke, it's bad; I know, sorry." She exhaled a plume.

"I thought we were just talking," I had said, realizing suddenly that I was in my first business meeting, and feeling ill prepared.

"Look, we both know that *Dusted* is got to bust someday . . ."

"Our sales are peaking."

Mandy squared me with her eyes. "Look kid, your backer isn't exactly the most responsible of individuals. He smokes too much pot and everyone knows his finances are a wreck."

"The Mack's always been like that. But he loves *Dusted*, he won't let it go under."

She had given a little laugh. "Believe me babe, when *Bop Cheese* gets rolling, he won't have a choice."

A flare of anger ripped through me, but I had stayed cool. Mandy stood quickly then, walking to her desk, bracelets jingling, to return with a slim stack of paperwork.

"I can pay you triple what you're getting at *Dusted*, babe. And I can give you something they never offered you," she baited.

"A free month of ballroom dancing lessons?" I had muttered.

"PPHAA!" she had brayed, adjusting her bra strap. "No babe: a dental plan. You come to work for me, and *Bop Cheese* will build you a brand-new mouth."

She had said that with a strange glint in her eye, one that made me scared, even though I couldn't figure out why. An instant later, she was next to me on the couch, her arm around me, and there was a contract lying on the table in front of us.

"Here it is babe, clean and mean, perfecto *absolument*. A year's contract: you sign, you write, you fix your mouth, and if you no like, you can walk, no problem."

I stared at the tight, neat wording on the white paper, as the burning Hollywood sun blazed from the other side of smoke-tinted glass windows. In my mouth, my tongue slowly ran to my back broken teeth, moving them silently apart and together.

"I even have an agent friend of mine at CCA who said she'd look it over for you," Mandy continued. "She's a big agent, Neil, and this is a big deal. It's time for you to play the majors, babe, no more hiding out in *Dusted*."

"Mandy . . . I, I . . ." My voice stammered as my tongue wound faster and faster round my shattered teeth. I thought of Flash and Stu, Terrance and the magazine, of the endless scraping for paychecks and the broken pieces still inside my head after all these years. Then I looked up at Mandy, her twinkling blue eyes blazing into mine, all of Hollywood glittering from the window behind her.

"Mandy, this is . . . uh, too much. I have to think about it all."

I watched a rage of rejection pass quickly, almost imperceptibly over her suntanned features, and then she smiled.

"Right babe, but don't think too long."

A second later, I was out of her office, down the elevator, closed up inside the limo, and zooming back to the airport. Between the limos, my hotel room, and the meetings, I had walked maybe a hundred steps total in Los Angeles, but they had been big steps; ones that could have changed my entire life, if I had let them. And as I gingerly ate my honey-roasted peanuts thirty-five thousand feet over the earth's surface, I had wound my tongue around the enamel remains in my mouth, thinking that working for Mandy might not be so much a sellout as a move of self preservation.

But as soon as I got back to New York, roaring down the Brooklyn-Queens Expressway in a battered old yellow cab, I knew I was where I belonged, broken teeth and all. Back in my compartment, there was a message on my machine from Stu, with a million assignments for the next issue. Flash had scribbled a note listing a dozen downtown parties that night, and there was even an old jazz mixed tape that had come from Terrance through the mail. As I popped it in the player and relaxed back into the cool brass flow, I knew there was no way I would ever get Bopped.

I left Beverly Hills and dug into the thigh-scorching inclines toward the Sunset Strip. Cars speeded past, edging me off the dark street, slamming their horns and laughing at my perilous climb; by the time I finally locked my bike in a back lot off the Strip, I was shaky with nerves, short of breath, and slicked wet with sweat. I waited awhile to catch my breath, spitting out curses at Sylvia and her car sabotage tactics, until I finally collected myself enough to round the corner toward the Black Adder.

Rage Against the Chili Pepper had founded the now famous Hollywood hang in the early nineties, as a lounge spot for the boys in the band as well as a moneymaking maneuver. Overnight, the Sunset Boulevard club attracted investors from all across the newly emerging Hollywood constellation; with Rage as the draw, every young rock star, brat actor, kid-prodigy director, and celebutante in Los Angeles seemed to buy stock in the Black Adder. Not a glamorous one of them had yet to hit thirty, but each had far surpassed the million mark in terms of net gross, and between their collective bank accounts, they had built up the Adder into a kind of media magnet/rich-kid clubhouse. Barfly photographers lounged on hand at all hours, not a night passed without at least one celebrity cameo or tabloid incident, and any musical act currently climbing the charts was bound to be found rocking the Adder stage.

Of course, the merely human were always welcome; it was their money that made the Adder move. When I rounded the corner of Sunset that night, the club's evening fodder were duly lined up out front, three deep and snaked around the corner, glammed and tanned to the point their day-job paychecks would permit. Towering bald bouncers draped in black designer suits stood like pillars before the door, lifting a red velvet rope to admit a few at a time. With no connections in Hollywood, and no hope of swift guest-list admission, I stood myself at the back of the masses, settling in for a wait.

As the line shuffled slowly forward, engine-revving cars crawling past on the Strip, muffled house music pumping from inside the club, I looked around me at the glassy-eyed crowd of poseurs and scenesters, hardly believing that of all the wide world, this glittered dead-end den was where Nile Rivers had decided to die.

My mind went back to the memorial service I had seen on TV while packing up in New York. Nile's hippie earth mother, who had been the prominent female figure in his life, rarely made public appearances, but she audiotaped a speech for her son's fans and peers who had gathered together in a Los Angeles park. Over the loudspeaker, her voice read out passages from an Indian holy book as the mourners stood, staring at an empty stage, and The Channel's TV cameras prowled throughout. The kids, even through their streaming tears, downcast eyes of woe, and clinging, group hugs, appeared aware of the camera's every move; it seemed to me staged, as if they were all trying to outmourn each other, in hopes of ending up on a *Decade In Review* special. I was glad to be in New York, alone with my thoughts, far away from them all.

But now in Hollywood, on line for the Adder, I wondered if anything happened here without its seeming staged. Before me stood a bandanna-wrapped rocker who looked as if his debut album was coming out next week; at his side, a makeup-caked Valley Girl who seemed like an extra from a video shoot in eternal progress. Hoping for a word with the natives, I reached out and tapped the rocker on the shoulder.

"Do you know who's playing tonight?"

The rocker turned and looked me over through red-streaked eyes. "Nah dude, just here to get loose."

"Yeah, me, too. I just got into town."

"Where you from?"

"Ireland," I lied.

He laughed. "You gonna get rocked tonight, right? All you guys do."

I nodded my head. "Hell yeah, that's what we do."

His girlfriend, slouching in front of him, took the last drag off a joint and crushed it out under a spiky white boot. The crowd moved forward, and we edged our way toward the velvet rope before the door.

The rocker lit a cigarette. "So why'd you come to L.A.? You wanna be a porno star?"

His girlfriend cracked up.

"I wanted to see where Nile Rivers died," I answered.

"Oh Christ . . ." He turned to the stone-baked Valley chick at his side. "Yola, this guy came all the way from Scotland to see where the River dried up . . . innn't that a trip?"

Yola rolled her eyes and nudged her boyfriend. "His band was playing out in Redondo Beach the night he died. I was, like, *so* pissed when I found out . . . that would of been totally historic; like you know, to have been here when it happened."

Just then the security guard raised the red velvet rope and waved us in. I followed the rocker couple down the steep steps into a crooked cement passageway, that fed us to a low-ceiling, red carpeted downstairs bar. The chattering crowd was packed tight, pounding music blanketing their bodies, the dim lights above casting shadows in the shroud of cigarette smoke that hung overhead. A lucky few had landed tables in the seamy throng, and through the haze, I saw their laughing, dazed, and jaded faces lit in eerie flickers from the low flames of wax-dripping candles. A massive-scale, slick-painted snake hissed grinning from the wall, its eyes glittering stones.

"So this is where it happened, Scotland!" The rocker shouted in my ear over a thundering guitar thrash that pummeled down from the stage upstairs. *"Your Buddha boy Nile drank down sixteen Scotch and sodas . . ."*

"SEVENTEEN!" his girlfriend corrected, shouting in my other ear.

"Whatever!" he shouted, grabbing on to my shoulder to be heard over the electric din. *"Drank 'em down, scored his smack, walked out the door and made himself a legend!"* A grin spread over his face, as big as the snake's on the wall. "THAT'S ROCK AND ROLL, SCOTLAND!"

He and his girlfriend became lost in a crush toward the bar, and I pushed past the pack of bodies to the stairs that led up to the stage. Red lights colored my skin as I threaded through the perspiring leather jackets and sticky silk shirts of the glam crowd, and the ratty T-shirts and three-day stubble of the slacker scenesters. Guitar power chords hammered down on me from the stage, cranked out though a screaming stack of amplifiers by a short, mop-headed white kid in beat-up sneakers, old corduroys, and a faded, oversize golf shirt. A sweaty girl with blond dreadlocks pounded wildly on the drums behind him, a cymbal-crashing beat that nearly swallowed the keyboard drones being fingered by a skinny, pale, absurdly tall woman wrapped in ski goggles near the curtain. I forced myself back through the half-dancing, half-pushing crowd, until I found a space against the back wall, where I sucked in a deep breath of stale, body-heated air.

"Yo! Scotland!!"

I heard the words over the wall of sound and turned to see the bandanna rocker from out front with a beer in one hand and a shot of whiskey in the other.

"Whooeee! Bet you don't have nothin' like this back home! Yo, check it out!"

He pushed closer to me and gestured with his whiskey toward a huge mirror at the back of the club, taking up almost an entire wall. "See that mirror back there?"

"Yeah!"

"That's the back room! Where the Pepper and all their homies hang, just watching us all. Inn't that trippy!"

"You ever been back there?!" I shouted back to the rocker.

"No way, dude! You got to be large to get behind the mirror! Only the Pepper and their crew!"

"They back there now?"

"I don't know! Supposed to be here tonight, I hear."

Just then I watched as a huge, bald albino bouncer planted next to the mirror wall put his finger to his earpiece. He nodded, then moved out into the crowd, bodies parting before him.

The rocker nearly howled in laughter. "There he goes: the only three-hundred-pound bald albino in captivity!" He jabbed his finger toward the pinkish head pushing through the crowd. "That's the cradle robber for the Rage! They only go for the young girls, dude . . . the little babies. Just like I'm gonna do it when I get my record deal!" He downed his whiskey and chased it with a swig of beer. "YO RUNNY R! LEAVE A COUPLE FOR ME, MY BROTHER! AHHHAAAA HAA!"

The bouncer stopped next to a duo of nubile young blondes, lowering his bald head to their height. Through the swarming crowd, I saw his lips moving close to the ear of one girl, who couldn't have been more than sixteen. A wicked grin spread across her face, and she turned in a quick swishing of hair, following the massive bald man through the crowd, leaving her overweight friend scowling in her wake. I watched as she stopped before the mirror; a moment passed, then a section of the silver wall slid open, swallowing her in.

"*Goddamn, Scotland!*" the rocker shouted to me, pointing his finger at the mirror wall with a demented grin wrapped round his teeth. "THAT'S WHAT I'M TALKING ABOUT! RIGHT THERE! THAT'S IT!"

It suddenly hit me that Flash might be behind the mirror, and I elbowed my way through the density of bodies, stopping at the back of the club. As the music raged around me, I watched myself in the shining surface, trying to see through my blurred image as it was shaken by the thudding thunder of the drums. Cupping my hands around my eyes, I leaned forward toward the glass in an attempt to see behind the reflection, into the space beyond.

A steel hand clamped down on my shoulder from behind *"Sir! You can't be standing there!"*

"I think a friend of mine is back there, I'm just trying to see in!" I shouted back as the albino bouncer spun me around to face his pink, watery eyes.

"LOOK! If you ain't back there yet, you *ain't getting back there ever!"*

"Can you just go in and check? He was supposed to call me, I missed him on the phone . . ."

"Don't even start with me, sir, not tonight," the bouncer intoned menacingly, his mouth a grim line.

"It's Flash! He's got a show on The Channel. He's my friend!"

He stared at me, unmoving, and I stood facing him. The song onstage ended, and applause exploded, laced with screams from the crowd.

"Will you please leave the club, sir?"

"WHAT!"

Somehow, his low tone came through to me over the shrieking audience. *"I said I'm inviting you to leave the premises."*

" 'CAUSE I TRIED TO LOOK IN A GODDAMN MIRROR?"

Another bouncer appeared, this one taller, bigger, black. He stood next to the albino and crossed his hands before him. "Do you understand the English language, sir?"

I looked at both of them for a second longer, then turned back to the mirror, half-hoping that Flash would dash out and save me. A power chord ripped out from the stage, carried on a drumbeat, and the crowd howled along as a new song began.

"Right this way, sir."

Defeated, I let the two giants lead me down the stair-case, through the packed downstairs bar, under the glittering eyes of the snake, and out the door. Without even a second look at me, they disappeared back inside the club, and I watched as the guard at the door raised the red velvet rope, letting in another to fill the space I had occupied.

Dumbfounded, I walked along Sunset Boulevard before the Black Adder Club. My eyes turned down to the pavement, tracing over the dirtied stones, realizing that one of them had been the place where Nile Rivers collapsed, ending his travels forever. Still bewildered from my ejection from the club, I squatted down under the dark electric light, running my fingers over the rough sidewalk. A few feet from me on the boulevard, cars floored past in a river of rushing metal, stereo selections pouring from open windows; speeding pop fragments, chased by exhaust, overcome by the next . . .

And then I heard the laughter, familiar and loud as always. I turned my head sharply and caught a glimpse of bright green, slipping through the ropes with an entourage that obviously didn't need to wait in line.

"FLASH!!" I shouted over the roar of traffic. I began running toward the door of the Black Adder, trying to reach my friend.

Faces from his surrounding crowd came clearer to me as I neared, and I recognized Runny R from the

Pepper, a few other band members, and a wave of platinum blond hair that stopped me with a shock.

"Gertie . . . ?" I muttered to myself, stunned to see the iconic young actress for the first time outside of a movie screen. As I watched, she giggled something to Flash, and they disappeared side by side down the dark steps.

"*Flash!*" I shouted, regaining my senses and rushing up to the velvet rope. A bouncer slammed his body in front of me.

"Back **away** from the door, sir."

"But my friend . . ." I half-explained, leaning down to see the bright green hair swallowed up in the Adder's shadows. "*Flash!*"

Suddenly, the albino appeared from inside. The huge man reached for the rope, and the crowd around us went silent, confrontation suffusing the air. His eyes, hostile pink pools in his mottled bald head, pushed me backward down the sidewalk, without so much as a word. As I slowly turned and walked over the glittered grime of Sunset Boulevard, I heard the sounds of laughter, jeering after me over the dull pound of music from deep inside the shadowed club.

4. flash

The phone rang three times in the dark, silent apartment.

"Yo."

"Neil, it's Terrance."

"Hey, whassup," I said into the mouthpiece, leaning up against the couch. I rubbed my eyes and clicked the light, illuminating Stu's room, cluttered with my mess.

"Haven't heard from you in a while. What you been doing, Samurai?"

"I don't know. Diving the Harbor, riding around, looking for clues."

He laughed. "Any leads?"

"Went to the Adder."

"Yikes."

"Yup. And I found out that palm trees aren't indigenous to Los Angeles," I said, recalling a fact I had discovered in a Harbor text.

"What does that mean?"

"It means that they don't grow here naturally." I pulled on my pants, inspired to dress now that I was actually talking with someone. "And that means that the one symbol I associated with this city isn't even authentic. This town is a complete sham."

"Is it getting you down?"

"Nah," I lied.

"How's the manifesto?"

"Going well," I lied again.

"Well yo, I'm with Flash over at the editing studio. It's not far away, maybe you should take a break."

"What are y'all up to?" I said, already searching for my boots.

"Flash shot some stuff for his show, needed extras or something. Said he called you . . . didn't you get the message?"

I scratched at my nose. "Must have missed it."

"Glad I caught you then. Why don't you come over? We're just off Melrose . . ."

As I pedaled through the nighttime Hollywood neighborhoods of dark, glassy quiet, cool grass, and silent security systems set ready to pounce, the emptiness made me feel as if I had been warped back to suburbia. My steady breathing and my bike's slightly squeaking sprocket created the only urban rhythms in the deserted neighborhoods, underscored only by the low roar of faraway boulevard traffic, or the occasional insectoid buzzing of a distant police helicopter.

It had been sunshine misery in Hollywood so far. Since leaving the Adder Club that night weeks ago, I hadn't met a single soul in Image City, aside from the cockroach in Stu's shower. The fib-riddled phone call with Terrance had been about the extent of my human connection; my old friend was starting at a new skate-board company set in San Diego, and between making the move and hanging with his wife, couldn't dig up much time. The New Guy called now and again, but it was a drain being idolized, and I wasn't much for the skate rat pack he rolled with. Flash I tried a couple times, but he was always busy; every so often on the answering machine I would hear his voice crowded by restaurant chatter, leaving an address of a party he was off to in the hills or Santa Monica or another exotic locale beyond the realms of my bicycle reality. He never offered a ride, and I never asked.

I knew what was happening, but my mind couldn't let me accept the fact that Flash was giving me the fade. Up until now, I had always been the fader, easing old friends from my life as I moved on to others. I knew the moves of a well-executed fade by heart: a calculated avoidance brought just to the brink of insult, only to be defused with feigned inclusion in last-minute, impossible parties, the ever-hovering "drink sometime next week" or a head-spinning, role-reversing: "*Kid, where you been? I was trying to reach you!*"

Up until now, I had never been the fadee, and Flash was the first who moved fast enough to overtake my scorching pursuit of a life ever larger. I had faded my friends from back home, as well as my pothead brother and for the most part, my family. Even in New York, I had relentlessly faded through a score of scenes and characters in a blaze of essence-absorbing madness. Once I knew all the jokes, once I had the patterns down, once I hit a wall and saw impending blockage of social or emotional flow, my weapon was leveled and set to fade, while I scanned the surroundings for the next lead.

And *Dusted* had been the pinnacle of my quest. Expenses paid, comped at clubs, listed at parties, and granted access to every edgy, young happening in New York, I imagined I had discovered all I had ever faded for. But evidently, there was more, and my old friend Flash had found it without me.

I found the editing complex easy enough, a low-lit, white brick building on an industrial block just off Melrose. Similar, windowless structures were lined up and down the deserted street, and as I wound through the parking lot, dodging broken glass and looking for a place to chain my wheels, I guessed that it was some kind of editing ghetto that I had ridden into. Satisfied with a link fence set back in the shadows, I walked cross the empty asphalt to the front door, pushed a button, smiled up at the security camera, and was buzzed inside.

A blond receptionist looked up from her fashion magazine. "Here for Flash?"

"How'd you know?"

"Only Flash's friend would show up at midnight on a BMX bike."

"How'd you know *that?*"

She shrugged. "Cameras all over the place." Raising a tanned finger, the receptionist pointed the way. "They're down the hall, number seven."

I walked down the newly carpeted corridor, past a brightly sparkling white kitchenette and a large, wooden-floored lounge with a basketball hoop, before rounding the corner to door number seven. I eased my way inside and stood for a moment, taking in the lair of technology I had entered.

How many millions of dollars had been sunk into the studio I would never know, but gazing at the gleaming rows of TVs, mixing boards, computer screens, and control panels in the room before me, I imagined that the dimes dropped on a mere couple knobs might be enough to solve my dental dilemma for life. Soft, dimmed track lighting downplayed the chaos of blinking lights from the spanning control panels, a freshly cleaned, maroon-colored carpet covered the split-level floor, and black lacquered tables shone spotless amidst deep, dark leather chairs.

I watched as a blue-baseball-capped guy, kicked back in a leather chair, called out to a small woman manning the controls.

"I wanna make sure that title holds long enough; wind it back for another run!"

The editor punched a series of buttons as I spied Flash's smooth crop of green hair just visible over a high-backed chair near the man calling directions. And then the images on the TV panels rewound, vanished, and appeared again in playback.

Within a familiar flurry of Channel-style editing, I watched my friend Flash on four TV screens as he rolled down a steep Hollywood Hills road on his skateboard. Retro spy-movie music raised in volume as he picked up speed, and behind him, Runny R suddenly appeared, pursuing in a vintage soapbox racer. Cutting quickly away, the camera pulled in on another Raging Pepper waiting in disguise at the bottom of the hill;

with a dastardly smile, the pop villain produced Pablo the lizard from under his coat, then tossed the hissing reptile before the now speeding Flash, in a slow-motion arc of imminent doom. But within a deft series of whip-lash camera cuts, the skateboarding TV host reached out, caught the lizard, and whizzing past, passed the creature off to a bewildered old lady on the sidewalk. The action suddenly froze, and a spinning title landed solidly on screen, recited by a whisper chorus of sexy female voices:

FLASH!

The collected crew in the editing room burst into laughter.

"Flash, this is *so* goddamn awesome!" the baseball-cap guy shouted. He shook his head in beaming satisfaction, sandy blond stubble sparkling on his sun-tanned face.

The woman at the editing controls nodded her head in agreement. "The Channel is going to flip over this, you guys."

"Look! It's NEIL!" Flash shouted as he caught sight of me leaning in the door frame. Grabbing hold of his armchair, he leaped over the back, legs flying high, and landed on the carpeting with a thunk, bounding past the editing boards toward me. "Glad you could make it, son! Where you been! How's the kids? And how's El Lay doing you?"

"Thrillsville, babe, thrillsville," I returned, falling instinctively into his world.

"Dynamite! Have you been eating well?" He reached back to a glass-topped table and snatched two items, holding them up before me. "How 'bout a soft drink and a carrot?"

But before I could answer, his attention snapped back to the TVs, which were rewinding through another series of blurring images.

"Wait! Stop there!" he called to the editor, crunching down on the bright orange carrot. "Bring up the opening shots again."

"I got it Flash," the baseball-cap guy said.

"Terrance, how 'bout showing the Samurai where the eats is?" Flash called over to our old designer, who I noticed for the first time, sitting back away from the equipment, still wearing the faded print dress he had donned to be the old lady in Flash's show.

Terrance kicked open a small, squat fridge on the floor with a worn and weary black boot. "Welcome to the big time, kid: free sodas and everything."

Just then, the tanned receptionist from out front poked her orthodontically perfected smile into the door.

"Um, excuse me, Flash? You have a call from Jamie at CCA."

"Check!" The star jumped up out of his deep leather chair and zipped toward the door, calling to us as he crossed the floor, "I'll be back in a flash, or my name isn't . . . isn't, uh . . ." He paused on the threshold.

"Flash?" I suggested.

"Thanks, Neil, I owe you one!" he shot to me, dashing out into the hallway in his beat-up skate sneakers.

I sank down into a seat next to Terrance, and we exchanged strange looks of recognition: the moment could have been sampled from *Dusted* just a year ago. My mind wound back to picture Flash, surrounded by the pile of magazines, demo tapes, and photo slides on his cluttered mess of a desk, busting fake karate kicks, singing stupid raps, and dashing in and out the door within a never-ending ring of phone calls.

"I called and left a message about the shoot. You didn't get it?" Terrance asked.

"Still haven't figured how to work Stu's answering machine," I lied. The message of course, I had heard, but I couldn't bring myself to be an extra in my friend's TV show.

"You been finding any work out here?" Terrance asked.

"Haven't been looking." I took a swig from my soda and flipped the script. "They pay you for today?"

"Nah, just the honor of being on The Channel," my friend said, laughing.

"Hmm." I played with my teeth, and envy rolled through me as I thought of Flash prime-posited in the thick of The Channel, deciding what millions of wanna-be hipsters would watch and wish they were.

The star suddenly bounced through the door, wearing rose-colored sunglasses and an Afro wig. "WHERE'S THE GAFFER? MY GRIP? AND WHO THE HELL'S THAT CHORUS GIRL? GET HER OUT OF THE PICTURE!"

Flash picked up a banana, waving it like a baton as he marched through the room in his Afro wig. "ACTION! CUT! THAT'S A TAKE!! HYYYAAAA!!!" With a yelp, he launched into a karate match with his director.

"ALRIGHT! Enough already," the director yelled, his face red and laughing. "It's a wrap."

Dropping the fight, Flash came closer and flopped down in a seat at my side, pulling off his Afro wig.

"Don't know about you kids, but I could use a belt of the sauce. Wanna hit the town?"

Terrance shook his head. "Sorry, y'all. I got to go home and act like a husband."

The TV star turned to me. "Neil?"

I watched as the images of Flash faded silently from the series of television screens before me and decided to take what I could get from my old friend. "Sure Flash, I'm down."

"What are we drinking tonight?" Flash asked me a while later as we walked through the door into a dark, stained-wood bar. I thought for a moment, looking around me at the Union Jack hanging from the far wall, the few leather jackets shooting pool, and the spinning silver disk shining from atop the CD jukebox, as it belted out an old sixties drug anthem. My friend had found us a hipster dive: not sketchy enough to be really thick, but chipped and stripped enough to feel real.

"I got the itch for ummm, a . . . Sam in a Sweater," I decided.

As Flash leaned into the bartender, I slid into an empty booth nearby, to await whatever a Sam in a Sweater was. The booze routine was a standard gig in our repertoire: I would invent the name of a drink, and then Flash would make up the mixture, explaining the improvised ingredients to the bartender. Over the years, I had drunk an unforgettable round of Savage Idiot Gods, had been pleasantly surprised by a tall, cool Junkie Panda, and on New Year's Eve in Atlanta, had been decked by the still notorious Semiautomatic Lebanese Drag Queen. Although the drink hadn't been an "official," as the bartender had refused to kiss the cherry, it was enough to turn me so green that a two-page photo documentary in the pages of *Dusted* had been devoted to the agony the deadly mix inflicted.

I wondered now what Flash was making up for me as he leaned against the bar, directing a confused-looking bartender amidst the various liquors. And as I traced my fingers over the carved names in the thick, wooden table before me, I also wondered which Flash would come back to join me with the drink.

Now that the cameras had cut and the audience was out, I had a fair shot of getting a friend instead of a cohost. While living together in New York, I had found that there were two Flashes: the one of songs and pranks, wigs and gags, and another quieter, reserved, somewhat distant one. The pranks I had been part of, and the songs I had shared, but the Flash without the flash was the one I had really bonded with. On so many late, quiet Fifth Street nights, my friend had listened in as I shared the snarled relationships of teeth, family, and writing that would wring my soul in tangles. My parents hated my work, my brother was too stoned to bother, and with no other connections in New York looking out for me, Flash had been there to care.

His past was never an issue; as far as I could tell, he and his parents got on fine, and there wasn't much to say. Flash talked vaguely about growing up in Hollywood, but for the most part, my friend was enviably rooted in the present. And the present, with all its confusion, we both shared equally. Talking to each other long after the parties had died, we had helped each other maneuver through the intrigue-littered landscape of downtown scenarios *Dusted* had drawn us into.

Without Flash, I imagined I might not have made it in New York, but now in Hollywood, as Flash executed an expert fade, it was becoming increasingly clear that I was a solo act.

"Two Sams in a Sweater," my friend said, appearing with two odious-looking highball glasses, purple umbrellas bobbing from the murky mix within. Grinning, he pounded them down on the thick, varnished wood, then slid into his seat across the table from me.

We clicked cheers and I hesitantly sipped. Grape juice, rye, and a few unidentifiables mixed in my mouth, but I was relieved to have only a slight convulsion as the concoction slid down.

Flash frowned in distaste. "Mmmm . . . now that's a drink for old friends."

Together we watched the pool game for a while, until I broke the silence.

"I was at the Adder the other night. I think I saw you."

"What! Really? Why didn't you say something!"

"I was on my way home and all," I explained, deftly short-handing the night's events. "But I have to ask: Were you there with Gertie?"

Flash grinned, looking down as he stirred his Sweater. "Yeah, we're seeing each other a little."

I raised my eyebrows, impressed. "Damn."

Over a decade ago, Gertie had been Hollywood's hottest child actress and was an icon for anyone my age. As a girl, she had starred in *Tooky*, a summer blockbuster about a cuddly, dimension-skipping baby dinosaur with magical powers, who had been stranded in a Los Angeles suburb. As kids, we had all cheered Gertie and the bug-eyed baby dinosaur, as they dodged

CIA spooks and built a makeshift time portal from scavenged garage materials, inadvertently reuniting the heroine's estranged parents in the process.

Tooky had gotten home of course, in a burst of inter-dimensional light and a swelling of orchestral strings, but Gertie had not been so lucky; a massive fame crashed into the little girl's life, shattering her childhood into a flurry of tabloid headlines. She legally disowned her parents, bought a Hollywood mansion at age ten, became an alcoholic by sixth grade, had a string of botched suicide attempts and wildly publicized drug arrests, and then disappeared for years into the hushed halls of rehab.

"Jesus, Flash. How the hell did you end up meeting Gertie?"

It was easy to see my friend's embarrassment as my envy suffused the air. "We had talked before, you know, when she was doing some of her comeback promo . . . *Dusted* folded too soon to do an interview, but, you know, we talked on the phone a few times."

"You were putting play on the star of *Tooky* and didn't even tell me?" I said, shaking my head in disbelief.

Flash shrugged and looked away. "I don't know, it wasn't anything really. But then I came back to Hollywood, and at some party The Channel was throwing, I ran into her."

"Well, it's good to know she's on the scene again. Man, she didn't have it easy."

It was currently impossible not to see my friend's new girlfriend, either chatting her way through the TV talk-show circuit, dishing to the day's primo entertainment mags, or starring in one of three indie films that had been released in the last two months. The little girl had grown into a classic Hollywood vixen, and like Nile Rivers, had shed her celluloid past to embrace an adulthood on-screen. But instead of ending up face-down in front of the Black Adder, the New Improved Gertie had triumphantly derailed her fate and was gushing to tell her tale of glitzy defeat and glorious, media rebirth to anyone who would point a microphone her way.

I sipped at my drink and scratched my head. "Look, Flash, I was thinking that maybe Gertie could help me out a bit," I began as an old acid anthem started on the jukebox.

"How do you mean?"

"I told you my manifesto starts with Nile Rivers, and I need to get in on his story a little more. Gertie used to roll with him, you know, young Hollywood crew. I was thinking maybe I could talk with her about it."

Flash stirred his drink. "I don't know. I'd have to ask her. But I doubt it; the whole thing kinda freaked her."

"It would be great though, for my manifesto," I pressed. "I really need to get something going in Hollywood."

"I don't know, Neil, I'll try, but she hates the press."

"I'm not the press, Flash. I'm your friend. And how can you say your girlfriend hates the press when she does an interview every time she takes a dump?"

A hostile flicker wavered in my friend's blue eyes, and I knew I had pushed it too far.

"Sorry. I'm just not used to her being your girlfriend. We used to joke about Gertie, remember?" I took a deep pull from my drink, feeling nervous.

Flash picked an ice cube out of his Sam and moved

it along the table with his finger, weaving a pattern of water. "So how are your teeth?"

Relief flooded me; with deft skill, Flash had brought us back to the old times. "Oh man, yesterday I got this funky little zitlike thing on my gum. I think it might be an abscess. I hope nothing happens; if I needed a root canal now, I'd be hosed."

"I bet you could get some teeth off of Mandy. You *know* she still wants to work with you."

"Come now . . . ," I answered, shaking my head as I finished my drink.

Flash started to sing:

> *Neil, oh Neil,*
> *do a* Bop Cheese *piece,*
> *So you can get some shiny new teeth,*
> *And some . . . um . . . um . . .*

"Some much needed dental relief," I chimed in, finishing his rhyme before dropping back to conversation. "C'mon, I can't write for *Bop Cheese*, they ran *Dusted* out of business."

"*Dusted* ran *Dusted* out of business," he corrected. "Do it under a pen name, why don't you?"

"Sam in a Sweater," I said, reaching for his nearly untouched drink. Something deep inside me couldn't stand the thought of a drink going to waste, no matter how terrible it was. I think this amused Flash and inspired some of his more sinister mixes.

He grinned and sat up higher in his seat. "Right, the adventures of Sam in a Sweater! We'll base a hit series on your zany escapades and touch the hearts of millions!"

"A *Bop Cheese* superstar," I answered, with zero enthusiasm.

"Bop the Cheese, fix your teeth, then go write a manifesto. It's a perfect plan! You'll be famous, with an award-winning smile."

"It's not that easy," I answered, wondering why it wasn't.

"Neil . . . ," he groaned, and I could see that he was getting frustrated. Then almost audibly, I sensed him give up on me. A song ended, and I finished the drink we had made up together, as we silently watched the pool game.

"You wanna go?" Flash said.

And like that, I knew it was over. The fade had been fully executed. In silence, we left the bar, and in silence he drove me back to Stu's.

"So call me up next week," Flash said outside the building. "I'm busy for a while, but you know, we should hang out soon."

"Yeah, OK."

I walked away from the car, and suddenly Flash called out to me.

"NEIL!"

I turned back, to see that he had jammed the Afro wig onto his head. With a grin and thumbs-up, he called out to me, *"Come of age, young man!"*

I heard his car phone ring as he zoomed off, and it wasn't until Flash was halfway down the shadowed street that I remembered my bike, still locked up in back of the editing complex. Envisioning the long trek through Hollywood to retrieve my wheels, I cursed bitterly to myself, then decided it would best be undertaken in daylight.

I entered Stu's, flipping off the blathering security system and heading straight to the kitchen. After the fade from Flash, I felt a deep need to pick up where the Sams in Sweater had left off and, luckily, had the goods to do it. Earlier in the week, I had picked up a case of **BEER**; the basic beverage, indigenous to California, cost $2.69 a six-pack and came in white cans with bold black stenciling that simply read: **BEER**. The taste was truly rank, but the price was right, and I decided that night I'd hang in the Harbor and drink it till I was **DRUNK**.

Flicking a light switch on the wall, I entered the teetering clutter of Stu's archives, marveling anew at the sheer volume of disconnected data he had amassed over the years. My eyes traced over the two entire walls of rough wooden shelving, laden with paperback novels, mismatched sets of encyclopedias, 'zines, VCR tapes, photo albums, and unproduced screenplays.

The demo tapes were stashed in cardboard boxes all over the floor, and stretching out my foot, I kicked one over and watched a river of translucent plastic cassettes spill out on the gray carpet around me. Choosing one at random, I pushed it into the stereo; after a short hiss, the bland production weakly filled the room, enhanced to optimum lackluster by Stu's lo-fi system.

> *They are in control,*
> *They own your soul . . .*

The lyrics began in an ominous growl, telling me nothing I didn't already know. I drank down half a beer in one gulp and picked up the tapes, one after the other, gazing at the names. Goin' Back to Kali, Captain

Mooey's Mess, The Abdo Men . . . witty bands of slacker youth with cute, clever names, but ultimately all the same. I imagined the dreams pinned to each cassette, and instead of feeling coolly superior, as I had planned, I suddenly felt as if I were sinking. All these young hopes, lost in an unmarked box at the bottom of the L.A. Harbor . . . and me, right along with them.

I walked to the stereo and punched in a Rage Against the Chili Pepper disc, listening to the familiar bass line ooze into the room. As Runny R's rhymes blended with the drum-rolling fills, I recalled the wild excitement of concert nights: distortion chords rippling through sweaty teen masses; rhythm sections plowing through walls of postpubescent madness; a stage diver dodging no-neck security and leaping blindly into the seething pit of fans, who would buoy him up and pass his slimy, tattooed body over their heads, before dropping him back onto the quaking floor.

Music had been such a simple way to define myself in the past, when identity only meant what band's T-shirt I wore. But that was all over now; the last few shows I had seen in New York left me hopelessly bored and unsatisfied. The singers that I once beheld as heroes now seemed juvenile in their amplified stage fury, screaming truisms to little kids who weren't old enough to buy cigarettes.

I slumped down at Stu's computer, almost turned it on to write, but instead finished my beer, got up, and walked to the kitchen. I pulled a frozen burrito out of the freezer, and slid it into the microwave. Passing the phone, an impulse hit me to call Flash, to try to deflect the fade he had aimed at me and make myself vital in his Hollywood world. Looking around me at the lonely apartment, stacked high with music and **BEER**s, I wondered why it wasn't filled with laughing young glamorous people, and what I had done wrong in my move to L.A.

As a suburb-stranded teenager, listening to Rage Against the Chili Pepper on my headphones while I composed my letters to *Dusted* late in the night, I had envisioned cities like New York and Hollywood as meccas of disco decadence. I was sure that if I only set myself in the thick of urban currents, a party palace of women and girls and endless shimmy nights would be mine. But here I was, in Hollywood with a beer-stacked pad of my own, submerged in the same murky isolation that had strangled me as a teen. I had left New York needing something new, but without my friend Flash to angle me into the scene, Hollywood was beginning to seem a closed set.

I opened the nearly bare fridge again, reaching for a beer that lay behind a few lolling apples.

"Don't you like to bite your happles?"

Milena's voice came back to me from last summer's London, and I wished she were here, waiting with me for my frozen burrito. As I slumped against the counter, a lonely Los Angeles was displaced by a whirl of London impressions. Milena's long legs wrapped around me in a soft, early-morning light, the smell of rich espresso brewing in the kitchen as we began the day with deep, leisurely love. Moving inside her, savoring the smooth friction in day's dawning, along with the feeling of freedom in a foreign city; London before me, mine to explore without the dulling gauze of routine that had shrouded New York . . .

And Milena hadn't been just another woman: she

was an archetype. When I was little, stealing nudie mags from my older brother, I assembled from the airbrushed photos a paradigm of the Naked Lady. I had been in bed with naked girls before, as well as naked women . . . never, though, had I gotten down with a Naked Lady. But one night with Milena, as I had watched her walking across the wine-colored carpet of her flat, I was struck with a shocking revelation. I blinked my eyes in disbelief when Milena came back to bed and kissed me. The full, perfectly rounded breasts, her long legs, curved hips . . . *I had been in bed with a Naked Lady*.

The microwave timer beeped sharply, bringing me back to Hollywood and an oozing cheese burrito, and at that moment, a realization struck me:

I could be eating *happles* with Milena in London.

Standing in the void of Stu's pad, I faced the fact that Hollywood was a desperately wrong locale to write a manifesto. A month was enough to know that the glittery city would be my demise; Jesus, a night at the Adder was enough to know why Nile Rivers had killed himself. Flash wasn't going to help me get in with Gertie for a word on Nile's death, and *Neil Before God* was a subversive act anyway—the motherland would have to be abandoned to get perspective. I needed travel to thrill my senses instead of the slow, air-conditioned embalming of Los Angeles. The Theory of East Jabip was suddenly making sense: any manifesto worth half its ink had to be written far, far away from the cloying, pop smear of American culture.

You're blessed, bro. If I were you, I'd just travel all over the world and write.

The words of Nile Rivers echoed in my ears, and I

rushed into the Harbor, excited to write for the first time since I had hit L.A. It was time to make an escape plan, and with a drunken lurch I moved to turn on the computer. But my movements were slurred from the **BEER**, and I knocked a junior encyclopedia from the desk, sending the heavy, white and maroon volume falling open on the floor at my feet.

As I bent down to pick it up, I caught sight of the heading where the book had opened:

JAVA

A series of photographs filled the pages, depicting the small Indonesian island. I leaned back in my chair, gazing at the ancient stone monuments, rice-terraced mountainsides, the rolling oceans, smiling, tanned women, and crowded cities filled with speeding, smoking mopeds.

Nile Rivers's faraway voice came into my mind again.

In terms of total cosmic depth, there's nothing like Southeast Asia.

A chilling tingle rippled my skin. Nile was talking to me! The hippie actor had perished, but his soul had returned to save me from the air brushed perils of Image City! And Java . . . it was perfect; my very own East Jabip, a foreign island untainted by lit history. In an awesome, drunken moment, a plan of action unfolded in my mind, the first one since *Dusted* had died: leave Hollywood for the exotic wilds of Java, roam the jungles with my manifesto, scribe a scribbled frenzy of exotic brilliance, and then trek back to civilization, to London, to Milena and her Naked Lady love . . .

Transfixed in the glamour of my drunken thrill, I stumble-walked with the encyclopedia into the main room, repeating the word softly to myself with almost religious reverence.

Java . . .

Java . . .

Java . . .

Why the hell should I stay in L.A. and hope Flash threw me some scraps to rewrite for his show? Why the hell should I stay here and kiss Gertie's rehabilitated ass to get a fifteen-minute chat about Nile Rivers? Why the hell should I do anything except what I really wanted to do? What I knew I could do. Rage Against the Chili Pepper wasn't punk. Flash wasn't punk. Getting **DRUNK** on **BEER**, knocking over an encyclopedia and then jetting halfway around the world was punk, goddamn it.

Neil Before God.

I threw myself down on the bed, the book held before my eyes at arm's length, the silence of the room solemn, surrounding me. I felt historic. I felt epic. I felt destiny coursing through my body and churning through my mind.

Java.

Milena.

Neil Before God.

It was all coming together.

Shaking in the impact of the revelation, I reached around with my tongue and pushed my three back molars apart, then back together. Apart, and together. Apart . . .

*   *   *

It was two in the afternoon when I woke up, surrounded by **BEER** cans, a child's *J* encyclopedia, and a spread of translucent demo tapes. For a second, I drew a blank on the night before, and then it all came back to me in a blur, as my aching brain began pounding savagely in my skull.

Groaning, I hid my eyes from the blazing Hollywood sun that tried to push its way through the drawn curtains. Every time I got drunk by myself, which seemed to be happening more and more often, it was always the same: I spent the night streaking into cosmic brilliance, inspired and dazzling, and the next day sweeping up the pieces of mind that had shattered in the reentry to reality. But this time I had gone even further than usual.

Java.

Jesus, it really was completely insane.

Two hours passed me by as I lay in bed. There was no reason to get up, really, as I couldn't make myself believe that this day would be any different from the sun-scorched, achingly solitary days that had passed since I got to Hollywood. There was no job to work, no leads to track down, and no ripe situations stretching out a hand to pull me in, either.

Sitting cross-legged in my underwear as I realized all this, I opened the child's *J* encyclopedia again, to gaze dumbly at a photo of the largest Buddhist monument in the world, far away in the lush hills of Java. Slowly, I shook my head again at the sheer insanity of last night's plans. And rubbing my sleep-sticky eyes, I groaned again over my aching head, as dust motes floated about the empty room. Reluctantly, I got to my feet and stood on the floor.

Java.

Come now, Neil, get real.

But then a realization came to me quietly, and very slowly:

I really had no other place to go.

5. bust a move

The day after I decided to meet destiny in Java, my fears crashed the scene. But picking through the coils of hissing doubts, I realized that I wasn't scared of going to Java, but more so of *not* going; of having to bear the knowledge of yet another sunken dream, abandoned in that murky wreck site inside me. Fate had reached down, into the dark doldrums of my Hollywood days to show me the way, and now it was my part to bust a move. To begin, I knew I needed one single motion, an irreversible gesture that would make it impossible to turn back, even if I should dream to.

So I picked up the phone. And taking a deep breath, dialed the number I knew I could never forget, no matter how far I flew, or how old I grew.

"Hello?"

She answered like I knew she would, like she always did.

Mom.

teeth

I knew that "Hello?" by heart: the perfect-pitched, domestic-android tone that she could click into in an instant. As a child, she could switch into that "Hello?" a mere heartbeat after slapping and swatting my head in a raging, frenzied fury and denouncing me as a no-good-ungrateful-son-of-a-bitch kid. (The logic of which I never turned against her, for fear of getting smacked yet again.)

"Hi Mom, it's Neil."

"Well. What a nice surprise. Hello, Neil."

There was a snarl of fury between my mother and me. I couldn't tell anymore whether it was about my writing, my dental neglect, or how I had broken my father's heart by skipping college, but I had lost interest in the case years ago. Anytime my mother and I tried to talk things out, we ended up screaming, and whenever we spoke about anything else, I felt a searing pain that came from ignoring our twisted past. I had long ago learned how to survive without parental support and felt that it was simply time for us to part ways, which was why I hardly ever contacted her. I had no idea what my mother felt about it all, and I doubt she did either.

"How have you been?" I asked, not really caring.

"Fine, Neil, just keeping an eye on your father and teaching away."

My mother and I had an unspoken rule to never talk much about our occupations. The tales of triumph over her Catholic grade-school regime made me sympathize with her rebel students, and from her end of it, my churchgoing mother honestly thought my chosen profession was evil. On occasions of righteous, Scotch-simmered zeal, she would even point out to my older brother segments of the one article she had read as "filthy," "vile," and "dirty."

Her voice was cold and clipped. "Been a long time, Neil. How's New York?"

"Wouldn't know. I'm in L.A."

"Oh, really? Thanks for telling me. Hollywood more suited to someone of your ambition?"

"Yeah," I said, not taking the bait, "but I'm not staying."

"Back to New York?"

"No. I'm going to Java."

"*Where?*" I could hear the italics in her voice.

"Java."

And as I proclaimed my destination to my mother, I knew there was no turning back. A private failure would be hard to bear, but a failure before my mother was not even a question. Once said, my plan would have to manifest, or only fuel my mother's next derision-filled denouncement of my life.

"Java," I repeated to her, feeling my strength gathering. "A small island in the Indonesian archipelago, and the eighth most densely populated place on the planet."

"Now just hold on a second. Where did you get the money to go to Java?"

"I'm going to do an article for a magazine out here. They pay a lot."

There was a pause in the conversation. In my mind, I could see my mother's fierce blue eyes darting side to side, up and down, searching wildly for the next strike.

"What about your teeth?"

Ouch.

"Yeah," I said with a sigh. "What about them, Mom?"

"Neil. Fix your teeth. Why are you going to . . . where are you going?"

"*Java,*"

My mother had found her argument now and had settled in comfortably on top of it. I heard her light up a cigarette across the country. "Why would you spend your money on some wild, ridiculous trip if you have the money to finally fix your teeth?"

"The last thing I want to spend my money on is my teeth. I'm young, I can travel. . . . When am I going to get an opportunity like this again?"

"Oh please Neil, just end it."

"I'll do it when I come back. I'll get some job in New York with a dental plan."

My mother exhaled forcefully through pursed lips. *"Why do you hang on to that stupid pain of yours? Why don't you want to fix it? What happens if you're in the middle of some crazy country and another one of your teeth dies!?! Have you thought of that?!"*

"There hasn't been anything serious in a while," I shot back.

"Oh for God's sake listen to yourself! Your mouth is a wreck!"

"Look, if I die tomorrow, you think I'd rather be in Java or a dentist chair?"

"Neil, that's a seventeen-year-old talking! Grow up! Do you know how much I've worried about you and that mouth? Do you know how many nights I've—"

"Mom, don't even try that with me. I **lived** through this whole thing. I lived with it right in your house, while you watched me suffer!"

She laughed with derision. "You were drunk. You were way out of line, Neil. You wanted to party and you paid the price."

"You're goddamn right I paid the price, and you will *never, ever* know how much it cost! You will never know how much it hurt! And don't you ever try and say you do! DO YOU HEAR ME, MOM?"

There was a moment of silence, then a resigned exhalation of menthol cigarette smoke.

"Oh Neil . . ."

"What 'Oh Neil'?"

"Why do you carry so much pain with you? Why can't you just let it go?"

The tears fell silently down my cheeks.

She went on, "You're going to hurt someone . . . either yourself or somebody close to you. You can't go on carrying all of that inside of you."

Unable to hold them, soft sobs burst through my choking breaths, and I cursed inside as my mother heard them.

"Just finish the job. Get your mouth together, please. You're young, you're talented, there's going to be other chances to travel."

I was crying too much now to tell her that I couldn't believe her. To tell her that this whole writing thing felt like one big scam, that one day the world would wise up and my ride would be through.

"Neil . . . ?"

"Whrmmfff," I managed to say. I felt like a kid, and I was really weeping now.

"Just please think about it . . . you can't go on like this. I know you're not happy. Find a dentist and at least make sure you're not going to have a tooth die in the middle of Indochina."

"INDONESIA!"

"Alright, OK." She sounded tired. "I've said my piece."

"Fine," I stammered, sniffling. "G'd-bye."

"Good-bye, Neil. Be safe. And try to enjoy yourself, I guess. I don't know what to say to you. I love you."

She hung up the phone, and so did I.

And for a long, long time, I just cried.

My teeth hadn't acted up in some time; the last nerve dying about a year ago, a painful reminder of the awful experience. If it happened in Indo, I would be sorry as hell and a twenty-hour plane ride away from dental civilization. Goddamn my mom . . . but she had a point. Cash was tight, but if Java was to be seized, I decided, I would need to be bold.

When my head came together, I made another long-distance call to another number I would never forget.

"Hello, Dr. Deal's office."

"Hi, Holly, it's Neil."

"Neil?! How are you love? Oh so good to hear from you. How's Hollywood?"

"Actually, I'm in the middle of casting for a feature film I whipped up on the plane ride. It's your star vehicle."

"Really? Oh, how exciting! I knew my day would come. I'll pick you as my leading man, naturally . . ."

"Hey Holl, I need to find a driller out here. Does Dr. Deal by chance know any dentists in L.A.? Is there like, some sort of secret brotherhood they all belong to?"

She laughed. "I don't know about that, but he might have an old colleague . . . or maybe somebody he went to school with. He graduated first in his class, you know."

Of course I knew. Holly let everybody know. "Really?"

"Yes indeedy. I'll have a word with him, Neil honey, and we'll get back to you later today. And get busy on that star vehicle!"

It was comforting to know there was a secretary at a dentist's office somewhere who thought I was the greatest. "OK. Thanks Holly."

"Bye-bye baby."

I slumped back in the shaded room, feeling memories come back, triggered by the double hit of Mom and the dentist. Since leaving home, I had made myself forget that spring night, so long ago, when pain had entered my life. But worn down from tears and BEERs, I was helpless to fight as the swirling imagery overtook me.

It had been springtime of my senior high school year. Nights were balmy and cricket thick, parties were exploding every weekend, and amidst the laughter and excitement of a pending graduation, the whole world seemed like nothing but a luscious future. I was feeling extrasmooth that particular Saturday night, as I had just announced to my parents that I was heading off to New York in the fall. Finally, I would be building my own life, instead of having my parents hammer their miserable one into me.

The local police force was notoriously tough on underage drinking and patrolled every weekend night, prowling through the suburban streets and creeping through the backyard shadows with a demented, deadly zeal for cracking teen vice. Dashing in a reck-less, drunken flight as soon as the goon squad stormed the party was just another part of the evening, and I had always prided myself on evading their clutches. At get-togethers, I would usually hang on the fringes of the crowd, near doorways and back stairways, so I could easily flee the fuzz should they descend. On this night, though, with New York visions spraying in wild-style graffiti through my loose and liquored mind, I forgot my place in the present. I was standing dead center in the middle of the living room, pouring a beer, when the shout of "COPS!!" boomed through the house.

Hundreds of teens scattered wildly in a blind panic, vainly searching for a way out as the police stormed in. Cursing wildly, I bounded through the chaos of colliding bodies only to find all exits blocked, and ended up trapped in the kitchen with a gang of quiv-ering girls, each one wringing her hands, crying, and screaming that their dads were going to kill them.

Police pounded through the front door, barged in from the back, and flooded up from the basement. Horrifying images flashed through my head: three months' license suspension, a thousand-dollar fine, my parents grounding me in their hell house for the entire summer . . .

And then I saw it: The Open Window. It was tiny, absurdly small, high up on the wall near the back hall, but I was skinny and desperate enough to go for it. All sound faded, the crowd parted, and I ran full speed toward my escape, just as a team of cops burst through the kitchen door. In slow motion, I leaped into the air and sailed headfirst through the window; the kitchen disappeared and half my body emerged into the freedom of the spring night. As I prepared myself for a tumble on the soft, lush grass past the patio, I almost started to laugh, it was so beautiful.

And that's when my foot caught on the sill.

In a flash of an instant, my body was yanked from its smooth flight and directed full force into a perpendicular impact with the pavement. My chin smashed down into the cement, and I heard a sickening crunch, then felt warm blood pouring down my chin as I somehow staggered to my feet.

"HEY! YOU!" a cop shouted, but I didn't stop, running instead through the backyard rhododendron, branches whipping against my face as rotating siren lights soaked the darkness around me. Crashing drunkenly through the tangle of branches, I spit hard little pieces out of my mouth, dimly realizing that they were my teeth as the sounds of the busted party faded behind me, and a ponderous ache settled grimly into my jaw, then started to grow. . . .

"OK, let's have a look-see."

I opened wide in the Hollywood dentist's office, hearing my jaw crack with a wet snap.

"Oooch, that doesn't sound too good," the dentist said as he peered into my battered mouth. "And all of these teeth were pretty traumatized by whatever it was you hit . . . looks like a root could die on you any day. What the heck happened?"

"I was in a martial arts tourney in Da Nang last

summer. Made it all the way to the final round before I got checked.''

"You don't say?'' he said with a smile as he adjusted the chair level with his toe.

"Well, to make an epic saga short, I went for a Drunken Lotus just as he backed into a Negotiating Monkey, and naturally, caught it full-on in the mouth.''

"Wow, must have been something.''

"Sure was, Doc. But I'm lucky. Almost came home in a box.''

He examined the damage further with a small, angled mirror on the end of a metal handle. "How many root canals have you had?''

"Six. A couple on those top teeth, then the ones in the back.''

"Open wider?'' He looked closer as I did what I was told.

"Nicely done. Good to see my old roommate's work is up to par. Deal just beat me, you know. I graduated second in the class, the son of a gun. Ah well, he's a good man, and that's a fine root canal he gave you. Quality work like that is rare these days. Lotta shysters out there.''

The Hollywood dentist picked up a long metal rod with a curved spike on the end and moved it into my mouth, striking up a conversation as soon as he did so. Dentists always pulled this maneuver and somehow actually understood the language it produced. His assistant started up the spit-sucking hose and placed it under my tongue.

"So you're going traveling, huh?''

"Yaarhg.''

I felt his rubber-gloved hands in my mouth and remembered when I was a child getting my checkups, and how my dentist had worked with bare hands, in those days before the deadly sexual disease panics.

"Where you off to?" he continued as he explored.

"Agdonasha."

"Indonesia! That's diving country!"

"Whar?"

"Best scuba diving in the world. You a diver?"

"Narhg."

"Too bad. Maybe you should get licensed out there."

"Mahbee."

"My advice to you though, is don't go anywhere until you fix these teeth. How long since the accident?"

"Fa yahs."

"Five years . . . hmm. That's long enough to assume that any nerves that were seriously traumatized would have died already. But you can't be certain about these things. I'd hate to have you somewhere in the middle of Indonesia needing a root canal. This fella back here . . . I don't like the looks of him."

He tapped my back molar, a tooth cracked down the middle.

"NUHHGHG!"

"Mmmm, that's no good, especially for traveling."

He peeled off his gloves and sat up on his stool, putting his hands on his hips.

"I'll tell you what. Why don't you get at least that one guy fixed up? We could even do it today. You're my last appointment, and you look like a young gun on the move; don't know when I'd get you in the chair again. What do you say?"

I was wary about having major dental work by a

mouth man I didn't know, especially one who referred to my teeth as "fellas" and "guys." Then again, this encounter could be a bit of divine intervention to save me from an ugly jungle dental episode.

"How long's the billing time?"

"I'll give you a month."

It wasn't hard to recall what it felt like to have my nerves dying under my teeth. How they fermented, the pressure of the festering pus building up in my jaw, and how I'd wake up in the morning with an agonizing thud in my mouth, a maddening, screaming torment amplified with the blood throbbing in my head.

And then the emergency appointment, the sharp sting and numb from the needle, and a burning drill, directly into the pounding tooth. The dead nerve reached, the rotten root slime erupting from the hole, mingling with bits of burning, drilled tooth and oozing over my half-numb tongue in a noxious, reeking cocktail. . . . It was a medieval enough scene in a dentally advanced culture such as the States, but if a root of mine decided to kip in down Java way, I knew I'd be doomed.

"OK. Let's do it."

"All right then!"

The Hollywood dentist seemed excited, whistling and rubbing his hands together as he collected the materials for my torture.

"Let's get down to business, here."

The assistant, a bored-looking woman with faint bags under her eyes and no smile wrinkles at the corners, moved closer to the chair. It was her task to take on much of the muscle work—no less vital than the dentist's finesse—and from my experience in the chair, I knew that a good assistant was just as key as a solid dentist. This one didn't look all that sharp, but it was too late to do much about it now.

"Open?"

I opened my mouth and the Hollywood dentist spread a green sheet over my face, isolating the tooth he would be concentrating on. The assistant pulled the light closer and the doctor jabbed a drooling syringe into my gum: I felt a sharp pain followed by a welcome numbing. And then the drill whirred into life.

I always found it strange to look at the dentist while he was working on me. Although inches away from my face, he was completely absorbed in the work of my mouth, leaving me free to stare openly at him. Examining my dentist, the flecks of grey coloring in his eyes, the individual hairs of his white eyebrows, and the pores on his tanned nose, it occurred to me that the only time I got to look at another human being this closely was in bed with a lover.

> Oooh baby, light the fire,
> I'll pour the champagne
> We'll be making love till midnight,
> if our backs don't sprain . . .

Lite hits pumped into the room from speakers recessed in the ceiling: this one an old seventies song about drinking piña coladas in the rain. I always thought it was sadistic to play those kind of tunes while you drilled a hole through somebody's mouth. If I ever became a dentist, I had decided long ago that I'd play speed metal at full blast.

As the Hollywood dentist dug deeper down into the

root and the smell of burning tooth filled the air, the memories came to me, as if they were being released from the cracked enamel itself. Painkillers wearing off at three in the morning and an agony so fierce setting in that it would wake me up from sleep, screaming into my pillow in the dark house.

When teeth are broken, a massive, grim pain completely fills the mouth, where everything feels bigger to begin with. The agony is lodged right under the eyes and ears; it's near the brain and the voice, so the soul itself feels ground into oblivion. All joy is sucked from life, the world appears in monochrome. There aren't any crutches, there're no bandages, no casts, so there's no clue to the outside world that a ferocious suffering has been wrought upon you.

As I had learned to cover the exposed nerves in my mouth with my tongue, protecting their raw nakedness from freezing beer or hot tea, so had I learned to bury the black memories of my dental anguish. The initial year was a grueling nightmare of reconstruction, but as time went by, I managed to force myself to forget how much it had all hurt. The thrill of New York helped obscure the past, and by the time I was working with *Dusted*, my teeth had even become a kind of joke.

Stu used to run a column updating *Dusted* readers on my dental work, and Flash once did a *Spotlight!* section on Dr. Deal, and for one of my birthdays, they ran a full-page ad soliciting our favorite bands to play in the *Teef Relief* benefit show. None of them responded, of course, but some concerned readers made donations. I pulled in eight dollars, three sleeping pills, five English pounds, and a tube of toothpaste.

But now in Hollywood, so many years later, it was

me and my teeth again. There were no *Dusted* deadlines to distract me, no Stus and Flashes to laugh with, no New Guy to make me feel cool, as he asked me again to crack my jaw. The magic and legend had seeped out of my mouth, so my fractured teeth weren't a punk badge of honor anymore, but just a broken set of awful memories; mine alone to taste for life.

"Well then, that couldn't have been too bad," the dentist said with a slight chuckle about a half hour later. "I've never seen anyone fall asleep during a root canal before."

"Yeah, well, I'm used to them by now," I said, my tongue rubbing the top of my tooth tentatively, feeling the work. The dental assistant slipped off my blood-spattered bib, and the dentist slicked a tan hand through his iron grey hair, rising to his feet.

"Glad you had the work done. I wouldn't of slept well sending you off to Indonesia with a set of chompers like that. Believe me, I still don't feel great: you need to get that whole business fixed up and soon."

He looked closer at me and then smiled slightly. "Now, call it a sixth sense, but something tells me that you don't have any insurance. Am I right?"

"Umm, yeah."

"Ah yes, too old for your parents' plan, yet still young enough to believe it'll take a silver bullet to get you. Marcie, give our young argonaut a statement at reduced rates, and a penicillin prescription, as well," he said to his sidekick, who was switching off the work light.

"Yes sir."

The dentist leveled his finger at me in a friendly way. "You have yourself a great time, and try to get some diving in, too. I'd kill to fill up a dive log in that part of town. And next time you see Deal, you be sure and let him know who fixed up that last guy there."

"OK, I will. And thanks again for squeezing me in and all."

"You bet. Bye now." And with a dazzling white, movie-perfect smile, the Hollywood dentist disappeared out the door.

A moment later, I was out on the burning, auto-choked boulevard, gazing down at my bill under the blazing California sun. My eyes squinted in the glare, fixing on the simple, computer-printed number as a fluttering shock rippled through my body. The very last of my *Dusted* earnings had just been swallowed up by my mouth, and I was now officially broke.

My fat, numb tongue lolled in my deadened mouth, and I wondered if I could actually bust the final, most painful move in my scenario. But then I thought of the glittering black snake in the Adder Club's shadowed din, of the empty, hazy days in the Harbor, of Flash's fade, fate's call, and the wrenching, bitter battle with my mother. I had no choice, I realized, as I pedaled slowly down the sidewalk.

It was time to cut the cheese.

Bop Cheese was just one small interest of the Eternity Corporation, a mega-glom corporate empire that had spent the better part of the past fifteen years buying up small chunks of the planet. Among their current holdings were about fifteen cable networks, a major movie studio, a video rental chain, two publishing houses, an international airline, the largest privately owned genetic-engineering facility in the world, and *Bop Cheese* magazine.

I still wasn't sure whether corporations like Eternity were evil or just human evolution, but I needed funding for the dentist as well as my Java quest, and they were the ones holding the bills. Approaching the familiar corporate plaza in the late afternoon, a cool spray of water lighted upon my skin from the sprinkling fountains, and I squinted at them in the dazzling sun. The hard, slick angles of black marble were ideal for skateboarding, and I wondered how often the marauding packs of Hollywood skate rats descended upon the plaza. If they showed now, laughing and wild, kick-flipping their boards in high speed, concussion-courting tricks, I realized sadly that I wouldn't be a *Dusted* dude in on the joke, but another hapless worker running for cover.

Swallowing the thought, I walked into the imposing, air-conditioned tower of black tinted window walls as a steady trickle of nine-to-five droids revolved through the doors. A skinny, balding man, who had been there last time I called on the *Cheese*, played a baby grand piano in the corner, his classical recitation echoing thinly in the hard echo of the cool marble space. I made my way past him to a central stone podium, where a kid my age in a cheap company blazer stood, manning the controls.

"Can I help you?" he asked.

"I'm here to see Mandy at *Bop Cheese*."

"Your name?"

"They call me Neil."

Security punched an extension number into a panel of digits and dropped his voice to a deeper octave. "Hello, a 'Neil' is here to see Mandy," he said, inflecting my name as if I were a species of some sort. Nodding, he hung up the receiver.

"Elevators on the right, fortieth floor."

I walked across the marble to a waiting elevator, stepped in, and noiselessly began to ascend. After the extraordinary dis I had given Mandy, I was more than a little nervous about how she would receive me. Traitor feelings came in stronger as the hushed car speeded me upward, even as I told myself there was nothing to betray but a silent stack of back issues, and this was all necessary for *Neil Before God.* My last bank statement had been more of a mumble, and I would need some serious green in a serious hurry if I was to get Java bound. Still, as the bell binged and the doors opened before me, I felt the eyes of some invisible, *no sell-out!* downtown chorus glaring balefully at me as I stepped out to seize the *Cheese.*

The massive red *Bop Cheese!* logo screamed at me from the opposite wall, and I followed its familiar letters into a waiting area, where a cute receptionist sat paging through a fashion magazine. Outside the tinted window ahead of me, I could see the sun dying down below the horizon, its late afternoon rays changed to strange, apocalyptic shades through the prism of pollution that hung over the valley. Suddenly, I felt as if I were living in a chain-smoker's lung.

"Hey. I'm Neil. I have an appointment with Mandy,"
I said upon reaching the desk.

"Oh great, you're here! Just have a seat and she'll be
out in a jiffy."

Sure enough, a jiffy later, the *Bop Cheese* office door
burst open.

"NEIL!"

The familiar estrogen-overload holler came from
deep within a cloud of perfume, and Mandy winked
as she zipped toward the elevators. "Come on, babe,
let's get outta this tank."

I followed the mind behind the *Cheese* out of the
reception area as she turned to me, flipping her blond
hair over her shoulder. "Oh, God, I don't know why
I do what I do. It's insane. It's worse than that, it's
*un*sane. Neil baby, do I look like a crazy lady to
you?"

Her wide-open, blazing blue eyes stared directly into
mine, as if expecting an answer. I smiled and shrugged
as we entered the elevator.

"OK, babe, forget it, I'll answer: I am crazy. *Mandy
is* un*sane.* Know that first and foremost and everything
will be easier."

Mandy's black convertible was a sleek, leather seat
affair, and she drove fast. The car phone rang three
times within our ten-minute, swerving sprint cross-
town, and I listened silently while she conversed
wildly, laughing, growling, soothing or scorching the
various voices that called upon her. A table was waiting for us the instant we arrived at the trendy Thai
restaurant she had chosen for business, and no sooner

than my first noodle-thick bite did the bleach blond Mandy begin to *Bop.*

"OK babe, first things first. Let's clear up the past."

"Well, uh, you see . . . ," I stuttered.

"Don't bother, babe, I'll explain. You came out to L.A. talking contract, and you walked out on me. Bad move. If you were any older and you weren't so cute, you'd be a nonentity in the Mandy Universe. But now *Dusted* is caput, you're here, and all is forgiven because you're going to write me one hell of an article. *Capisce?*"

"Sure, Mandy, I ca peace."

"Timing, babe. Timing is everything, and you hit it dead on. You know, of course, the Chockapolacka festival is kicking off in Vegas next week . . ."

Of course I knew about Chockapolacka; it was impossible for anyone with a television set and half an eyeball not to. Flipping through The Channel at any hour, Chockapolacka could be seen advertised every other nanosecond as *the* event of a young consumer's lifetime. The all-day, all-night music affair was the "alternative" rock scene's annual tour, which hauled its way, stadium to stadium, around the country every summer. Every band with a music vid hit in the Alternaverse was on the bill, jamming out for thousands of disaffected youth with disposable incomes, every one of them laying down fifty bucks a ticket in the name of punk.

"So here it is, Neil: I want to send *you* to Las Vegas to cover Chockapolacka for *Bop Cheese.* We've already got the photographer; he's shot for *Buddha Smoke,* knows you, loves your writing, can't wait to work with you. You two together. PHAA! It'll be unreal. I even phoned in reservations already, because that town is going to be *packed* for Chocka!"

"It sounds great Mandy, but I'm gonna need my cash on acceptance, not publication."

"For you babe, no problem."

"And um, what do you pay?"

"It's our feature piece, Neil. Five thousand words, five thousand dollars."

A cash register sounded in my brain as I quickly calculated just how far I could float on five balloons.

Mandy eyed me for a while over our dinner. "*Dusted* was a lot of fun, wasn't it?"

"Yeah, it was."

"It's too bad it didn't last; really, I'm sorry for you guys. I guess you've got to think about taking care of yourself and those teeth." She lit a cigarette and smiled. "And you don't have a trust fund to fall back on, babe, like your pal Flash."

The sounds in the restaurant, the clinking forks and scraping chairs, the soft sound track of night-life music and the clatter of dishes being prepped and pushed out of the kitchen, all of it faded away, replaced by a low buzzing noise in my ears as I stared at Mandy's glinting blue eyes.

"*What?*"

"I said you don't have a trust fund to fall back on, like your pal Flash." She brushed her hair back with a jingling flick of her bracelet-heavy hand, then started to laugh. "Neil, baby, don't tell me you didn't know!"

"N-no," I stammered, reaching for my drink.

"Babe, his father is *the* biggest plastic surgeon in Hollywood; mommy's got her own law firm . . . kid was born and raised Hollywood. Quite a racket his parents run, too: she divorces 'em, and then he gives 'em a face-lift so they can bag the next one." She laughed again, sipping her iced tea. "Great people, we've done dinner, they're a riot."

The last of Mandy's drink slurped upward through her straw, and I stared out the widow, to the cars glinting past in a speeding flow down the boulevard. But the cars I didn't see: Flash's grinning face danced before me, his laughter running circles round my shock-rocked mind. From far away across the table, I heard my new editor's voice.

"His father must flip over those tattoos! And he's got a show on The Channel? And Gertie, too? Phaa! We should all be so glamorous."

"Y . . . yeah, yeah we should," I said, pulling my senses back to the restaurant, to the table, to Mandy. I smiled with all the strength I had. "But I guess some of us have dental bills."

"Phaa! Babe, I love ya. Did I ever tell you about the root canal I had in Florence? Forget about it." Mandy waved her hand and took a thirsty swig from her mineral water. "Neil, I got a feeling this is just the start of something rad, fab, and all that. You with me?"

I smiled weakly and raised my beer, which evidently didn't serve as sufficient confirmation in the Mandy Universe.

"C'mon babe, I want to hear you," she said with a bullying grin.

"I'm with you, Mandy," I said, swallowing my samurai code of honor.

She raised her glass of sparkling mineral water. "We need a toast then. What to?"

"To punk," I said wanly, raising my beer.

"Perfect, babe! To punk!"

I clicked cheers with my new editor, and as my tongue rubbed slowly over my freshly derooted tooth, I heard the taunting sound of Flash's Hollywood laughter ringing in my burning ears.

6. chockapolacka

As I threw a pair of socks into my backpack, I watched a frizzy-haired girl on Stu's TV, holding a microphone in the empty Las Vegas stadium. Far in the background, techies could be seen scuttling across the distant stage, gaffing, adjusting, and tweaking amidst the towers of metal scaffolding and coils of electric circuitry. The trademark Chockapolacka banners, massive sails depicting brightly colored fractal patterns and ancient religious symbols, rippled wildly in the wind above them. Soon, the familiar, universally despised face in the foreground began to speak.

"Viva Las Vegas! HEY! Johnson here at the grand kick-off of this year's Chockapolacka, which promises to be the woolliest one of 'em all! Yessirini, this here gambling mecca is crawling with punks . . . you can hardly turn around without getting your wallet chain caught on a nose ring! Haw! I mean, come on people, Alternative Rock has never seen anything like this before!"

Johnson's personal security detail, tall black men in double-breasted suits, stood stolidly at the edge of the screen. They had been employed by the network after Johnson's personality proved to be almost lethally obnoxious; in New York, she had been decked twice in the street, and at the spring-break special in Miami, the video host had been hit by a brick and a used condom. After taking steps to protect their investment, the network went on to double her hours. Johnson, I imagined, was a priceless asset. Through her revolting magic she had drawn together a disparate demographic in the fast bond of mutual hatred.

And I supposed she and Flash were colleagues now. As I set the security system, hoping the neighborhood thieves wouldn't be suspicious of the Ice Sports Channel for three days in a row, I recalled the strained talk Terrance and I had had about him the night before.

"Yeah, I knew Flash was rich," Terrance had said over the phone.

"Why didn't anyone tell me?"

"Why does it matter?"

"I don't know . . . it just does. Damn, me and Flash starved on Fifth Street, and he had loot all the time."

"Look, far as I know, his parents don't grease him any. Flash is doing it on his own."

"But don't you feel weird?"

"About what?"

"That . . ." My voice trailed off, but inside my head, I screamed the rest of my thought: *THAT HE DIDN'T SAVE DUSTED!! THAT HE DIDN'T HELP ME FIX MY TEETH!!*

"Neil?"

I exhaled. "I don't know. I just feel weird."

"Maybe you could ask him at Chocka."

"How do you mean?"

"You didn't talk to him?" Terrance went on, "He's doing some of his show at the concert."

"Hey, what do you know, a reunion."

"Yeah, I guess it is. Me and the New Guy are going to Chockapolacka too, for *Buddha Smoke*. You need a ride?"

My heart sank further into a messy ooze of bad feelings. "Nah, the *Bop* copped me a plane ticket."

"Nice."

"Yeah."

There was a silence between us, and then I cleared my throat, even though it didn't even need to be cleared. "Well yo, I got to get my stuff ready. I guess I'll see you there."

"Yeah, take it easy, Cheesy."

Mandy had set me up in the King Arthur, a newly constructed medieval theme hotel/casino, with knights in armor walking around, a Merlin magic show every night, and other *ye olde* type accoutrements, all housed in a massive, cartoonlike castle. Crossing the moat and entering the main portcullis, I checked in with the fair maiden at the front desk, then went straight up to my room for a regulation disco nap. I had a long night of wry, detached observation ahead of me and needed all the snooze I could catch.

"DUDE! NEIL! You in there?" an excited voice shouted from through the door, the moment I lay down. With a quiet growl, I walked across the room and opened the door.

"Whassup cuz! Chockapolacka YEOW!!"

Standing barefoot before me on the King Arthur carpet was a sun-dazzled, grinning guy with a mop of shaggy blond, beach-bleached hair hanging completely over his eyes. A scratched pair of designer ski shades hung round his neck, and his baggy, faded pink shorts only half-covered a collection of scabs and scratches I imagined he had picked up while skating. Extending his hand, the stranger introduced himself. "I'm Ray. The photographer. Got your room number from Mandy."

"Hey, how's it goin'."

"Dude. Totally psyched to be working with you. Come down to my room?"

"Yeah, sure." I shut the door behind me and followed Ray down the fluorescent-lit hallway to a room identical to my own, except for the tough looking chick who was sitting near the TV. I took in her jet-black hair, braided tightly in two tails behind her, the sharp green eyes outlined in black, and the striped red and blue tank top, cutoff shorts, and battered skate shoes that completed her look.

"Neil, this is Barb, my girlfriend. She's kinda my assistant, too."

"Assistant?" Barb cut in. "Please, I'm more like your mother. You were halfway through last week's shoot before I noticed the lens cap was still on." She gave a curt wave. "Nice to meet you."

I turned back to Ray and noticed that he was at work packing up a long, well-used bong that had been hiding behind the chair.

"Dude, we could get *housed* for this. Vegas is, like, a zero-tolerance state," the photographer said, pushing a pinch of thick, green buds into the metal pipe. "I picked up an ounce of killer Santa Cruz hydroponic on the way down. . . . That's like, ten years here."

He took a hit, then passed the bong on to Barb. She took a strong, deep pull, then held out the blue plastic tube to me. I passed it back to Ray without taking my share.

"Dude, you're not bakin'?"

"Nah, when I smoke I just get paranoid and hungry, and then I get a boner."

Ray exploded in laughter, busting out a billowing cloud of Santa Cruz hydro. "DUUUUUUUDE!!! IT'S NEIL! WE'RE CHILLIN' WITH NEIL!!!"

"He's been a *Dusted* fan forever," Barb said, speaking in soft, sarcastic tones, as if Ray were her special kid brother. "Don't worry, he'll calm down."

"Hell no, woman, I'm just gettin' up! We's with *Dusted* Neil here, and we's gonna party, even if he does get a boner!"

He passed the bong my way again, and I waved it away with a smile.

"Don't sweat him, Ray. He doesn't want to smoke," Barb told him.

"All right, chill. Yo, how's your chomps dude? That was like, my favorite part of *Dusted*, when you used to go off on your teeth."

My tongue ran instinctively over the old ruins. "They're all right."

"I had some cavities and all when I was little, but dude, nothing like you. But I knew this skater cat in San Pedro, he was busting out this nose grind down like, three flights, and he totally clocked, like—BAM!— right on his face. His teeth were like, spread all over the cement. I mean, like spread, dude, like all mushed . . . it was so sick. I found his front tooth, dude, root and all, and that bad boy looked like a golf tee. I mean, we only see this little bit, but those suckas run deep." The photographer took a hit, held his smoke, then slowly exhaled a hazy stream into the air-conditioned room. "Dude, teeth are gnarly."

Feeling a dental flashback coming on, I walked toward the window to escape. The sun had dropped down behind the desert mountains hours ago, but a dazzling ecstasy of electric lights blazed up and down the Strip, illuminating Las Vegas before me. I watched as a steady stream of people flowed along the dirty sidewalk below: packs of scowling young Alternates in ripped jeans, nose rings, goatees, and dyed hair pushing past gangs of overweight, sunburned senior citizens, in a surreal cross section of America's past and future.

Only half of me was watching, though, as a dark jag of buried memories ripped through my mind, triggered by Ray's story. I forced them down as always, far away back in my brain, but the look on my face must have betrayed the struggle.

"Dude, I saw on TV somewhere that teeth are like, the best source of DNA in the body."

Barb turned from me and glared, eyes jabbing, at her boyfriend. "Maybe we could change the subject?"

Ray saw me by the window and stopped. "Aw, I'm sorry." He scratched at his leg. "That was ignorant."

"No, it's cool," I said to him.

"It's just . . . I really respect you, Neil." Ray said softly, holding the bong idly at his side and looking up at me through his hair. "Like suffering, dude, it makes you strong."

It was silent for a while, and then Barb got up and quietly began to pack up the photo gear.

The stadium appeared like a white, glowing bowl of electrical alchemy in the distance, the faint explosions of drums and droning guitars growing louder the closer Ray, Barb, and I rolled in the photographer's van. As Ray turned the wheel into the lot, looking for a space, the headlights beamed over the roving posses of Alternates shuffling about, looking like extras killing time between takes of some epic-scale music video.

Thanks to The Channel, kids who lived hundreds of miles apart, who had never met or communicated, milled about looking as if they had all borrowed each other's clothes. With their faded punk T-shirts, cut flannels, black boots, backward baseball hats, tattoos, dyed hair, pierced noses, oversize jeans, and wallets chained to their belts, it was as if an entire generation had fallen victim to some weird strain of schizophrenic rebellion, in which each was trying to look different in the exact same way.

Barb, her boyfriend, and I approached the gate, skipping the lengthy line of ticket holders and flashing our *Bop Cheese* All-Access Passes to the security goon with smooth nonchalance. As a rope was raised and we slipped into the stadium, I noticed a gang of dorky, zitty guys look on in longing.

"There's a way to get laid with one of these things, right?" I said to Ray, flipping over the laminated card as if to find instructions on the back.

"Totally dude. Flash it at some little Alternate spank and you'll find out why they call it *all access.*"

Following a pathway through the stadium's wood-chip garden, we soon entered the arena, passing through a sticky cement antechamber of a million spilled beers, then emerging into the cool night of the open-air stadium. Conversational tones were immediately crushed by the storm of Chockapolacka's legendary sound system, as the three of us, standing atop a stairway leading down to the floor, stared in awe of what lay below.

Bathed in a blaze of white sulfur lights ringed around the stadium, a roiling, sweaty sea of Alternates churned to the sonic avalanche unleashed upon them from the stage. Not a single scrap of safe ground seemed visible as the teeming thousands clashed and bashed at each other's bodies. As I watched from far above, a young face would every so often become clear to me: contorted in anger, giddy with glee, revved in manic excitement, or frowning in frustration as arms lashed out, boots kicked up, bodies went down, and the pummeled were rescued. Sporadic punks were launched spontaneously in the air, passed overhead and dropped to the dirt, and lithe young girls surveyed the scene from atop their boyfriends' tattooed shoulders. Gazing on, I half imagined my old teenage self somewhere in the din of it all.

"Damn, I haven't been to a show in a *while,*" Ray said slowly, taken back by the bedlam.

"If one of those pre-pube losers lays a hand on me, they're gonna find out what punk really is," Barb snarled over the noise.

Her boyfriend loaded another roll of film and wound the camera. "Dude, you ready?"

"Yeah," I answered. "Let's do it."

The noise was a deafening din, the crowd a sweaty mess, but by circumnavigating the stadium wall, we were able to make it backstage without getting hauled into the violent stew of teenage frustrations. Our *Bop Cheese* All-Access Passes had the goon at the gate lift a velvet maroon rope for us, and we walked up a set of stairs, behind the amp system, to find ourselves backstage, in the Chockapolacka Players Club.

"Anyone need a beer?" I asked.

"Sure."

Through the crowd, I spotted a kiddie pool filled with beer, ice, and champagne on the far corner of the large, wooden platform that served as backstage. I walked through the thick crowd of rockers, techies, groupies, and hangers-on, all chatting and laughing as the echoed sound of the onstage band filled the night air. The mellow mood, illuminated by strings of soft red beach-party lights, was cut only by the intermittent flash of press cameras, and the sharp, roving beams of light from The Channel's video crew.

"So what's the *Dusted* Neil plan of attack?" Ray asked me when I returned with the beers.

"Probably just chill back here for a while. I mean, it's a mess out front, and the beers are free."

"Are you gonna interview anyone?"

"Nah. I usually just walk around and watch things, then make stuff up."

"Well, I gotta catch some pics, so I'm gonna go peruse the stadium." He checked his film in his side pocket, smiling and excited to be backstage. "Barb, wanna come?"

"I'm gonna hang. I have like, zero tolerance for the teeny punks."

"All right then, I'm out. Meet back here in a bit." He leaned over and gave his girlfriend a kiss on the cheek.

"Have fun, hon," she said after him as he shot us a grin and twisted through the crowd toward the stairs.

Barb turned to me. "Hey, I'm really sorry about Ray. You know, with your teeth and all back at the hotel. He can be an idiot." She rolled her eyes and shook her head, causing the shining black braids of hair to slap lightly against her bare shoulders.

"Nah, it's not just him. Everybody talks about teeth around me."

"Serious though, I feel for you. I had like, two root canals, and it floored me for a week. You must have been through hell." Her eyes focused then on a point somewhere behind me. "Hey, isn't that your friend?"

I turned to see Flash standing with Runny R and a gathered crew, laughing and joking before a hand-held camera.

"Looks like he did in the magazine," she said. "Maybe he could hook us up with the Pepper, so Ray could get some shots."

I swallowed a cold flow of beer. "I don't know. I mean, I'll ask. But he looks kinda busy now. He's doing his show, you know."

We stood for a while in the laughing, lounging, celebrity-thick crowd of Alternaverse luminaries, while the music from the stage thundered out into the stadium.

Barb turned to me. "So how did that all go down between you guys, you know, with *Dusted* going broke."

"We're still friends," I said quickly. "I mean, it's different now. Flash has got his own groove going."

"Yeah, right. Getting famous as we speak, and the kid's already loaded."

I almost choked on the beer. "How . . . how did you know?"

"Hollywood is like, so small," Barb said with a dismissive wave. "I grew up there." She laughed a little. "Still recovering, too. City's built for cute little blondes. Sucked for me."

"So you knew Flash?"

"I didn't hang with him, just like, knew him from around, seeing him at shows and all. He went to Oakridge for a while, which is like *the* private school for every hard-core Hollywood power kid. But then he ditched it and dyed his hair, switched to a public school in the Valley. Started hanging with the skater crew."

From across the way, I watched Flash talking with the cameraman, who I now recognized as the director I had seen in the studio.

Barb laughed again, taking a drag from her cigarette. "I always thought that was funny. You know, *Dusted* was always like, utmost punk, No Sell Out and all that. But Flash was a total rich kid." I watched her glinting eyes narrow for a second, and then she shrugged. "It's cool though, whatever. Be what you want . . . but he's still Oakridge to me."

Over her shoulder I saw Flash moving away from his crew now, cutting through the crowd toward us.

"I'm gonna check out the show for a while," I said to Barb.

And before my old friend and I could cross paths, I slipped behind an amp stack, past a trio of technicians, and made my way to the side of the stage. A loose group was gathered just on the wings, watching the latest electrified act of fury wailing out in the desert night. Relieved to have dodged Flash, I joined them, crossing my arms over my chest and leaning back against an unused sound monitor.

I gazed out below the stage, to the thousands upon thousands of sweaty young faces upturned in raw adulation, desperate and frenzied. A crush of guitars shuddered through the night, as a sweat-soaked lead singer flailed and wailed mere feet from where I stood, his blood-rushed face contorted and twisting in riff running growls. I sipped my beer, disinterested, imagined some young punk packed down thick in the teen melee, eyeing me in envy on my backstage perch on the edge of the Alternaverse.

But as the songs droned on, one hit after the other, and another glam-furious band replaced the next, I found myself sinking into envy for those in the sweaty mass below me. My mind recalled a million similar teenage nights as I thrashed wildly in some concert pit, and I wished back for that life. Standing at the very edge of the music, as if by being closer I might catch it all again, I watched on as the Alternaverse's reigning prince of moods released a lushly orchestrated suburban-angst anthem into the night. Ecstatic screams of solidarity from the gathered thousands erupted up to meet it, and I envied them all, envied a time when it took noth-

ing more than a Rage Against the Chili Pepper stage
rush to give my life meaning.

"NEIL!"

I turned, and Flash was there.

"What are you doing here?" he said, the same instant
his eyes focused on my stage pass. "BOP CHEESE!
ALL RIGHT!" He raised his hands for a high five and
I met them.

"Whassup, Flash."

"Chocka rockin' man! MAN OH MAN! IT'S NEIL!"

Flash had his wig on now, and was holding the
super-8 camera he had been running around with,
catching candid footage for his show. Not only taping,
Flash was being featured live backstage along with
Johnson in coverage of the event. Followed by her camera crew, the notorious video host had been stomping
the scene all night in her big black boots, letting loose
with an arsenal of snide asides and obnoxious laughter,
assaulting anyone she could get her microphone under.
A closed-circuit line connected her cameras with two
massive screens on either side of the stage, and between Flash's antics, and her brutal, backstage sarcasm,
the two had provided comic relief to the masses out
front, as well as millions of viewers across the country.

From behind Flash, a familiar white b-boy shuffled
up at his side. Flash turned and spoke. "R, do you
know Neil? We used to work together at *Dusted.*"

"Yo, s'up," Runny R muttered, nodding his head.

I gazed at him for too long, my mind calculating the
number of times I had listened to his lyrics and wished
I was in on his grandiose world of fat beats and females.

"How's the article going?" Flash asked.

"What? Um, great. You know, *Bop Cheese.* How hard can it be?"

"It's cool, though, you know, getting the work."

"Yeah," I said.

We stood for a moment, and I felt an explosion of questions, accusations, and screams struggling inside me: *Oakridge, trust funds, plastic surgeons, the Palisades . . .*

But before I could speak them, Flash suddenly burst in. "HEY! What are you doing later? I mean, after the show?"

"Uh, no plans. Why, what's going on?"

Runny R pulled up his oversize jeans and muttered from beneath his beach hat, "Yo Flash, come on, I gotta get ready."

Flash turned to me, walking backward as he followed Runny R. "Sorry! I got to get back to work! But hang around! I'll meet you!"

"Where?" I shouted over the music.

But Flash didn't hear me, just started a song I could barely hear over the sonic jam of guitars:

> *Meet me later on!*
> *And we will do no wrong!*
> *We'll . . . uh, um . . . ?*

I followed him to try to ask again, but backed off as I saw Flash closed in by the Pepper groupies near their trailer. My eyes caught Gertie among them, legs crossed, sipping a mineral water, dressed up in a black evening gown like pop culture royalty. I watched as rockers, young actors, and others came by to pay their respects and could hear her high laughter, loud and often, over the jam on the other side of the stage. Suddenly, she broke away and ran, chasing after Flash and grabbing him up in her arms, covering him with kisses as he fought to escape.

Barb appeared at my side, handing me another cold beer. "Jesus, you'd think they were in fourth grade," she said in disgust, motioning with her head toward Gertie and Flash.

I snapped the top and drank down the cold fluid as Barb gazed around us at the cute and famous, idling on couches, semiposed for pictures, as they casually chatted. "What a bunch of duds, huh? No one's having sex, no one's doing drugs, and they're not even dressed well. I mean, backstage is completely unglamorous and mundane."

She lit a cigarette, exhaling the smoke long and cool, and I was just about to mention Gertie when I was cut off by a familiar bray of stomach turning laughter.

"HAAWWWWW HAWWWW!!!" The harsh bray sprayed through the party chatter behind us, and there was no need to turn to see who was there.

"Oh Jesus, Johnson," I muttered.

Walking right to us, the VJ planted herself before Barb with a smarmy, girlish grin.

"Excuse me," she began, "I know you're not familiar back here, so I understand why you wouldn't know the rules. But you happen to be in violation: smoking is not permitted backstage at Chockapolacka." Her blue eyes glimmered from behind heavy horn-rimmed glasses, and I could see through the cake of studio makeup on her face that she was sweating.

"You've got to be kidding me," Barb scoffed, staring her down.

"I'm no kidder! It's the rules. The fellas in Rage

Against the Chili Pepper are allergic to cigarette smoke and well, I'm glad too, because as we all know, that secondhand smoke is a killer-diller!"

And without a moment's more hesitation, the VJ quickly licked her two fingers, reached out, and extinguished Barb's cigarette.

I saw rage, pure and primal, surge up in Barb's blazing green eyes and wondered if The Channel would spring for Johnson's reconstructive surgery. A low murmur of *awwww!*'s went out from the backstage party, who had ceased conversation to become spectators of the emerging event.

But instead of exploding, Barb calmly dropped the dead cigarette at the feet of the grinning video host. Gazing icily into Johnson's eyes, she reached into her bag for another one, placed it in her mouth, and flicked the lighter as she spoke.

"Lick a tit, babe. This is a friggin' rock show."

The backstage gang let loose with a low round of *ooooooo!*'s

Johnson smirked. "Would that be *my* tit or *your* tit?" she said, grinning, to her foe. "Because if it's yours . . . I don't know. I just can't stand to get hair caught in my teeth." She spun away and walked toward her crowd.

"Mayday! Mayday! Ice-cold dyke in the house! Johnson requests backup!" the VJ shouted wryly, moving into the midst of her wildly laughing groupies.

"That's right, run away, you no-talent tart! They only keep you on the goddamn Channel so everyone can have someone to hate!"

"WHOOOAAA!" Johnson let loose in mock fear, backed by her laughing posse of Alternaverse stars. "Aren't *we* sore we're not famous!"

Barb threw out her cigarette and began to stalk toward Johnson. I started after her.

"C'mon Barb . . ."

"Watch out! Here she comes, big bad smoker!" Johnson shouted, edging deeper into the famous crowd.

I reached Barb and put my hand softly on her shoulder. "Forget it. If you deck her, The Channel will probably sue you. She'll be reruns in a year, anyway. "

"She inn't gonna live that long. The bitch dies. Tonight."

Barb started forward again, and I looked over to Johnson's protective posse just in time to see Gertie clear the smile off her face and emerge from the pack, striding gracefully toward us. Placing herself before a simmering Barb, the movie star spoke in sweet, pleading tones.

"Come on now, I know you don't want to get in a fight."

For a moment, I lost my place in the scuffle, rendered literally speechless at being next to Gertie after all these years.

"Please, don't," Gertie begged, lightly taking Barb's arm. "Johnson can be terrible. But you don't want to do something you'll regret."

"Outta my face, blondie," Barb muttered, fazed not in the slightest that she was growling at the star of *Tooky.*

"Fine," Gertie said, backing away, her hands up. "I was just trying to help you . . . I doubt you're coming across well on camera."

"*What?*"

As if breaking from a trance, Barb looked around her, noticing for the first time Johnson's cameramen, who had been recording the action all the while. Just then, Ray rushed into the scene, out of breath and wild-eyed.

"What the hell's going on! Barb, Jesus, you're up on the screens out in front of the stage!"

"I . . . what?" A stunned look came over Barb's face, and from the other side of the stage, an entire stadium of Chockapolacka fans began to laugh uproariously.

"Looks like Johnson got another one! And don't she look baaaaaaaddd!" a faceless voice intoned, the words echoing out over the stadium. A surge of laughter rolled from the stadium bowl.

"Yer famous now, sister!" Johnson shouted with vicious glee at Barb, her eyes widening in shock. A mounting wave of cheers and screaming rose up from the crowd, drowning the noise out even backstage. A chant began.

"JOHNSON! JOHNSON! JOHNSON!"

"You . . . BITCH!!!" Barb finally shrieked, plunging wildly into the crowd of Alternaverse stars after Johnson.

"Get her offa me! Get her offa me!" The VJ screamed as a raging Barb grabbed hold of a thick clump of her mousy brown hair, raising a clenched fist high in the air.

But before she could connect, security swarmed in, yanking the writhing, screeching Barb out of the tangle of bodies that had gathered round to shield Johnson from her attack.

"THAT'S RIGHT! GET THAT SLUT OFFAA ME!!" Johnson shouted with wicked glee. "Murray! KEEP THE CAMERA ON!!"

The lights swung toward Barb, following her humiliating struggle as she fought in vain to get free. "LET GO OF ME YOU BASTARDS!!"

They dragged her away, past the smug crowd of famous faces ringed around the jeering Johnson. The bright, shining light from the cameras illuminated the VJ in wild detail as she leaned over the railing, shouting after her decimated opponent.

Come on girl! You want some more! You want some of this!" she shouted after Barb, clutching her microphone and flexing her skinny arms. From the stadium, a massive roar went up into the desert night, as the Alternates watched Johnson's victory on the towering, close-circuit screens from either side of the stage.

And suddenly, a riff everyone knew by heart ripped out from the sound stacks, as Rage Against the Chili Pepper rushed the stage in their headline spot, driving the thousands of Chockapolackers into an utter, roaring frenzy.

Instantly forgetting the fight, the backstage party raced to the wings, and I ran the opposite way, after Barb and Ray. I scanned through the now empty backstage, then busted toward the lone security guard standing near the ropes.

"HEY!" I shouted as Rage Against the Chili Pepper hit rhyming stride over the bass-heavy beats. "WHERE'S THAT GIRL?!? THE ONE IN THE FIGHT!"

"She's outta here!" he said with a derisive nod, jerking his thumb toward the roaring mass of fans pushing and mashing on the screaming stadium floor.

I bolted past him down the steps, where a crowd of zitty teens were gathered, hopeful for a brush with fame.

"DUDE! BACKSTAGE! GET ME IN!" a skinny, wobbling, drunken kid slurred, reaching out for me as I pushed past him from the stairs.

"Move it!"

"*UGGGGMNNM!*" I saw his face go green, and felt a warm, wet explosion smack against my skin, then looked down in shocked revulsion to see the young punk's puke seeping down my side.

"YOU LITTLE . . . !" I screamed, drowned out by booming drums as the kid collapsed down on the trampled grass, heaving up chunks of cheese dog. The moshing crowd tore me away from the stairs, and I turned, pushing violently through their sweating masses, scraping the hot, reeking vomit on the soaked shirts of those crushed against me.

Fury roaring through me, I tripped through the crowding, teeming teen bodies until I finally reached the stairs. Bounding up three at a time, Rage's ego-blown raps piercing through the PA system all around me, I ran through the rocking stands, outside the stadium. A spraying fountain, empty now of splashing concertgoers, promised me relief in the wood-chip-strewn garden. As I headed for it, reeking of hot vomit, I wondered ruefully how I would parlay tonight's events into a quirky *Bop Cheese* piece that would make everyone laugh and wish they were me.

"Neil!"

The old, familiar voice stopped me dead, just as I reached the water.

Terrance.

Of course my old friend would have to see me now, in order to make my night the utmost in humiliation. Loathing the inevitable encounter, I turned to face him and felt my misery double as I saw the grinning New Guy at his side.

"S'up?" Terrance said, reaching out to shake my hand. "We were just catching some air. Jesus! You reek!"

"Yeah," I muttered. "Some little Alternate punked on me."

"Damn," he said, laughing. "That's ill. PHEW!!"

Terrance waved his hand before his face as he backed away. I took off my *Bop Cheese* All-Access Pass and dipped it in the water, rubbing the chunks of punk barf off its laminated surface before turning, holding it out to the New Guy.

"You want this?"

Astonishment lit his eyes. "Uh . . . sure! I mean, if you don't need it anymore."

"You're not sticking around for the Pepper?" Terrance asked.

I shook my head. "Nah. I'm done here."

"Wow, thanks, Neil," the New Guy said, taking my pass by his finger and letting it dangle at his side. I knew he was grateful, but I could already see his article in my head, edited in typical *Buddha Smoke* style. The elder draftsmen of the magazine, eager to pass on their craft, would patiently, gently guide their new scribe to skillfully coax forth the sneering juvenile contempt from our encounter. I knew the *Buddha* would tax me hard for cutting the *Cheese*, but this was going to be too good: a pukey Neil hands off his *Bop Cheese* All-Access Pass to the New Guy. Jesus, his first article was going to be a cinch.

"We saw Ray," Terrance said.

"Know him?"

"He used to skate, yeah. Said he was taking his girl-friend back to the hotel, said he'd be back for you."

"OK, thanks. Guess I'm out," I said, extending my hand for slaps.

"Bye, dude," the New Guy said.

"What are you up to later on?" Terrance asked.

"Nothing," I said, stripping off my shirt and holding it under the running water. "Just want to finish this piece and get out of here. I'm leaving, man."

"Ditching Vegas tonight?"

"I mean I'm leaving Hollywood. I'm out. Done."

"Oh." Terrance stood silently for a second, rubbing his bald head. "Where you going?" he said softly. "Back to New York?"

"No, I'm splitting the whole scene. I'm going to write *Neil Before God* in Java." I wrung out my shirt and slipped back into it.

"Rad!" The New Guy grinned.

"Where's Java?" Terrance asked, frowning.

I was suddenly impatient, angry even. "Southeast Asia. You know, near the Nam, Thailand, and all. Look, I gotta go man."

"OK. I don't want to hold you up." Terrance looked at me, then down at his beat-up black boots. Behind us, the sound of yet another Rage Against the Chili Pepper hit boomed out into the black night.

"Take it easy, cheesy," Terrance said, wrapping his hand around mine in a soul shake. "And good luck."

"Yeah, good luck Neil," the New Guy copied.

A smile flickered across my lips. "Thanks."

Before anything more could be said, I turned and walked fast toward the barbed-wire-fence exitway. A loose gang of fat security guards were leaning against their posts, laughing and talking with each other around a trash can full of confiscated booze.

"ALL EXITS ARE FINAL!" one of them yelled as I raced past.

Standing at the edge of a nearly endless cement expanse of automobiles, I realized that I couldn't stay here another minute waiting for Ray to come back. Behind me, the concert raged on, booming out in echoing thunder from the stadium; across the dark distance beyond, I saw the shimmering, sparkling electric lights of the Strip. Still fuzzy from the beer I had drunk backstage, I calculated the distance and decided it couldn't be that far. The ride over had been less than twenty minutes, and it had been by a circuitous connection of roads. If I cut straight through the desert, I figured I was certain to hit my medieval theme hotel within an hour.

Using the light of the Strip as my marker, I cut boldly through the parking lot, out into the dark wasteland. As I walked on, the heat of physical effort began burning off my beer buzz, and clearheaded, I cut my way across the rocky, silent terrain, illuminated enough by moon glow to keep me from falling. By the time the stadium had faded into silence behind me, I felt all of the snarled thoughts in my head—about Flash, about Barb and Oakridge, about the sickening backstage scene I had witnessed—becoming lost in the rhythm of motion.

The hours passed, and I realized that I hadn't had a walk so long since the sticky spring mornings right after my accident, and the epic hikes I took between my dentist's office and high school. I remembered now, as I tramped through the dusty Las Vegas desert, the old family dentist who had first treated me in the early mornings before school. I remembered seeing my X-rays for the first time after the accident, as his aged, liver-spotted hand pointed out various points on the ghostly grey images of my shattered mouth: the ominous black spaces welled in the grey gum line, and thin, hairline cracks spidered through the white teeth. And as the dentist pointed out each trauma, he had laid a price tag on me: $300, $450, $600, until the numbers had lost their meaning, and I felt the weight of inescapable debt settle down on top of me, heavy as the stone pain pinning me to the chair.

My parents had no dental insurance, and after I'd rejected my father's offer for college, he seemed to take an almost sadistic glee in watching me sweat out the astronomical sum of mouth damage. The family dentist could only fit in the lengthy, near surgical work in the very early mornings, and as my mom and dad both worked, neither of them had time to wait around while I had my dental nerves rewired. Groggy from sleep, I would be dropped off at the dentist's office not long after dawn, left to endure the torture and then find my own way to school. My face a numb frown, the taste of cold metal and blood still lingering on my tongue, I would try in vain to hitch rides from the blank-faced commuters blurring past. But no one ever stopped for the lone dental derelict trudging the roadside, and I was forced to walk the miles to school every day, my freshly smashed mouth a grinding ache all the way. . . .

Exhausted and still trudging through the dark, dusty desert, I realized that my eyes had played a cruel, nasty trick on me. My legs were aching and burning, the hip joints aching from the march, but for all my walking, the blinking lights of the Strip seemed no closer. Anger flared through me, and suddenly I felt as if I were still that broken-mouth kid on the grey strip of suburban roadway, passed by car after speeding car. For all the writing, for all of New York, for all the world that I had sucked down in a travel-mad frenzy, I was still broke and walking alone.

"Pick me up!!" I screamed into the black night. *"God-dammit! Pick me up!"*

Without warning, hot, bitter tears of anger flooded my dirty face, and the distant lights blurred before me. Angrily, I smeared them off my face with filthy, rough hands and stumbled on as the sobs overtook my body. Was it for Flash? Was it for Barb? Was I crying for the Terrance I left behind or for those stupid kids scrambling and screaming in the stadium or was it my Scotch-soaked parents or that old family dentist or my squalid, *Bop Cheese* existence . . . Or maybe I was crying for those days of dental dementia, so long past, but never farther than the touch of my tongue. I didn't know anymore, and I didn't even care, I just wanted out of the desert, out of the night, out of my life and into the heavy, kissed nothing of sleep.

At some point, a switch inside me flipped. My heart, my head, my tears, it all clicked off and I became a ragged machine of pure motion, walking doggedly through the dust to the lights. Some more time passed, but I couldn't know how long I had staggered when I finally stepped out of the still, shadowed desert, into the electrified frenzy of the Strip. Shell-shocked, dirty, numbed and near delirious, I found my medieval-theme hotel and walked directly through the lobby gambling games, oblivious to the chingling change and card-calling dealers, the buxom, fair maiden waitresses, and anxious, luck-hungry players all around me.

I had just reached ye olde elevatore and was inches away from pushing the button when I saw them round the corner.

Flash was decked in a sharply pressed, jet-black tuxedo, his hair bright green and freshly dyed. Gertie was at his side, in her black, lowcut evening wear, a string of pearls dangling round her neck. Runny R and the boys had long since quit the stage, ditching the b-boy getups for lush, wine-colored velvet tuxes, and sleek women surrounded them, curved bodies hugged tight in glamorous gowns. Easy laughter lilted between them all, as Johnson, wearing a garish purple prom dress, tagged along with her camera crew.

It was she who spotted me first, standing before their evening elegance, a vision of desert dirt, tear stains, and dried vomit.

"Hey, isn't that the *Dusted* guy?" Johnson shouted. "*HAHAWW!*"

The crowd looked my way and broke up in laughter, but I saw worry on Flash's face, just before he turned sharply on the VJ. "Shut up, Johnson!"

"What? What'd I say? You said that guy's from *Dusted*, right? It looks like he's really into his work!"

The red heat of absolute embarrassment burned through me, and I saw Flash murmur something to Runny R, who herded the crew down another dimly lit aisle of the casino, their giggles and hushed words swallowed by the sounds of dancing change and spinning roulette wheels.

My old friend came toward me quickly, a look of

concern on his face, Gertie at his side. "Neil, are you all right?"

I avoided his eyes, staring at his shining, polished black shoes while I tried to find a lie. "Yeah, yeah. I just . . . I was out at some party in the desert some people were having . . . uh, after the show. I got a little fluxed out and, you know, wandered around for a while."

Gertie, the gorgeous, famous, blond movie star, her body on perfect display in customized Hollywood finery, put her hand softly on my arm. "Are you sure you're OK?"

A roaring cheer went up from a blackjack table nearby. "Yeah, just need a shower, some sleep. I'll be fine."

"Forget the Z's, kid, we're in Vegas!" Flash said, grinning. "Shower up and come on down; we'll wait for you."

"No, really. I just wanna sleep."

"Neil and Flash Do Vegas!" he pressed playfully.

And as I looked in Flash's bright blue eyes in the low, casino lights, I saw that something inside of him genuinely wanted me to join him. I almost smiled with him, but then I looked at his tuxedo, and at the smooth string of Gertie's pearls, and thought of Runny R and Johnson, of their velvet tuxedos and trailing camera crews. A hidden trust fund somewhere behind it all . . .

"Thanks and all, but I really just gotta crash," I said to him. "Maybe work on my piece of *Cheese* while it's still fresh."

My friend's tone lowered just a touch. "OK. Guess I'll see you back in L.A."

"Maybe. But, uh, I'm leaving pretty soon. I'm going out of the country, to write my manifesto."

"EAST JABIP!" Flash exclaimed, grinning at me before turning to Gertie. "Neil's working on a manifesto, *Neil Before God*. It's gonna be the best. He's gonna write it in East Jabip."

"Great. Can't wait to read it." The star of *Tooky* played her manicured fingers through her pearls. "Um, we should probably catch up with everyone, Flash, before they all go broke."

"Yeah, I don't want to keep you," I said.

"We should get together before you go," Flash said, slipping his arm round Gertie's slim waist. "For our parting moment."

"Yeah, we should," I answered, knowing already that we wouldn't.

We stood facing each other in the casino, the sounds of money all around us. I felt my tongue nervously working my broken teeth, as all the questions and accusations I had for my friend tangled themselves in knots in my tightening throat. Everything was tainted now, I realized, all the laughter, all the memories, all the adventures I had shared with Flash seemed false and fleeting; a ruse he had played while his trust fund matured.

"C'mere you!" Flash suddenly shouted, grabbing me tight and hugging me. From the corner of my eye, I saw Gertie's lip curl in dismay as the dust from my desert walk pressed into her boyfriend's black tux. "I'm gonna miss you, kid. And I want you to write one hell of a manifesto!"

"Sure, Flash."

He pushed me at arm's length, still holding my

shoulders. "You're the Irish Samurai, and don't you ever forget that."

"I won't."

Gertie checked her silver watch again and switched her weight from one high heel to the other, sighing loudly.

"Bye, Flash," I said.

"Bye, Neil," he answered.

And with that, my old friend turned with his date, and the glamorous young couple walked away through the gambling games, under the hushed, golden lights of the casino.

7. a cheap flight

"Glad to see the old jalopy is running smooth. Very considerate of you, Neil," Stu said, eyeing the side mirror and pulling into the next lane. The wheels marked a steady beat over the segmented slabs of highway cement as we thrummed over the freeway to the airport.

"Wasn't much wrong, really; only cost a couple hundred clams. I needed to get around town for my Java gear."

"*Neil Before God,*" Stu said, shaking his head slowly as a speeding convertible overtook us in a roar. "Funny that the funding for the ultimate manifesto of our generation is coming from *Bop Cheese* magazine."

"Really."

After leaving Las Vegas, it had taken me only a week to pound out a *Bop Cheese* masterpiece. Pulling out my usual bag of tricks, I had been blithe as all hell, brilliantly obscuring any actual feeling in yet another piece that would make everybody laugh and wish they were me. Of course, Mandy had loved it.

"NEIL! Classic, babe! Everybody in the office is *dying* over this," she had gushed only hours after I faxed it off. "You're coming in here to talk more biz! Pronto, babe, pronto!!"

"What about Monday?" I had said, withholding Java. "I need to pick up that check."

"Sorry babe, out to Palm Springs this week. The issue's to bed and Mandy needs *rest!* But your check will be here, like I promised, babe. And we'll talk soon, hear?"

Of course, we didn't talk, as I had screened her calls through the answering machine, listening to her excited voice detail further features in the Mandy Universe, while I quietly assembled the equipment for my quest. I had left Hollywood without so much as a good-bye.

Stu flipped the radio, skipping over speed metal and Spanish hip-hop to land on an old seventies rock anthem.

"So what was your favorite place on the trip?" I asked over the roar of hot wind through the open windows.

"Rome was cool. I kicked off a piece of the Colliseum. And we had unbelievable sex in Greece."

"I'm going there."

"Now hold it. Just because we did doesn't mean you will. There were a lot of variable factors coming into play."

Since he had returned from his honeymoon, Stu had that Don Suave poise and relaxed, energized aura of a person who was being incredibly well laid. The last night I had stayed over, docked on a moldy futon mattress in the Harbor, I had heard the young couple reaffirming their nuptials on pounding bedsprings all night long.

"No, I mean Rome," I corrected. "I'm going to live in Italy."

"Why?"

" 'Cause that's where all the Italian women are."

Stu dropped down a gear as a black low-rider with tinted windows raced past. "Have you talked with your telecommunicatively deprived Italian girl lately?"

"Milena. And she isn't a girl; she's a woman." Slight apprehension tightened inside me, as I thought of the three letters I had written her while in Hollywood, each without an answer.

"Whatever. Have you heard from her?"

"Yeah," I lied. "After I pen my manifesto in Java, we made escape plans for Rome, to live a bilingual life of bliss on mopeds."

Stu smirked. "Why does everything have to be so international for you? Why can't you just date some girl from Massachusetts?"

"American girls are lame."

"Well, European chicks are probably more like you, anyway: armpit hair and messed-up teeth."

"That's only the Brits, and I already made a vow to never date a girl with teeth worse than my own."

"You know, no one's forcing you to go all epic. Could just stay in Hollywood. Between *Buddha Smoke* and the *Cheese*, I'm sure you could keep yourself up over the poverty line."

"Yeah, well I really got to leave the States to write."

He turned to me. "Ah yes, the East Jabip manifesto protocol."

"That's right."

"So why don't you go to Ireland instead of friggin' Java? That's your homeland. You could find out where your great-uncle Barney came from. Damn, that piece you wrote on him was one of my favorites."

Early on in my *Dusted* days, I had written a history-thick profile on my great-uncle Barney, who had grown up with my grandfather in Ireland. Recalling the brogue-thick tales he had told me as a child, I had laid down a rambling weave of family and Irish history, pleasing my parents and Stu, but never getting much in terms of reader response.

"I don't know man, that place scares me. What if it's just like one nightmare Thanksgiving dinner?" I said, remembering the Irish aunts and uncles, gathered together in dour, Scotch-sullen celebration around the turkey.

"Come on, Ireland is a magical place, everybody knows that."

"So's Java."

We rode on in silence for a while, the sun burning down over the speeding highway. I looked at Stu as he calmly piloted his bitchin' T-roof, and wondered what would become of my former editor. He had recently taken a job with our old rivals at *Buddha Smoke* and put away any notions he had of writing the screenplay he was always alluding to. With Terrance at the skateboard company, Flash at his show, and me heading for Java, all of us were accounted for.

"What about Flash?" I suddenly heard myself say.

"What about him?"

I desperately wanted to ask Stu about the rundown on our old friend. As soon as I thought of Flash everything twisted ugly inside me, getting confused and angry, then guilty at feeling angry, but ultimately angry again. I needed to hear another voice who had known him, but now with Stu, I felt scared to speak, for a reason I couldn't quite reach. "I mean . . . what about his show?" I managed, choking down the un-formed glut in my throat.

Stu slid us off to the right and rolled down a ramp to the airport. "The Chockapolacka tour?" He shrugged. "Good gig."

I waited for more, but Stu only drove, staring dead ahead. Silently, he navigated the maze of incoming and outgoing terminals as I scanned the signs, searching for my airline.

"What are you flying?" Stu asked after a while.

"Air Narud."

"Air Narud? Jesus Christ, Neil, you even fly weird airlines."

"What can I say, it's a cheap flight." I spied the sign and pointed it out. "There, the last one."

Stu pulled in to the curb, and we both sat in the idling car for a minute.

"Well, I guess this is it," I said.

"Yep."

I got out and went around to the back, pulled my backpack from the trunk, and walked back to the open car window. Leaning down, I looked in at Stu.

"I don't know what's going to happen now that *Dusted* is all over," he said, gazing ahead. "But wher-ever we end up, it was really great working with you."

"Yeah, I feel the same way."

I stood for a moment, my pack on my back. My fingers hooked on the windowsill.

"You were one of my favorite writers." Stu was looking down at the steering wheel, pushing his thumbs over it as if he were trying to rub something away.

"That's touching, Stu. But *Dusted* wasn't exactly a literary cavalcade."

"No, I mean, you're one of my favorite writers. Anywhere. And working with you . . . I just feel lucky to have had a front-row seat for a while," he said softly.

"Thanks," I said, feeling I should say more, but not knowing what.

There was a moment of silence between us, and I was nervous suddenly, about leaving.

"Well, I guess you better get a move on if you want to get to Java by suppertime," my old editor said.

"Yup."

"Good luck with *Neil Before God* . . . and watch out for your teeth, huh?"

"Yeah yeah."

We looked at each other for a while, and I grinned.

"Neil . . . ," he said, shaking his head. Then he shifted into gear, pressed the gas, and was gone.

Indonesia

8. jakarta

The raw thrill of pure motion raced through me as I roared out from Jakarta's airport in the tiny taxi van, eighteen hours after leaving Stu at LAX. As the short, tan skinned, chain-smoking driver floored the speeding, stripped-down craft over the tar-strip highway, the tropical heat blasted through the wide-open side door; I gripped my knees tight round my backpack as the first trickles of sweat began rolling down my temples.

Outside, a row of towering, faded billboards blurred past my eyes, each boldly lettered corporate logo glaring down like a coat of arms planted in conquered grounds. The image of Flash's grinning, green haired visage beaming from some future ad flew through me, but I shook him violently from my mind. I was a million miles from his Chockapolacka world, and heading out farther, beyond the frames of his television screens to find *Neil Before God* land. My fingers played over the nylon surface of my backpack, and I felt the hard outlines of the spiral notebook I had picked up on Sunset Boulevard, mere hours before my flight from America.

Inside my mouth, I felt my tongue slowly perusing the new work that had been sunken in at the back of my bite. There wasn't much difference to be felt; just a tiny porcelain plug filling the hole the Hollywood dentist had drilled. But the tooth felt safer, like a bomb that had been defused, and some mental strain had been drained out with the bitter pus of the rotting root. As much as I hated my mom being right, I was glad she had talked me into the chair. It would be just like my mouth to sabotage *Neil Before God,* killing off a tooth in the midst of my first prepositional phrase.

I gazed ahead to the red sun that hovered like a bleeding eye over the looming, smoking city of Jakarta and felt the first nerves rattle through me, as I realized how much of a move I had actually busted: Hollywood was half a planet away, and I was off on an authentic Epic Quest through my own personal East Jabip. Suddenly, it all seemed insane, or as Mandy would tell me, *un*sane. The L.A. editor had actually laughed when I alluded to *Neil Before God,* and maybe through her braying haws and jingling bracelets, there had been some bleach-blond knowledge I should have heeded; maybe the best thing a kid with no cash flow or bloodline *could* get was a chance to cut the *Cheese* . . .

I felt sweat soaking into my shirt as the driver hit the highway and accelerated, the whine of humming tires rising a tense octave as we gained speed. Panic zigged through my skull, and in a desperate second, I nearly shouted at the driver to wheel around and dash me back to Hollywood.

"Losmen?" the driver called back to me over the rush of heated air.

I swallowed my fear and nodded my head. *"Losmen."*

It meant hotel, and it was the only Indonesian word I knew, having picked it up at the airport. I hadn't bothered with a guidebook, and I didn't even have a map; the only reference points I had taken with me around the world was a currency-exchange table, and the old, thick pages I had ripped from a child's *J* encyclopedia. I pulled them out now from the back pocket of my army shorts, to gaze for the millionth time at the faded fifties photography.

The pictures of the timeworn stone monuments, the Buddhist temples, the Hindu deities, and the scaled planes of lush rice patties had drawn me here all the way from Hollywood. But the one that had gripped me tightest was an ancient, hallowed structure, which was the largest Buddhist monument in the world. My eyes scanned again over the pyramid levels of carved friezes that lead up like stone steps to a sculpted span of enraptured Buddhas. Weathered by the passing of a thousand seasons, it was set dead center in the island of Java, and from the solitude of Stu's L.A. Harbor, I had built it into a kind of stone spiritual magnet, pulling me into its field of power.

That's why the old *J* encyclopedia had fallen open to the Java page, why *Dusted* had folded, and Mandy had gigged me with the cash to catch a plane to Java. The Fates had conspired to bring me to this tiny island, far from the buzzing hype, so I could sit down and manifest *Neil Before God*.

The driver downshifted and yanked us off the highway, spiraling down a curving off-ramp before hurtling into the teeming city streets of Jakarta. I refolded my encyclopedia pages and slipped them back in my pocket, holding tight to the wooden slat of my seat, facing out the open door as we roared into the thick, smoking clog of traffic.

Rounding one last turn in the ramp, we suddenly bucked into a seething density of human beings that I had never imagined possible. Crowding the sidewalks, dashing through the street traffic, piled into buses, zipping by on mopeds, or packed into cheap tinny cars, the mass of short, brown-skinned people pushed through the sweaty urban throb. Our van slipped into the chaos, melded with the vehicular blur, hurtling along with the droves of mopeds, motorcycles, trucks and scooters in a river of revving engines.

Slamming into lower gear, the driver swerved a hard left turn, flooring us through a maze of tin and wooden shacks. Left turn, right turn, straight ahead through the crooked complex of poverty, picking up passengers with no signals, no beeps, just a swerve of the driver's wheel and another near miss. An old man, his body braced against the bucking vehicle, moved forward and handed the driver a few pink and white bills, then disappeared out the door. Three turns and a dashing stretch later, we escaped the shantytown and plunged into another clogged ventricle of the heaving city.

"Losmen?" I asked again to the driver. He nodded his head, distracted, as he swerved and speeded through Jakarta, and I wondered if I was even communicating at all.

And then I saw him: the tall white guy loping through the crammed streets, three heads taller than the Javanese around him; a fellow traveler. As we passed by, I eyed his dusty, travel-worn backpack, shaggy, dirty hair, and faded African-print pants, comparing them to my fresh, new boots and feeling like a weekend Ulysses in comparison. Part of me wanted to leap out and wring directions from him, but before I could find the words, the driver speeded on, suddenly veering to the curb and slamming to a stop.

"*Losmen,*" he said, jerking his head toward a narrow strip on the left.

I had been in many travelers' ghettos before, and looking through the heated haze, I recognized Jakarta's equivalent with a rush of relief. Young people with backpacks and mismatched, journey-worn clothes wandered amidst the strip of cheap rooms and restaurants, their paths overlapping on their various global journeys. Excited to join them, I yanked my gear off the metal floor and moved to the open side of the van. I dug into my pocket for the roll of Indo scrip I had changed back in Los Angeles, but then stopped, suddenly paralyzed in the gunning taxi.

"*Losmen!*" the driver said again, impatiently.

But I was hearing different words, coming across a cheap speaker system set somewhere in a travelers' bar, and they froze me in my place:

> Gots a dive watch so I can drop deeper,
> Got mad connections but I don't wear a beeper.
> Runny R is the teller, so ladies, y'all step up,
> Deposit, withdrawal, your body go bankrupt!

"No . . . ," I muttered. "Jesus, no."

I stood hanging in the door frame of the van, hearing

Runny R's multiplatinum, sneering Rage rhymes, mocking my ridiculous attempt to escape the Chocka-polacka Universe. My stomach turned as I peered through the exhausted, soot-shrouded air, into the ghetto of white Euro faces and lumbering backpacks.

"No, another *losmen!*" I blurted to the driver, dashing back to my bench like a kindergarten kid scared of school.

"*Losmen!*" He repeated, now visibly angry, as the clamoring crowd of cars honked about him.

"No!" I shook my head, motioning him forward. "No good *losmen!*" I needed to be somewhere badly, I was exhausted and starving, but I sure as hell hadn't dragged myself through nine time zones to hear a god-damn Runny R rhyme.

Exasperated, the driver slammed into gear and gunned back into the burning-rubber snarl of traffic. And as we hurtled on, I realized with a dim shadow of dismay that my travel high was already wearing off. Jet lag was hitting me full force, and I sank against the wall, hungry now, desperately wanting to find a bed. Outside, it was getting darker, and I gazed with dead-ening eyes into the blurring anarchopolis passing by.

And you haven't got a trust fund to fall back on, babe, like your pal Flash.

Mandy's words came again, with the laugh and snort she had framed them in, from deep within her cloud of perfume. My mind filled with a tangle of curses, and I imagined Flash on a set somewhere in Hollywood, witty and punky, with Gertie winking from the wings. And I suddenly wished I could reach back and yank them from their climate-controlled lives, throwing them down in the burning smoke of this foreign traffic with me, careening blindly, with no fame or trust funds to light the way.

Flash . . . Why didn't you tell me? Why didn't you clue me in that you were just visiting? That the rebel lifestyle I was clawing through was nothing but a passing phase for you? Why didn't you warn me that I should never count you as an ally in the *Cheese* wars? Flash, why didn't you tell me you *were* the *Cheese*, just rolling through the dust for a thrill? That once it got dull, you would leave me behind, an unemployed pile of words, beer bottles, and broken teeth, while you went on to become a show?

The van battled its way through the grating traffic, veering past collisions by bare inches, and I struggled again to the front, balanced on shaky legs. Desperately, I shouted over the roar of surrounding engines.

"Losmen!"

The driver grunted, slamming the brakes and cutting right as a truck jumped in front of us, and I fell backward onto the gritty metal floor. Darting out with my hands, I desperately gripped the bench, pulling myself to my seat in the jerking vehicle. And then for a long time, I simply sat, gazing blankly at the blur of the foreign city as a steady passing of passengers flowed in and out the door.

"Losmen!" the driver barked back to me, sometime later.

I looked up from my empty trance to see what I already knew: he had taken me back to the travelers' ghetto.

"No good," I said to him wearily, shaking my head.

The driver, shrugging, ditched us back into traffic. A paranoid fantasy oozed into my mind: Flash and

153

Mandy, Johnson and the Chili crew had set up this entire scenario. They had hired the driver, set up the speakers at the travelers' ghetto, and rigged this rattling, tinny van with secret cameras all around. I imagined a million vid kids staring at The Channel, their dull faces bathed in flickering TV light, laughing dumbly at my ordeal while Johnson and Flash provided wry, irreverent commentary.

Brakes screeched sharply as another driver stopped suddenly, just missing a little kid in pajamas who scurried across the road. With a grin on his face, the child jumped into our van and scrabbled toward the back. After he sat down, he watched me for a while, then slid closer on the bench to speak.

"Hello. English?" he said tentatively, his little voice barely audible over the urban turmoil.

"No, American," I hollered.

"Ah! American! Very good, America very good." He gave me a thumbs-up and nodded his head, smiling. Weak headlamps from passing cars and scooters streaked over his soft skin, highlighting his smudged pajamas in dull yellow.

The driver shouted something back in Indonesian. I watched the kid listen, then nod his head and scratch at his hair.

"He wants to know why you don't like *losmen*."

"Tell him I want to find Indonesian hotel, in a different part of the city. Not expensive. But no other travelers."

"Hmmm." The pajama kid started to speak, but then stopped, screwing up his eyes as he tried to concentrate on the right words. Then he began speaking Indonesian to the driver, who nodded his head and said something quickly, then slowed down as another family boarded. The little kid jumped across and squeezed in next to me.

"He will take you to a place. Very good." He smiled and gave me another thumbs-up.

"Thank you," I said. "Thank you very much."

"No problem," he said, speaking the foreign phrase with slow, deliberate care.

It was dark when the van dropped me off with my new guide, and after paying for us both, I followed the excited pajama kid over the hard, soot-stained sidewalks of a near deserted street. The night was hazy and hot, the air smelled of rotting vegetables and gasoline, and as we moved farther into the neighborhood of twisting alleyways, the ferocious roar of Jakarta traffic faded to a faint, diesel rumbling. My blue backpack weighed heavy on my shoulders as the child led me on, and I realized ruefully that I had brought too much to travel with.

"Here!" the pajama kid suddenly said, ducking around a corner and leading me to a dark square cut in a cement wall. I followed him into a dim, stagnant courtyard, where mosquitoes buzzed over a small pool of brown water, and dead night heat hung heavy in the air.

A sour-looking old man shuffled toward us in flip-flops, a faded batik shirt hanging over his bent shoulders, exposing his sunken chest and potbelly. The red ember of his cigarette glowed and died with slow, deliberate draws as he looked me over, finally nodding and motioning me to follow.

Past the murky fish pool, I dragged my pack behind him to a line of thin wooden doors on a crumbling cement patio. The old man pushed one open and clicked a light, revealing a tiny, yellowed room with a single chair, an electric fan on an old wooden bureau, and a thin, sagging bed. I nodded my head, threw my pack in the corner, and the old man shuffled off. The pajama kid remained, smiling in the doorway, and I reached into my pocket for a few bills, but then remembered how heavy my backpack was.

"You like American music?" I asked.

"Hip-hop!" he called back gleefully.

Snapping the latches of my backpack, I dug deeply, past my notebook to a plastic bag filled with cassettes. I had spent a solid week listening through Stu's legendary record collection, filing through every riff, rap, and jam that had rocked our world during the *Dusted* days to compile five memory-soaked tapes. I thought the tunes might keep me company as I roamed Java, but now, my shoulders aching, they just seemed to be weighing me down.

"Here," I said, holding out the cassettes in the dim yellow light.

His eyes went round as he slowly reached for them.

"And here, I don't need this, either."

I wrapped the headphone cord in a tight circle around my black tape player, then placed it his hands.

"It's yours, thanks a lot." I sat down on the bed and began to unlace my boots. The pajama kid stood, motionless in the doorway, the booty held loosely in his hands.

"Bye-bye?" I suggested, waving my hand.

For a moment more he looked dumbly at me, then

suddenly hugged the tapes and player to his skinny body, spun around, and ran out the doorway.

"Bye-bye, mister!" I heard him call out as his little feet scampered away over the dusty cement of the courtyard patio. I closed the skimpy door behind him, stripped off my sweat-soaked shirt, and fell down into a dark, heavy sleep.

9. neil before god

I left Jakarta and crisscrossed Java for days that blurred into weeks and soon enough melted into a month. At some point, I put the *J* pages away, giving up a direct quest for the Buddhist monument, and giving in to a random roll through the nameless villages and palm-tree roads. Slumped in crammed bus seats, sleeping in the flat slat beds of local *losmens*, wandering through monkey forests, rice terraces, and loitering in ancient temples, my life slid into an aimless, joyless drift through the hot, dusty island.

My notebook, still empty of words, was none the less worn. The blank edges of its white pages were gritty with dirt, the cover creased and folded from being drawn out each night, stared at, then shoved back, deep down into the bottom of my pack. I sat alone with it in the warm nights, lit in weak yellow from low-watt bulbs as gecko lizards scurried across the ceiling. An easy, dark quiet permeated every village, where I drank beer from tall glasses, smudged thick with the fingerprints of past travelers. More empty than at peace, I whiled away the nights in an untroubled solitude, gazing at the pages of my unwritten manifesto.

My parents, I imagined, would be satisfied. Even though they had no knowledge of *Neil Before God*, they would be against any attempt at me sorting out my past in print. Dad read spy novels, my mom, historical biographies; anything else was a waste . . . or worse, a threat. Our battle over my words had started with my first article, and even though they never read another, my parents' cold judgment had haunted me with every piece I wrote since.

Two years back, when I had first moved in with Flash, financial troubles for our backer, the Mack, were whacked worse than ever. *Dusted* had finally hit its stride, with nods from key players all across the pop pantheon, and rising demand for issues. Musicians and actors held sacred in the eyes of hipster youth were suddenly available for *Dusted* interviews, calls were coming in from rival mainstream magazines, even a few ad agencies had leaned in to see what we were about. But tax time came round with an audit on the Mack, and in a panic, he put the mag on hold to straighten the snarl of alimonies, palimonies, loans, and kill fees that made up his life.

For a month in New York, Flash and I were left to starve. In two weeks our savings bottomed out, and at the end of the third week, the black beans, spaghetti, and pasta sauce that had somehow sustained us were gone. With the last of our pennies, Flash bought a jar of peanut butter and three dozen day-old bagels, and it was then, in the early blooming of a hot New York

City spring, that the Great Bagel Famine hit Fifth Street.

Sitting in the tiny compartment, gazing dully at the walls, we gnawed on onion, poppy-seed, and pumpernickel bagels, as our laughter and sense of romantic adventure slowly trickled away.

"This is noble, Neil," I remembered Flash convincing me as he pulled off a piece of garlic bagel, spreading cheap peanut butter over its hardened mass. "This is punk."

I had just moved into the compartment and had nothing in my tiny room but a blanket, a pillow, and a scratched, red milk crate that propped up my sticker-covered computer. My green-haired friend and I had long since run out of jokes, and as we waited in a deadened haze for word from the coast, I decided to do the only thing I could. Closing the door, I settled in my tiny room before my computer, slowly pulled the keyboard onto my lap, and began to write.

For five delirious days, my fingers crept across the keys. Drifting through a realm of reality eons beyond hunger, I traversed the imagery inside me, exploring the grim snapshots from the suburbs my karma had cursed me into, my later escapades on the urban pavement, and the dreams of possible futures that meandered through them all. Empty and hollow-eyed, I wound the words around a day-by-day account of the Bagel Famine, stopping only for thin, black sleeps or a few shuffling steps to the kitchen for yet another stale, rock hard poppy-seed.

And then one day, the phone rang. As I heard Flash screaming with joy in the empty kitchen, I smiled from the sea of papers I had submerged my hunger in.

"Neil! The Great Bagel Famine is over!" Flash shouted, running to my door. *"The Mack sold off his old skate park! We're liquid, kid, liquid!"*

I looked up from the scattered thrash of papers and bagel crusts to see a look of dazed wonderment over my friend's face as he stood in the doorway.

"Jesus, Neil," Flash said to me in a dull whisper, sinking to the floor beside me and slowly picking up a scribble-edited page. *"What did you write?"*

By the time it was cropped, chopped, and made sane, the rambling dream recount of the Great Bagel Famine was a fifteen-page epic masterpiece of starvation in the name of punk. It was my first feature, the voice I had been struggling for, and although I didn't know it at the time, the first inkling of *Neil Before God.* With a unanimous motion by the magazine's founders, my wild-style spree of words was made the centerpiece of the new *Dusted.*

Stu placed me on the magazine masthead overnight, assigning me three major stories for the next issue. The day I cashed my first check, Flash stole a plastic crown from the toy store, knighted me as New Jack Poet Warrior, then took me out for a wild, whirling night in Alphabet City. Terrance immersed himself in the layout, drawing up old artwork he had never shown anyone, explaining to me in a long, handwritten letter that what I had chronicled was everything *Dusted* had ever meant to him.

When the piece was finally published, the positivity only amped louder, with responses from readers all over New York and around the country. Whenever I went out that spring, I saw copies of the mag circulating at scenester coffee shops and dim downtown bars, as "The Great Bagel Famine" became a cult classic.

People I had never known wound up next to me in bars, quoting my words, buying me drinks, asking me questions about the crazed family portrait I had etched in ink: the church mom who slapped me across the head on the way to mass, the pot-dealing brother who smoked me out in the mornings before elementary school, the Scotch-sipping father who refused to lend a hand when my teeth were smashed . . .

But as the free drinks came round, and readers' letters poured in praising my ways, I was uneasily keyed in to an icy silence from home. Even though I had mailed them a copy, my parents never responded to my article, and for two months, their silence grew in an ominous, deafening thunder, eventually overriding the dying buzz of the downtown denizens. It wasn't until my punk lit triumph had finally become old news, and I was sweating out my next assignment, that I received a thin, simple letter from my father. In his tight, left-slanted script, he invited me home for "a chat."

I got a terse greeting from my mother at the train station the night I arrived, and then we drove in silence back to the house. Along the curving roads, my mom steered her car beneath the canopy of leafy branches, past the private schools we couldn't afford, the loping golf course where I caddied, the old church we had filed into every Sunday, and finally, the still, quiet lawnscape of my old neighborhood.

My father was in the TV room when I arrived, sitting in his red leather chair near the door. He didn't even look at me or stand up to say hello, but just clicked off the TV and pointed to the sofa. I sat down, and my mother entered the silent room, placing herself near my father.

For a long while, the three of us sat in the deadly quiet.

"Well?" I finally said.

My father spoke. "Your mother and I were not amused by your article."

"Low blow, Neil. Really low," my mother intoned, slowly shaking her head.

"That wasn't—" I started, and my father cut me off.

"No, you said what you wanted to say in your magazine, Neil. Now it's your mother's and my turn."

I settled back into the couch and heard the flint of my mother's cigarette lighter being struck. Menthol smoke filled the room.

"Your mother and I, you know, we worked very hard on this pithy little suburban existence you so despise," my father began. "At first I didn't think my own son could have possibly written that story."

I sat up, clicking into fight mode. "How could you have known? You never bothered to see a word I wrote up till then!"

He ignored me. "I showed your mother the article and said, 'Would you imagine the poor, stupid saps who had to raise that ungrateful bastard kid?' I had myself a laugh, until your mother said, 'Why, Dan, we *are* those poor, stupid saps,' and showed me your name at the bottom."

"Dad, it wasn't—"

Again, he cut me off. "You really did it, Son. You really showed us up."

"Like a kick in the gut, Neil," my mother said slowly, shaking her head, gazing down at the carpet.

I looked across the room to the blank television set, seeing the three of us reflected in its curving, grey glass like some twisted soap opera.

"And there's going to be consequences."

"Consequences?" I repeated. "What are you going to do? Ground me? Sorry, I don't live with you anymore."

"That's good, that's great!" my dad said with a sickening smile. "And get used to it, kid, because you won't ever be living here again. Your mother and I have decided that someone of your talent and ego couldn't possibly fit into our small, humble thatched cottage here. So I hope, for your sake, that your brilliant writing career *really* takes off, because you're on your own."

"GOOD!" I nearly shouted.

"Easy," my dad threatened, iron anger in his voice. "You just calm down now."

I sat, breathing burning breaths, pushing my teeth with my tongue: apart, together, apart, together, apart, together . . .

"And there will be no writing about us, *ever*, Neil," my mother added, frigid and righteous.

I raised my gaze to stare down her piercing blue eyes. "What is that supposed to mean?"

My father glared at me. "Just what she said. It means *you don't write about us.*"

My mother blew out a thin stream of smoke. "Frankly, the way you write, I can't imagine that anyone would want to be in your articles."

"Go to hell!"

"YOU WATCH YOUR MOUTH AROUND YOUR MOTHER!" my father thundered, getting halfway up out of his chair and jabbing his finger at me.

My mother frowned and shrugged her shoulders. "You don't write clean, Neil. You're angry, your language is filthy, and we don't want to be associated with it."

"Whatever I want to write, I write, and you can't tell me what to do anymore because you don't own me!" I screamed in their empty shell of a home.

My father held up both his hands, his voice oozing with sarcasm. "Oh, no! We wouldn't *dream* of standing in the way of your artistic vision, Neil. We're just poor, dumb suburbanites . . . what do we know? You're the genius. And you're as free as a bird to write whatever your little heart desires." He took a nasty drag on his cigarette and snubbed it out in the ashtray. "But just don't expect us to be around if you do."

I made a choked, awkward noise I had intended as a laugh. "Is this a threat? Are you going to disown me or something?"

My father settled back into his chair. "That's up to you."

Suddenly, tears were fighting to get out, making it almost impossible to talk. "Oh, great. So we'll h-hh-have one of those st-stupid Irish grudges and never talk to each other again."

"If that's the way you want it, Neil," my mother concluded.

And then I couldn't hold them off anymore. I wept, holding my head in my hands, as my parents watched on. The tears flooded my eyes, pouring down my cheeks, and my parents watched on, saying not a word.

It was the same way they had watched so many years ago, as the strain and pain from my teeth ground me into a black, hostile hole before their eyes. I would never forget those silent summer dinners, crickets whirring beyond the screens, as I sipped soup or scrambled eggs, my ragged, contused jaw cracked just wide enough to allow the thin trickle of nourishment. My father, sitting grimly at the head of the table, atop every dollar that could have paid a dentist, but instead saving sadistically for a college education I never wanted. And my mother chatting away about the neighbors and the news, and the stupid inconsequentials of her daily living as if everything were pretty and fine.

"Same as my t-t-teeth," I stammered softly.

"What did you say?" My father pushed, snapping at the bait.

I raised my red, tearstained face to look him in his murky, angry eyes. "I said it's the same as my teeth, *Dad*, I was on my own then, so why should it be any different now?"

"Oh please, Neil, the teeth again?" My mother laughed, shaking her head ruefully. "Is that all you're going to say for the rest of your life?"

"Grow up, will you?" my father said, disgust and anger in his voice. "If you want to get drunk and high and God knows what and go jumping face first out of windows, don't ever expect your mother and me to pick up the pieces. Then or now, that stands. *Period.*"

"I was YOUR KID!"

"And you still are. And if you want to go on being our kid, you play by our rules."

I somehow pulled myself together, wiping the tears from my face with the back of my hand. "So is that it?"

"Yes Neil," my mother said without a trace of softness in her voice. "That's it."

"You are free to go, illustrious author," my father said. The sick, sarcastic smile was back on his face.

A moment passed. Then I lifted my head, and I stood up. I went into the kitchen, called a taxi, picked up the bag that had been packed for the weekend, and walked out the front door.

We hit level road and the driver gunned into gear, pulling out to pass a few families piled high on mopeds and a lumbering truck stacked thick with raw, reddish wood. We were deep in the island countryside, rumbling over muddy, mottled roads past endless rice-paddy terraces, the hand-formed walls and wayward sloping brown pools dotted with the conical hats of barefoot farmers. For a fleeting moment, I thought of Flash and the air-conditioned editing rooms, which seemed light-years away as the tropical scenery passed before my eyes. The wind blew hard through the rattling bus windows, and sunlight flickered through speed-blurred palm branches as the driver floored the gas, chugging steadily along to take the pole position on the winding roadway.

Halfway past the truck, I looked ahead to see the looming figure of an oncoming bus, speeding toward us in the opposite lane. My body tensed, and images of flaming wreckage and charred, bloodied bodies exploded in my mind. But at the last minute, the lumber truck tapped the brakes, our driver veered into lane, and the charging bus pulled out by a hair, avoiding catastrophe by mere inches. The pilots beeped and waved, smiling to each other, and I relaxed back into my seat, wondering again if the Javanese obeyed a higher traffic law that my Western mind could never conceive.

I reached into my side leg pocket for the peanuts I had bought at the last roadside stop, pushing three past my sun-chapped lips. I ate slowly and cautiously, mushing the hard, sweet nuts on one side of my mouth before spreading the flavor over my tongue. Toothpicks had slipped my mind when I left the States, and I was stuck in Southeast Asia with a vital need for these simple tools. It had taken me a maddening week of tongue tactics to liberate a chunk of peanut besieged in a cracked back molar, and from then on, I had fed myself with care.

Finishing my snack, I took off my sunglasses, wiping beads of sweat from the tinted glass. A little boy across the aisle watched as I fogged the lens and rubbed them on my shirt.

"You wanna try?" I said with a smile, holding them out.

He smiled shyly and slowly reached out for them in response, taking them from my hand and sliding the oversize black glasses onto his tiny face.

"HEY!! MR. COOL!!"

"HA HA!!"

"MOVIE STAR!"

The bus was filled with shouts and laughter from the brothers, friends, and little cousins who leapt up from surrounding seats, jeering and grabbing for the sunglasses as we rumbled over the bumpy road. The kid fought them off, laughing, giving me a big smile and thumbs-up from behind my shades in the midst of the playful melee.

A young Indonesian woman was sitting before me, smiling faintly as she watched the giggling kids passing my glasses between them. The bus rumbled on into the gathering dusk, and she turned to look at me several times, as if to speak. She seemed anxious, and I pretended not to notice her discomfort when she finally found her voice.

"Excuse me. Hello, how are you?" the girl said softly and carefully.

"I am fine, thank you. How are you?" I responded in slow English.

She thought for a moment, then spoke. "Good."

We rode together in a smiling awkwardness as the bus rattled on through the curving roads of the countryside. I looked closer at the girl, with her soft, brown eyes, thick lips, and black wave of shiny, well-brushed hair. She was neatly dressed in white jeans and a blue-patterned blouse and seemed to be half my size, although close in age. I wondered for a while what to say next, but as the bus rounded a curved and eased to a stop, she turned to me.

"Would you like to come home with me?" she asked suddenly.

The answer came automatically. "Yes, I would."

A look like gratitude passed over her face, and I followed her through the aisle, taking my sunglasses back from the laughing kids and dragging my heavy pack through the thick crowd, some of them smiling at the embarrassed girl and teasing her lightly.

"Bye-bye, movie star!"

Their jeering chorus called out the windows as the bus faded into the darkness, and I looked around to find myself standing with the small Indonesian girl on the edge of a quiet, poorly paved road, a tiny village of houses visible not far away.

"My name is Ehrlina."

"I'm Neil."

"It is good to meet you."

"It's good to meet you."

Ehrlina exhaled a nervous breath, relieved that the exchange had gone well, then led me down the road.

"Hello, mister!" a little boy piped, speeding past on a bicycle as we entered the village. On a porch nearby, a group of teenage girls were brushing each other's hair. They giggled, some hid their faces, some waved, and one girl called out *"How are you, mister?"* which sent them all into bursts of laughter. An older man strolled by with a child and his wife, and I watched the small girl's eyes widen in fright at my tall, white, alien presence. She scrambled for cover behind her father's sarong, and her parents laughed gently, the mother speaking calming words in Indonesian. As we passed, her little face peeped out from around the patterned folds, staring in awe, then dodging back under cover as I waved.

"I will take you to my home, where I am living," Ehrlina said to me. She turned down a narrow, angular pathway through a cluster of dwellings, and I followed, until we stopped at a cement patio laid before a small home. I set my dusty pack down at my feet, and she disappeared into a dark doorway; I waited, listening to the soothing night noises of birds and insects as I gazed up at the stars hanging bright in the clear black night.

Ehrlina appeared from the small house she had slipped into, a bashful look on her face, followed by three older women. They were short and smiling, dressed in sarongs and T-shirts, and nodded in satisfaction at the stranger brought to their doorstep. The eldest, a wrinkled woman with a scarf wrapped round her head, reached up in the air and said something, causing the others to laugh.

"She said you are very long," Ehrlina explained.

The village children appeared suddenly, from around every corner of the surrounding buildings. Cute little boys and girls swarmed the patio, the bold venturing near, the more timid hanging back near the women. We stood in the night, gazing at each other, the little children hiding their faces when I met their eyes, or coming close then running away, giggling hysterically as they dashed back to their friends, hugging them tightly and laughing.

One of the little girls looked at me and touched her nose, saying something in Indonesian. Everyone laughed and began touching their nose, repeating her words.

Ehrlina turned to me. "They think your nose is very good," she explained.

I touched my nose, moving the tip back and forth, and the gathered group burst into fantastic laughter. Lowering myself down to a little kid clapping excitedly at my feet, I placed my face close to his. He reached a tiny, tentative hand out to my nose, touched it for a bare second, then ran away to hide behind his mother.

I joined in with the laugher, beaming, happier than I had felt for a long, long time.

"I would like you to come in and meet my grandfather."

We walked over the patio into the quietly lit home, and I ducked my head beneath the low frame, entering a simple, sparsely furnished cement-floored room. A barefoot, elderly Indonesian man sat in a chair, wrapped in a sarong and smoking contentedly beneath a single pool of lamplight. He looked up as we entered, gesturing to a small couch with a welcoming smile.

"Hello," I said to the man.

"Allo," he said slowly.

Ehrlina spoke to him in Indonesian as I sat on the couch, and the older man nodded his head, then spoke gently back to her. She thought for a moment, translating. "He asks me why you go to Java."

"To write my manifesto."

He nodded as if he understood.

"Manifesto?" Ehrlina repeated, grappling with the word.

"Yeah. It's like a book."

She spoke in Indonesian to her grandfather, then turned back to me. "You write a book? What about?"

I shifted in my seat. "I don't know. Teeth, God, Hollywood, stuff like that."

Ehrlina nodded her head and the old man said something to her. "Where in Java do you go?" she translated.

My original mission returning, I reached into my side short pockets and pulled out my encyclopedia pages. For a moment, the Harbor days came back to me, the heavy loneliness of **BEER** nights, microwave burritos, and an endless din of demo tapes. Then I found the picture of the monument and passed the page over to the old man. He nodded approvingly before handing the thick, folded page on to his granddaughter.

"This place is very near to here," she said, looking at the photo. "A small ride on the bus in the morning. You would be there in the day."

"Good, tomorrow then."

The three of us sat together in an easy, soothing silence for some time. There was no music, no TV, no distractions or entertainment save for the smoke rising in thin trails from the old man's cigarette. As I watched it curve and billow, forming ghostly, abstract script in the pool of lamplight, my mind flew back to my father, sitting with a similar cigarette in another part of the world, along with a Scotch, a newspaper, a chattering television, and a ringing phone to crowd out the silence.

"You leave tomorrow?" Ehrlina asked me.

"Yes."

"Oh."

A vision rippled in my mind: dropping my manifesto, cutting all contacts to the Chockapolacka world behind me, and staying here in the village to marry Ehrlina. Becoming a farmer, my fame-hungry past fading in rhythms of soul-cleansing labor, as I worked the good Javanese earth. . . .

Ehrlina cleared her throat nervously. "You are smiling. Something is funny?"

"No. I'm just happy to be here."

"Yes, this is a good situation," she agreed.

I looked up to see the older man snuffing out his last cigarette. He got to his feet, and I did too; we shook hands, and then he shuffled away into the back. Ehrlina led me to a small door and opened it.

"This is my room, where you will be sleeping."

The space reminded me of my Fifth Street compartment, small and close, without much area to move in. Taped to the wooden dresser near the door, I saw a magazine picture of bad-boy Javanese metal rockers, pulled from some kind of Indonesian *Bop Cheese*. I placed my pack down on the floor, and we stood, looking at each other.

"Thank you so much," I said. "This was really a beautiful night."

She looked at me a bit bashful, her lips curving in a smile, then looked down at the floor. "Thank you."

A clumsy silence passed. Around us, I heard the quiet noises of Ehrlina's home settling down for the evening: soft trails of conversation, shuffling footsteps, the trickle of water in the courtyard, and finally, the last evening prayer call from the mosque, faint and melodious, rising into the night sky.

"Good night," Ehrlina finally said. "I will see you on the morning."

"Good night."

She left me then, and I slipped under the covers, exhausted and content, curling up like a baby to make myself fit in her tiny bed.

A knocking on the door not long after dawn had me up and dressing, somewhat bewildered in the chilled, tranquil morning. Chickens ran outside, and the first prayer call began from the mosque. I entered the living room to find Ehrlina, sitting with two muddy, thick glasses of sweet Javanese coffee. She was wearing a freshly pressed shirt and a white-brimmed hat with a bow around the top, dressed up as if for a special outing.

"Good morning. Did you sleep well?"

"Good morning. Yes, thank you."

We sat together and sipped at the thick coffee in the wan morning light. I asked Ehrlina about the bus to the monument, and she nodded her head, saying it left from the end of the village road. Then her grandmother and mother entered the room in sweaters and sarongs, sitting down and regarding me benignly, murmuring to each other in Indonesian.

I sipped the coffee slowly, savoring its sweet thickness on my tongue as the four of us sat together in the early morning light. I met Ehrlina's eyes and quickly looked away, my gaze wandering randomly around the small room, until it finally rested on my backpack near the door. In the soft light of early dawn, I saw the hard angle of my notebook pressing against the stretched nylon of the pack, and a sudden, tremendous need to run from Ehrlina's home rushed through me. I hurriedly swigged the last of my coffee, and just as I reached the bottom of the tall glass, felt a single grain of coffee from the bottom find its way into my broken back molar.

"Damn," I muttered under my breath.

"What's wrong?" Ehrlina asked, frowning.

"It's my teeth." I dug with my tongue back toward the grain, only to lodge it deeper. With a sigh of defeat, I stood and walked to the whitewashed wall where my backpack leaned waiting, then hoisted it over my shoulder.

"Good-bye," I said to the older women. "Thank you so much for having me."

They smiled and nodded, understanding my actions if not the words. I ducked my head and walked out of the door, and Ehrlina followed me out to the small patio. We stood for a while in silence.

"I will never forget this day," Ehrlina said eventually. "I am very happy today."

"I am, too. Thank you for having me."

I noticed that her mother and grandmother, along with a few little kids, were watching from the windows. I watched as Ehrlina concentrated, then heard her speak what she must have rehearsed all through the night.

"I feel that you are the bold man I have never met before."

Hesitating for a moment, I leaned down and gave her a kiss on the cheek. An astonished look appeared on Ehrlina's face, and she brought her hand to where my lips had touched. I heard a collective gasp from the onlookers, which changed to laughter as I began to walk quickly away. Before turning the corner of the home, I looked back to see Ehrlina still standing there, hand on her cheek.

"Please forget me," she called to me, confusing her English in this last moment. Then she turned and ran inside.

I walked fast through the narrow maze of houses until I reached the village road, where a bus appeared almost immediately. I jumped on board and showed the driver the picture of the monument, and he nodded his head, pointing to a seat right behind him. The rattling old vehicle bucked away under the rising sun, taking me off toward my destination.

I cursed softly to myself, winding my tongue around to the back tooth, where the chunk of coffee from Ehrlina's was now wedged fast.

"You noticed, I am sure, that the steps up to the top are very steep, very high," the Indonesian tour guide began in a soft, even voice. "They are very difficult to climb; not like ordinary steps. That is to show that the way to Enlightenment is something not easily done. The very top of this monument, where we now stand, is the level symbolizing of Enlightenment."

A group of Australian tourists, red faced and sweaty, slowly gathered around the base of the topmost Buddha on the monument. A small Indonesian tour guide, in a freshly starched blouse and pressed skirt, threaded through the heaving, sweating crowd and placed herself before them, smiling softly to gain their attention before she continued speaking. The long climb to the top had taken its toll, and the sunburned group was swallowing air in deep, desperate gulps. The men pulled handkerchiefs from their pants pockets and mopped their soggy brows, as the women exchanged looks of mock suffering and fanned themselves with maps and brochures.

" 'Scuse me love, is there anywhere up 'ere in Enlightenment to get a lager?" a portly Aussie with ointment on his nose joked. The group laughed as one, and the guide chuckled along politely with the doomed souls.

I slipped away from the crowd and found an empty

crevice at the edge of the monument, looking out over the brown, tree-steeped mountains in the distance. The sky was a bright blue, with wisps of clouds drifting high over the carved monolith of stone that rose up, serene and awesome, from the dark Javanese earth. It had taken me all morning to get to the top, up the giant steps leading pyramid-like to the level stone surface, where a series of circularly situated Buddhas sat poised in eternal meditation.

And now, far away from the touring groups, I sat down at the foot of one archaic, serene figure. Uncapping my pen, I opened the notebook I had taken with me halfway around the world and stared at the first empty page.

Neil Before God

I wrote in heavy, dark letters, then sat still in the shadow of the Buddha, gazing at the title over again. A soft breeze blew, playing at the edge of the page, and then a rush of imagery reeled in my mind, taking me away from the monument. Sweaty, screaming crowds of Chockapolacka, my mother's and father's baleful glares, the sickening crunch of my chin smashing the pavement, Flash's bright green hair, Milena's full red lips, the whir of my bike chain in the empty Hollywood night, Nile Rivers in a tape cassette, springtime blossoms during the famine on Fifth Street, suburban pot smoke and the pain in my mouth like frozen stone . . .

Just wait Neil, you'll end up behind a desk like everybody else.

My mother's damning prediction came back to me

through time, and I remembered the night I had left home as a teenager. My dad, of course, had been working late, my teeth were aching, and my stomach was burning from all the aspirin I had been taking to ease the pain. In the warm spring night, the suburban sounds of crickets and cicadas whirring from the surrounding darkness, I had packed away a few belongings from my childhood room as my mother had watched on ruefully.

"Why don't you just stay here and caddy? You can get all the fall tournaments in and probably make enough money to fix at least part of your mouth," she had argued.

"*Dusted* is just starting up a New York office, I have to get in at the beginning," I repeated for the eighteenth time that day.

"Neil, I can see the pain in your face. You can't leave like this."

I frowned as I wrapped a rubber band around a fistful of pens. "It's going to hurt wherever I am, and I'd much rather be aching in New York City than aching around here."

"What are they going to pay you?" she had shot at me.

"I don't know."

"Why didn't you go to State School? What kind of job are you going to get without a college education?"

"Pimp."

"*You watch that mouth around your mother!*"

When I thought the conversation had finally ended, and my mother had used up every doubt and discouragement in her seemingly endless arsenal, she came back into my room, a drink in her hand, a cruel smile on her hard lips.

"So you think you're going to New York to become a big somebody, is that it?"

I spoke softly, avoiding her hateful eyes as I finished packing. "Yes, I do."

My mother stood for a moment in the door frame, staring at me with an expression of bemused contempt, inhaling thinly from her cigarette. And as I unfolded and refolded another shirt, I heard her blow a stream of menthol smoke through tight, pursed lips and then utter her farewell:

"Just wait Neil, you'll end up behind a desk like everybody else."

The click of a tourist camera pulled me from the past, and then I heard a few French words laced with laughter; looking up, I saw a beaming young couple in well-traveled army shorts, scuffed boots, and faded T-shirts walking toward me. With their deep tans and battered backpacks, they clashed heavily with the brightly colored, well-managed outfits of the older bus-tour Australians around them. I watched as the two stopped at the base of a Buddha nearby, the man pulling a map from his bag, spreading it out on the stone pedestal. His girlfriend brushed her long brown hair from her eyes and followed as he traced along a line with his finger. A moment passed, and then I closed my notebook and walked to them.

"Pardon, mon français n'est pas bien, mais où est-ce que vous travelez?" I asked, remembering a butcher version of some French Nadia had taught me back in New York.

"We have just come back from Sulawesi," the young Frenchman answered, thankfully in English.

"Sulawesi is a good spot?" I continued, easing myself into a conversation.

"This is an excellent place. Very beautiful."

"I'm Neil."

"I am Stephan, and this is Cleo," the man said.

"Hello." Cleo spoke a heavily accented greeting, nodding her head with a smile. She wore cutoff shorts, boots, and a faded blue T-shirt with rolled-up sleeves, hanging loosely over a well-toned body. Her boyfriend had short crew-cut hair and strong muscles, clearly visible through his unbuttoned, checkered shirt. He looked like the type who could lash together a sturdy, makeshift shelter, then track and kill game. Next to him, I felt like a boy.

"And where have you been?" he asked.

"Just Java."

Cleo murmured something in French, and Stephan placed his hand on her long leg, absently stroking the smooth skin as if it were his own. With an ache, I wished I were him.

"We were scuba diving in Sulawesi," he said, pointing it out on the map. "Really, this is some of the best diving in the world."

Indonesia, that's diving country . . . The words of my Hollywood dentist came back to me in the echo of memory.

"Do you scuba dive?" Stephan asked me.

"No. But I want to start," I said, the idea gripping me.

"If you have the time, you should get licensed here. It is the most amazing diving in the world."

"Do you know a place?" I asked excitedly, suddenly overcome by the notion.

"We have just been studying for our dive-master class in Pang, on the west of the island." His thick, calloused finger pointed out the spot. "There is a school taught by an American named Roy. You could get licensed there if you would want, and then be diving."

"Stephan?" His girlfriend pointed to a statue across the way and pulled at his hand, speaking in French.

"Would you mind watching our things?" the dive master asked, sliding the map under my notebook as he was led away.

I watched them move through the crowds of tourists, rugged and young in the brightly colored, overweight throng. Shouldered video cameras scanned slowly from every figure around them, and I looked on as Stephan took off his battered running sneaker, holding it up to his eye as if he were filming. He aimed at Cleo, and she dissolved in laughter, then walked to her boyfriend, lacing her arms around his muscular body. Alone, I took in the young lovers, a fond breeze rippling their travel tousled-hair in the warm glow of afternoon's end, a series of light, slight kisses flurrying between their lips.

As I regarded the couple, I felt a sudden surge of regret for running from Ehrlina. Why didn't I bring her with me? Why hadn't I asked? She was dressed for a special day and I hadn't even asked her to share it with me. She had taken me into her home, and all I could do was run away . . . And what about Milena? What was I waiting for? Why didn't I go to her?

Stephan glanced my way, and our gazes locked for a fleeting moment across the stones. Then my eyes darted down and bored into my empty notebook, and hot shame ripped through me, as if I had been caught in some kind of perversion. For a long while, I kept my head bowed, but I couldn't help from hearing the foreign voices of the couple on the wind.

Before me, the white page of my unwritten manifesto lay open and empty.

Just wait Neil, you'll end up behind a desk like everybody else.

And suddenly, I was filled with a loathing I had never before felt for my work. My mother was right: I was stuck behind a desk as surely as my father had been. It didn't matter if my office was halfway around the world, atop a Buddhist monument in the jungles of Java; I was still trapped. My tongue ran slowly back along the fractured ruins of my mouth, and it was then that I saw *Neil Before God* for the first time. Not for its shining unwritten brilliance, or its future cultural triumph, but for the endless collection of empty rooms its words tried to fill, and the vacant, lonely nights its scribbled pages desperately attempted to write away. Flash had Gertie, Mom had Dad, James had pot, Mandy had *Bop Cheese,* Stu had marriage, Ehrlina had home, Stephan had Cleo, and I had my endless, absurd task; a swamp of dark memories I could safely stew in, keeping me from ever taking hold of something new.

"So, I think they are making us to go." It was Cleo's deep, accented voice that brought me out of my empty pages a short while later. In the long shadows of the Buddha, I looked up to see her before me, arms reaching overhead in a delicious stretch, her tall, healthy body extended, lean and gorgeous in the glow of the setting sun. The tourists were dissipating in the background, and Stephan was meticulously folding up his map on the base of the Buddha.

"I'm going diving," I announced.

"That's very good," he responded, sounding distracted.

"Yeah, I decided I really need a vacation. I've been

here working, you know, working really hard. And I just need to relax, that's what I've decided." I took a quick swig of water and wiped the sweat from my neck. "What's the place called again?"

"Go to Pang. Find Roy and tell him you met Stephan and Cleo. He will remember us," Stephan answered, slipping the map into his pack.

Cleo pointed to her thick, black dive watch, saying something about the time in French.

"Good-bye then. Good luck," Stephan said as he slipped his arm over his girlfriend's shoulder.

"Bye-bye," she said waving, as they walked away.

"*Au revoir*," I returned.

"Your French, it is very good," Stephan called back over his shoulder, and I heard Cleo laughing.

"*Comeand tiemyshoe, s'il vous plaît?*" I said after them, remembering a dumb joke I had made up with Nadia in New York. They disappeared down the steps, and my mind wound back to the big-boobed Belgian girl, clouded in pot smoke in her spacious, upscale New York City apartment. I suddenly wished I had her address, so I could send her a postcard, a letter, anything at all to connect. I squinted in concentration, trying to recall her street number, but then remembered I had left for Hollywood without even a good-bye.

Milena, then—my mind seized her memory. I got up with an excited rush and began walking across the rough surface of interlocking stones, toward the sun creeping down behind a distant mountainside. I would island-hop like Stephan and Cleo, maybe even buy a map, diving my way across the archipelago in the azure sea. And when I'd lost myself for long enough in the swirling schools of colored fish, I'd go to Milena, to London, where we'd start what we had begun a year before. A new city, new faces, a place to lay down a whole new groove and . . .

I hit the top of the stairs and suddenly remembered my manifesto. Turning back, I looked at the empty, abandoned notebook at the foot of an Asian deity, its cover blown open, pages flapping in the evening wind. Instinctively, I began back toward it, but then stopped.

I heard my mother's contemptuous laughter echo in my ears, and then it mixed with Mandy's, was overcome by Flash's giggling Channel antics, and then all was drowned out by the roaring jeers of a thousand Alternate drones in a Las Vegas stadium. All along, the mockery had hounded my attempt to write my own script, and now they would be winning, crushing the unformed words that rattled endlessly in my head.

I started back.

But then a violent fist squeezed tight my insides, and I knew with a blazing certainty that I couldn't spend another second in the sticky, solitary web of black bitterness that was my past. I spun around, leaving the empty, flapping book behind me as I began running across the timeworn stones. Evening's breeze blew colder on my skin as I threaded through the ring of silent Buddhas in the dying light, past their serene faces and the gentle curves of their smoothly carved limbs. In my head, I felt my tongue winding back to the last molar, prodding at the chunk of coffee that had stuck fast at Ehrlina's. Pulling and pushing at the fractured enamel, I cursed myself again for forgetting toothpicks, as I made my way hurriedly down the steep steps of the ancient, deserted monument.

10. pang

It took me a few days to find Pang, a dazed little village on the sleepy, tranquil sea of Java's western coast. Dropped off by a smoky bus, I followed a dusty sketch of a road through a cluster of tiny shacklike dwellings, past an old red gas pump and a single merchant's hut, until I reached the beach. My boots slid as I trudged through the blackish sand, scanning the silent, still shoreline in the blazing midday heat for a single sign of life.

Just as I decided the French dive masters had duped me, I spied a white-tiled bungalow set back from the beach in the shadow of a lone palm tree. Squinting at the weathered wooden sign, I breathed a sigh of relief and walked across the burning sand toward Pang Dive.

"Hello?"

It was breezy and cool inside the dive center, a pair of large, standing fans gently humming as they swiveled side to side on opposite sides of the white-tiled room. A series of bright blue coastal maps were posted on the walls, along with underwater photographs of grinning divers and psychedelic tropical fish. Sparkling new face masks and snorkels were arranged under the glass counter, and sleek, brightly colored wet suits hung up on display near the window. Through the open back door, I glimpsed racks of tanks and vests hanging to dry outside, like space suits waiting for their astronauts.

"Hello?" I called again.

"Hang on," a sleepy-sounding American voice called from somewhere in the back. "I'm gettin' there."

A tanned, lanky, but potbellied man appeared from a doorway behind the counter, wearing nothing but a purple bikini swimsuit.

"What can I do you for?"

"I want to be a diver."

"I see." He scratched at his thinning, bleach blond hair. "Well, you caught me at a bad time. Season's pretty much done, and I'm heading to Kalimantan in a week for an expedition."

"You're Roy, right?"

"Yeah, how'd you know?"

"Stephan and Cleo told me to come here."

A warm smile spread across his face. "Ah, Cleo and Stephan. Wonderful young couple; and dive masters, both of them."

"They said you'd certify me."

"They did, did they?" He frowned for a moment, then reached a decision. "What's the name?"

"Neil," I said, extending my hand.

"OK, Neil," he answered, with a handshake. "You're

a friend of Cleo and Stephan's, and I'm not leaving for a few days. That'll be enough time to get you certified."

I grinned in the white room. "When do we start?"

"Tomorrow morning. You a swimmer?"

"Yup."

Roy reached under the desk for some papers, then clicked his pen and slipped on a pair of bifocals. "Good enough. There ain't much more to it than that."

I slept through the heat of the afternoon in Pang's lone *losmen*, sweating under the slow circles of the ceiling fan in the simple, white-tiled room. Sunset drew me down to the beach, and when I walked through the blackened sand, I found that the deserted village of Pang had come alive.

Fishermen in cone hats were hauling in their boats from the sea, pushing the wooden craft up onto the beach. Strong black nets, thick with fish, were spread out on the damp sand by the women who had come from the village to help their husbands. Little girls ran laughing around their fathers, and farther down the sandy strand, young boys prepared their kites, a few already up, flickering and flapping as they dived and circled in the strong, seaside winds.

As I sat in the sand, I remembered the kites my mom used to buy: cheap plastic ones for James and me every summer when we went to the seashore. It was an annual vacation all through my youth, over the last two weeks of August. We would get a rental house where Dad would read his spy novels and Mom did her crosswords, while James mastered the latest boardwalk arcade games, and I spent all day near the water from dawn until dark. Swimming in the ocean, bodysurfing, building drip castles, meeting kids and being friends for a while until the waves pulled us one way or the other.

But my favorite time on that beach of my youth was when my dad would join me in the waves. He never hit the water until late in the afternoon, when the sun's rays had died and evening was closing in on the beach. I remembered how excited I would become when I saw him on the sand, pulling off his blue golf shirt and swimming out toward me.

"Gotcha!" my dad would growl, grabbing on to my foot as I shrieked in delight, trying to kick away from him. We would wrestle in the salt water of the Atlantic, laughing and ducking the breaking wave, my dad's big back greased up from sun lotion, his tanned face unfamiliar without his glasses.

And after what seemed like never long enough, my father would wipe the salt water from his eyes and say, "OK Neil, ready to go to the moon?" It always meant my father had had enough, and it was our last game before he swam to shore. He would take my hands, and I would balance, standing on his shoulders, while he sank down underwater. Then I would wait there on my father's shoulders for what seemed like forever, shouting out in the fading sunlight:

"To the moon! Send me to the moon!"

And finally my father would burst up from the sandy bottom, letting go of my hands and sending me flying so far through the air, then splashing down laughing into the green-grey waves. The surf would tumble me along in its churning tunnel, the sand swirling around me until I swam up from underwater and found the surface. I'd look back then, over the crashing waves to the beach and my father, who would wave at me, smiling, before pulling on his blue golf shirt and walking away over the emptying beach.

I suddenly wished that he could be there with me. Not the old Dad, the dour, Scotch-drinking Dad who had been laid off by the company he had dedicated his life to; not the Dad who was sent out looking for work at the age of fifty; and especially not the Dad who had his two little boys grow up into a pot dealing burner and a snagglepuss, college-dodging writer. No, I wished the old Dad was there with me, relaxed and tan, calling me Neil-O and kissing my Mom in the little kitchenette of some rental house by the beach. The big Dad swimming out to me in the ocean, taking me upon his giant, sunscreened shoulders and sending me flying to the moon.

The engine whined high, and the flat wooden boat skipped over the waves, smoke rising into the clear sky behind us. Gusts of salt water sprayed up into the air, baptizing my face in the Javanese sea.

The two days of testing passed in a simple series of equipment quizzes and oxygen tables, ending with a practice dive in the little pool out back of the center. Roy kept insisting I had dived before, as I breezed through the various skills and swam casually through the warm water. This day would be my first ocean dive, after which I would be licensed and free to roam the sun drenched Indonesian archipelago, sans manifesto and the ghostly prisons of memory trapped in its empty pages.

Roy moved next to me, squinting his eyes against the sun and rushing breeze, and shouting over the motor:

"You ready, Neil?"

A grin overtook my face as I nodded my head in the jumping boat. "Hell yeah!" I yelled over the whining engine.

He laughed as the boat pilot cut the engine, slowing us to a stop in the sparkling sea. Roy and I began prepping for the dive, arranging our weight belts, fastening the fins, and spitting into our masks, spreading the saliva with our thumbs to keep the glass from fogging. When all was ready, we moved to the side of the bobbing craft. After a thumbs-up to Roy, I held my regulator in my mouth and then rolled over backward into the water.

A soft depth charge sounded from my body's submersion in the shimmering blue, and as gravity let me go, I was surrounded by a flurry of silver bubbles. My inflated vest brought me to the surface, but I held my head in the water, gazing down at the fabulously colored fish that swirled and swarmed below me, my freckled arm looking pale and skinny, the black arm hairs waving in the wavering current. There was a tap on my shoulder, and I picked my face up to look at Roy, floating next to me.

"Ready to explore the ocean blue?" he asked.

Bobbing up and down in the warm water, with the aquamarine sea surface spanning awesome all around, I realized that I had never seen the world from this angle before. The Javanese coast was far behind, and as tides pulled me gently this way and that, I felt like a little kid again—happy at the seashore.

"Yup," I answered, grinning.

"Remember, we're in no hurry. The fish aren't going anywhere. Just relax, and let's take our time and enjoy."

I pushed the regulator past my lips and bit down on the rubber, inhaling the cool air from my tank. Roy sank out of sight and I depressed the valve on my vest, releasing short, sharp bursts of stored air, following him down into the sea.

The bubbles rumbled past my ears as I turned my eyes first to the shimmering green depths, then to my teacher. He gave me a thumbs-up, and I flashed one back. With the regulator in his mouth, and the mask over his face, it was impossible to see Roy's expression, aside from his pale blue eyes staring up at me and slowly blinking as we drifted down. His blond hair waved weightless around him, silken with the sunlight shining through, as all around us spirals of silver bubbles chased each other to the surface. The sun sparkled and dazzled through the undulating seascape in pinprick rays of piercing light, and I knew that I was finally where I belonged: a warm, wordless universe where all I had to do was breathe and float.

But as the first striped fish swam past my face, I felt a sharp ache grip my tooth. As I let more air out of my vest and dropped down lower, the pressure got tighter. Roy drifted down ahead of me and I prayed for the pain to pass, even as I felt it clenching harder. Sinking farther down in the sea, my heart thundered in my chest as a black vice slowly crushed into my teeth, threatening to splinter my entire skull. Helpless to stop it and sinking faster, panic swarmed my senses as I kicked up towards the sun, so far away.

Need to get out. Neil . . . out . . .

I tried to scream for help, but the words strangled themselves in my tightening chest, and I sank, like a hammer into a sea once green and shimmering, transforming before my eyes into a black, murky ooze . . . The pressure pounded my tooth, and I felt as if I were being swallowed by my own agonized mouth, down into a primeval sea of dental despair. I began to panic.

I had ignored my dentist . . . The Great Work . . . God, if I had only listened! My only chance was gone forever . . .

Wait . . . THERE!

Motion caught my eye, and my head whipped up, where I saw shafts of shining lights cutting through the gloom, dropping down closer to me. And as they came nearer, I saw that each light was a single point, a man, a diver, descending down to meet me, lifelines to the surface.

I tried to call out, but my voice was killed in the black liquid, and I watched, helplessly silent as the divers moved closer, their forms softly glowing white as they slowly came into view. They were a crack team, I could tell, their bodies muscular and fit, hard and lean, their cool, capable faces illuminated in sharp clarity behind the silvered glass of their face masks. And as they began to pass by, I realized they were no ordinary divers, but dentists.

Scuba Dentists!

Polished picks and angled mirrors gleamed from the equipment belts rigged around their waists, drills hung securely in sidearm holsters, emergency nitrous canisters banded crisscross over their strapping chests . . . I heard the static and crackle of radio communication between them as they slowly glided past, taking no notice of me as they dropped farther into the dark depths.

Help me! I'm the one! Right here!

But they moved on, their bubbles of clean air rising silver and shimmering around me in the blackness. None of them stopped or even looked at me, and I screamed and cursed, flailing in the water, until the last scuba dentist dropped smoothly past me, eyes on the men below. Extending myself with everything in me, I somehow reached out through the heavy depths and just managed to brush his taut, muscular arm as he drifted past.

The dental diver turned and looked at me with a quizzical frown as he glided down past me; I tried to speak, but the words clogged in my throat. With a burst of air, the scuba dentist stabilized his weight and floated to my side. He stared at me with clear blue eyes set squarely in his clean-shaven, chiseled face, an expression of guarded concern lit white in the illumination of his equipment.

Savagely, I pointed my finger at my tooth. He nodded his head and pulled a series of laminated charts off his hip, flipping through them in the slightly undulating current. Not able to wait, I grabbed his shoulders, screaming savagely.

HELP ME!!!

"OK, OK, I want to help you," the scuba dentist's voice came sharp and clean over his radio set. "But you have to calm down and listen to me." He put away his charts, securing them once again on his hip. "I know about your case, but we can't proceed on the Great Work down here."

BUT I NEED HELP NOW!

He gazed steadily at me. "Neil, listen to me. I know you are in intense pain right now. However, we can't risk an open-heart root canal at this depth."

Risk a WHAT?!

The dental diver saw the look of furious incomprehension on my face. "It's beyond your teeth, Neil. The infection has gone to your heart, and it's moving towards your soul. You're in a lot of danger, and you're going to have to get yourself to the surface before anyone can save you."

HOW?!

"I can't help you now." He glanced down to see the rest of his team, already dropping out of sight. "We're on a mission that's bigger than your mouth and my mouth put together, Neil. Bigger than everyone's mouth in the world. I'm sorry, I'm under orders."

And with that, the SCUBA dentist saluted me, released a short, sharp burst of air from his vest, and dropped at a dizzying speed into the darkness below.

NO! COME BACK!!!

I screamed and screamed, but no sounds came out of my throat as I fought savagely in the blackness, flailing my arms and feet and reaching for something, anything to help pull me out. Helpless, I thrashed in the depths, my heart hammering, my breath becoming ragged and burning, until finally, exhausted, the fight slowly seeped out of me, and I had nothing to do but give in, sinking ever faster into blackness.

*   *   *

"NEIL!!"

My eyes slowly opened under the burning tropical sun.

"Are you all right?"

Roy was bent over me, panic and fear contorting his face, seawater and sweat dripping from his brow.

"Can you tell me what's wrong?"

I looked at the abandoned dive equipment strewn about me in the bottom of the wooden boat. Flippers, respirators, face masks, tanks . . .

"My teeth . . . they hurt . . . real bad when I went down . . . The scuba dentists . . . couldn't help me."

Roy spoke clearly and sharply. "Are you all right now? Is there any pain, Neil?"

I felt my skinny, dripping body, lying limp and white on the bottom of the boat. "No, I'm fine," I said, slowly recovering my senses. My hand went to my mouth, and I stroked the side of my jaw, the excruciating pain now vanished completely. "It was my teeth . . . like a clamp on them, real bad when I went down . . . but they're fine now," I answered, confused.

Roy exhaled a long breath of pent-up tension and leaned back against the side of the boat. "Jesus, Neil, you had me scared. You blacked out down there."

We sat for a while in silence, the azure Javanese sea lapping softly up against the sides of the white wooden boat.

"Your teeth, huh?" my instructor asked.

"Yeah."

"And they hurt worse the farther you went down?"

I nodded my head.

Roy spoke with slow certainty. "Then it was a tooth squeeze."

I stared dumbly at my instructor as he pulled the mask off his forehead. "It's a pretty rare condition," he continued. "I've never seen one before, but it's in the book."

"*A tooth squeeze?*" I repeated, in disbelief.

Roy turned and rooted through his equipment bag as I blinked under the blazing blue sky, incredulous.

"*A tooth squeeze?*"

"Here. Take a look," the dive master said, holding out an open page. Numbly, I pulled myself up in the dingy craft and took the book, squinting to read the words under the glaring tropical sun.

Air spaces rarely exist in the teeth, but may occur in cases of extensive dental work, where small bubbles of air can be trapped beneath fillings. Increasing pressure pushing in on this small air space during descent causes what is known as a "tooth squeeze." In most instances, the discomfort prevents further diving. In extreme cases, lapse of consciousness can occur, leading to emergency situations.

I cursed bitterly, slowly closing the book and staring down at the brown water pooled in the boat's bottom. "Goddamn Hollywood dentists."

Roy shook his head slowly. "I'm sorry. It's a damn shame."

"But . . . I wanted to be a diver," I barely managed, my voice a husky whisper.

"What can I say, Neil?" Roy said with a sigh. "Not this time."

A single tear rolled down my cheek, and I gazed around me at the massive indifference of the sea.

The next morning, I left Pang. It took me three days by bus to reach Jakarta. There was a flight for London leaving late that night, and I found a seat on the near empty plane, dimly lit and cold with air-conditioning. Wrapping myself in a blanket, I gazed blankly out a black window all the way to Europe, while my tongue softly pushed at my broken teeth.

Apart, together, apart, together, apart . . .

London

11. a whole 'nother trip

I had stayed in the Alfred Hotel for a stretch last time I was in London, before moving in with Milena. It was a fairly notorious backpacker's crash set in the center of a large, gently curving street near the Earl's Court tube stop, and I didn't have any trouble finding it again. Fifteen hours after jetting Java, I walked through the familiar whitewashed doorway into the cruddy reception room. Looking around at the archaic soda machine leaned against one wall, the TV blathering from the corner, and a mixed-up assortment of institutional furniture supporting a handful of slouched and smoking telly gazers, I was glad that I wouldn't be staying long.

At the desk stood a guy about thirty, mustache, worn flannel shirt, smoking a cigarette. "Good day kind sir, do you seek lodgings?" he asked me as I approached.

I slid my backpack down to the floor. "Yup."

"Very good. But I must take pains to warn you that our polo stables are in a state of disrepair, and the Presidential Suite is currently occupied."

A tall smoker with bad skin gave a laugh. "He'll be lucky if the toilet takes his crap."

Jet-lagged from the flight, disillusioned from my doomed diving experience, I had no desire for chuckles. Quietly, I reached for my passport, dropping it down on the desk before me. The deskman didn't bother taking it, though, eyeing me for a speculative moment instead.

"India?" he guessed.

"No."

"Thailand?"

"No."

"Israel?"

"No," I answered, tired and annoyed. "I just back from—"

"DON'T SAY IT! I'll get it yet." He folded his arms across his chest, stroked his mustache for a moment, then slowly smiled. "Indonesia."

"How did you know?" I asked, a slight wonder cutting through my mood.

The room burst out into laughter at my surprise. "Gordon got another one, Bridget!" someone called into the hallway.

"Well let's just call the bloody press!" an irritated female voice shouted back.

Gordon pulled an old logbook out from under the desk. "How long do you plan on staying?" he asked, entering my passport number into the register.

"Couple days," I told him, even as I imagined running to Milena that very night.

"Ah, sure, couple days. That's what they all say. Old Alfred has a way of sucking people in. I remember when I came here, full of sap, my whole life before me . . ." His voice trailed off in a sigh. "But now look at me. And look at her," he said, nodding his head toward a scowling girl my age as she yanked an ancient vacuum cleaner into the room.

"Oh piss off, Gordon!" she snapped.

"She was a traveler, like yourself. Should have seen Bridget when she first checked in. Like a breath of fresh spring air; a pretty smile on those once rosy lips . . ."

The Alfred lounge gallery broke out into raucous laughter.

"ALL YOU WANKERS BETTER SHUT YER BLEEDING HOLES OR I'LL SPIT IN THE JAM EVERY MORNING FROM NOW TILL BOXING DAY!" Bridget screamed, jamming a plug into the wall and drowning their jeers in the deafening roar of her cleaning machine.

Gordon handed me a key and shouted over the racket. "Yes, Bridget is in charge of breakfast here, and she does have the power to spit in your jam, so be sure and stay on her good side!" He gave me a salute. "Be seeing you!"

I left the lounge and walked up toward the crooked, creaking stairs, away from them all.

Within a single grey week, I realized that London this time around would be a whole 'nother trip. Last summer's sprawling stone city of delight had been drizzled away by a cold, dark rain, spitting down on me from the moment I arrived. The charged thrill of

travel had been lost along with my abandoned manifesto, and as I wandered the wet cement streets, digging at my tooth with a newly acquired English
toothpick, I realized I had reached a kind of dental
homeland.

Each passing subject's mug showcased yellowed
teeth, rows wrenched into wicked overbites, woefully
crooked bite lines, and grins interspersed with gaping
holes, stained brown blotches, or blackened-out, rotten
nubs. It was as if the entire island had been rear-ended
at a red light, and the whole populace had been sent
flying face first into the "boot" or "bonnet," or whatever the hell it was the Brits called the dashboard.
Wincing at every smile, I avoided any pleasantries that
might coax one forth from the natives and made a solemn vow that I would never, ever seek out an English
dentist, no matter what the calamity.

Even the Alfred had taken a distressing, downward
dive in the year I had been away. In the short time I
had spent there before meeting Milena, the run-down
rooming house had been home to an excited crowd of
intermingling nationalities: young backpackers wandering the globe, eager to meet and trade travel tales
late into the night. But now, with summer gone, a grim
stagnation gripped the hotel. Most metal bunks were
vacant, and the mismatched lobby furniture supported
a slouching cast of rumpled drifters and forlorn for-
eigners, silent and smoking, staring blankly out the
rain-patterned windows.

In the nights, as I lay on my sagging metal cot, listening to the snoring, sputtering sleep of the strangers
bunked about me, I tried to call the courage to meet
Milena. She was mine, I knew, but fear clamored my

senses as I counted off all that had changed since our first *happle* together. With no *Dusted* backing me up across the Atlantic, and no manifesto to give me meaning, I felt skinny and pointless: it wouldn't be a pen-wielding Irish Samurai showing up on the gorgeous Italian woman's doorstep, but a homeless, broken-toothed kid.

I had been marking time for the past few days in the news agencies, perusing through the scenester English mags, seeing where my style might fit in. No qualms oozed through my stomach as I jotted down titles of glossy, vapid, perfume and cologne-scented magazines, only a blank consent to reality's grim demands for survival. Whether it was *Bop Cheese* or Brit cheese didn't matter anymore: my once noble ambitions had dwindled to a faint desire to keep breathing. Milena was prime in my mind, and I'd write what was needed to fall asleep at her side.

The springs creaked wretchedly in the bunk above me as a thick, wet, rattling cough ripped through my Pakistani roommate; I shivered, listened to the cold rain outside falling harder, suddenly feeling mad for fleeing the lush tropics of Java. Behind my closed eyes, I saw the azure ocean swelling against bleached beaches, the languid bodies stretched out on patterned sarongs, bronzing in the rays of a blazing sun . . .

But Milena.

She was the sole reason I had abandoned Java's dreamy balm for this isle of gloom, and manifesto or not, I *knew* she would still have me. Confidence came as I brought back the first night we had made love, remembering the heated, playful passion we had shared. How I had asked her to speak Italian in my ears, and how Milena had laughed, refusing. But I had pressed relentlessly with kisses, my lips tender and persistent against her skin, until finally she blew out the flickering candle and laid her body on top of mine.

"OK, I don't mind to speak for you, but there must be dark. And there is nothing I can think to talk, so you must tell me what you want to hear."

"Hmmm . . ." My mind went blank, so I began scanning around the bedroom of Milena's Camden Town flat. And just visible in the corner, beneath the streetlight glowing through the window, my eyes picked out a pair of black, lace-up disco roller skates. Smiling, I had nestled my lips through the soft scents of her luxuriant dark hair and whispered in her ear, "Tell me about your roller skates."

"*No!*" Milena had burst out laughing and shut her eyes, shaking her head from side to side as she pushed me away. "You are mad! Do you know that? Are all American boys so mad as you?"

"Your roller skates, Milena. Tell me all your secrets about them."

And after a long moment, when her laughter had faded, Milena had slowly put her arms around me and taken me on top of her, bringing my mouth close to her lips with a gentle hand. She tenderly kissed my ear, running her wet tongue in slow, heated circles, then began to whisper, ever so deliciously, all about her roller skates. Her Italian came at first in short, pressing breaths, but as we moved together, the words came faster and faster, her foreign tongue flickering hot exotic syllables deep into my being as our passion exploded, bright white lights in the darkness . . .

Another racking cough brought me back to the Alfred, and I exhaled my breath, not realizing I had been holding it. I felt my body relax in the sunken mattress of the bunk, as I assured myself that Milena was ready and waiting in her world of *happles* and roller skates. I smiled, knowing now that I would go there, as a blessed, welcome sleep pulled me into its heavy hands. And the last thing I was aware of before sinking into black was my tongue, working almost on its own now, digging softly after the piece lodged deep in my broken tooth.

It was Saturday night and London was charged. I joined the crowd of scenesters descending the steps into the underground, finding my place on the crowded train car as it clattered through the dark tunnels. The heat of weekend expectations saturated the train as we rattled beneath the London streets, heads bobbing with the curving car. I watched a red faced kid laugh wildly with his raven-eyed sidekick, saw a black man buried deep inside a dark coat, nodding to his friend and smiling, gold front teeth gleaming in the light. The train stopped, a few got off, a few more got in, and a weary old man wrapped in a drab coat, weighed down with bags of groceries, searched for a seat. I gave him mine but avoided his tired eyes, turning instead to two giggling teenage girls, their tight young bodies bound in hard-core leisure wear, the night theirs for the taking.

Despite the humming excitement, I felt a weariness deep inside me. Ever since I had left my parents' house with a shattered mouth and my mother's curses, I had been picking myself up and down, city to city, round the world, looking for home. My manifesto and its promise of instant salvation had for so long kept me moving, but after abandoning the pages in Java, I felt dangerously close to caving in. As I glanced up at the colored lines of the underground map yet again, I realized that this train ride to Milena's was the last length of some manic, global marathon that had cost me nearly everything I had. Reaching into my pocket, I took out her address and gazed at the numbers again, seeing an equation to fill the holes in my life.

The train rounded a fast turn and bodies wavered, leaning into each other. From an unseen corner, a man belted out a drunken song, joined by a few others for a throaty verse before they faltered, staggered, and broke down into loud, liquored laughter. I tried to let their spirits catch me, but somewhere inside, a tiny, trembling fear was writhing. Even with Milena only moments away, I couldn't help but be wary of London. After the entropy of the Alfred and the cold, continuous rain that spit down on me from the brooding English skies, I wondered whether that glistening city of last summer, sprinkled with Milena's kisses, had been nothing but a hallucination. And reeling and rolling with the underground car of rowdy English subjects, I couldn't help but remember my great-uncle Barney's warnings about this island, which I had listened to as a child long ago.

On Thanksgivings, my father's clan had gotten together in New York at my aunt Nancy's, and when dinner was over, everyone would gather on the living room sofas, sipping Scotch and remembering the Tough Times. How Grandfather had died not long after immigrating, how Grandma worked as a maid in the big houses to feed the family, how my dad and Uncle Rory had dug through the sofas for bus-fare change, how the Church donated a turkey every year at Christmas. Then they recalled the Protestant kids who weren't allowed to play with my dad and his brothers, the endless weekends of caddying at the country club, the bare scholarships to prep schools and college . . . And ultimately how they had all risen up, every brother and sister, grinding through the struggle for their own chunk of America.

But after the regulated amount of time was spent in sullen, Scotch-soaked silence, one of the older cousins would yank the group out of their painful memories with a sharp, snide arrow of deftly aimed sarcasm, and a sudden, roaring rush of laughter would turn the evening's tide. New drinks were poured, the music got louder, the jabs, the jokes, and the stories began. And that was when my great-uncle Barney would pull me, the youngest cousin, aside, and give me my lessons.

Uncle Barney had grown up with Pappy in Donegal and was our only living link to Ireland, my grandma having died when I was little. He had thick, knotted hands, a heavy brogue, and a white, floating eye, which kept most of the other cousins at bay. But Uncle Barney was my favorite of all the relatives who came together at Thanksgiving. He was the only one who would tell me tales about the grandfather I had never met, and the tiny Northern town of Carrygalen they had left behind for America.

From school, I learned of the English as a proper, civilized, noble race, all grammar and Parliament, theatre and tea. But on Thanksgivings, as all the drunken uncles and aunts carried on in the next room, Uncle

Barney would give me *his* English lesson: the genocidal horror of the Famine, the savagery of the Black and Tans, the cold evil of absentee landlords, and a twisted history of oppression, murder, deceit, and treachery.

Inevitably, at some point in this dark tableau, my huge, rich, drunken uncle Rory would overhear us and belt out:

"The history of the Irish is the history of a bunch of losers, and the best thing Pappy ever did was get the hell out of Donegal!"

He'd laugh in his big bellowing laugh, and just about everybody except Uncle Barney would join in. A moment later, my dad would suddenly take notice of the same old Irish tape we listened to every year: brogue brothers in sweaters singing ballads of woe. He'd shout over the laughter Rory had sparked:

"Is there a single record in this house that isn't about Ireland?! Jesus, it's Thanksgiving, let's find something we can be thankful about! Even Christmas music if you have to! Anything but Ireland!"

They'd laugh louder and Uncle Rory would join him, shouting again, "Best thing Pappy ever did was get the hell out of Donnegal!"

Every relative would join in the roaring laughter, a few kids would be hurried off to mix drinks for their parents, and Uncle Barney would lean down next to me and say:

"Don't listen to your uncle Rory. He's a stupid drunk ass. It's important you know your Irish history, because I know when my wee ones went through school, the teachers didn't tell them the truth about the English."

He'd lean over his cane and squint toward some place in the distance, while his floating eye mysteri-

ously perused the room, and start in about the Irish
flight from famine to America: "They called the boats
the English ran 'coffin ships' because so many died on
the passage. Worse than the slave ships ever were. The
blacks had to be sold, but the Irish, they weren't worth
nothing to no one—"

"What are you doing over there, Barney? Recruiting
for the IRA?" Uncle Rory would shout. "C'mon, the
kid's not even twelve! And they gypped Pappy out of
his pension, anyway!"

My dad would put his hand to his mouth and shout
over the rolling laughter of his brothers and sisters,
"He's yours, Barney! Take him and make him a soldier!
That's one less to put through college!"

"Well, if he's a triggerman, the first one he's going
after is you, Rory, you big drunk ass!" Uncle Barney
would counter, barely heard over the rollicking laughter.

Uncle Rory would throw his hands up in the air.
*"Do it! Do it! My taxes are a mess! My marriage is collaps-
ing! And you know what? It's all the English's fault!
HAAAA HAAAA!"*

His deep laughter bellowed through the entire house,
and everybody would become swallowed up in it, except Uncle Barney, who would lean closer to me and
almost whisper:

"You don't pay attention to him, Neil, he's full 'a
muck. And he's terrible with his whiskey. It's the devil,
it is. You look out for that stuff when you get older,
hear me? And you look out for the English, too."

The train stopped at Camden Town, and I came up
from the underground in a surge of urbanites spilling

onto streets packed thick with young Brits. Gangs of slicked players prowled out of pubs, hipster couples strolled hand in hand, and young beauties tossed their heads back, laughing with their girlfriends. Night music poured from club-lit doorways lining the way, held in by a visual chaos of concert posters clamoring over the walls all around. Rastas offered smoke under their breath, hippie craftsmen pushed beads and bracelets, and through it all the flirtations flew, with wide-open wings or fledgling flickers, in the cool night chill.

Rounding the familiar corner, past the furniture-piled secondhand store and the vintage rockabilly record shop, I savored my moment, clutching tight the *happle* I had bought earlier. Moving toward Milena, my shoulders shifting side to side against the flowing throng of young Londoners, I felt as if I were treading the last steps of a thoroughly worn life. The past had passed, and it was on to the new; I stepped up to Milena's familiar black front door, poised on the brink of my future.

I knocked.

I waited.

I heard footsteps.

The door opened.

My mouth dropped.

"Yeah?" A smoothly dressed, young black man in a dark pin-stripe suit and long, braided hair stood impatiently in the door frame.

"I'm . . ."

"What's that?"

"I'm looking for Milena," I managed. Behind him I caught a glimpse of the bright white kitchen, where I had passed a long-lingering, raining day with my love, sipping tea and learning to say "I want to lick your toes" in Italian.

His face quizzed. "Who?"

"Milena . . . I . . . I . . . she lives here."

"Milena?" He thought for a moment, looking down at his polished, silver-buckled boots. My eyes followed down to the wine-colored carpet, where she and I had made fast, hard love on a Friday before the movies; sharp, red burns on my elbows, on my knees for days.

"Oh right, must be the bird was shacking here before me." He suddenly smiled and leveled a finger at me, heavy with silver rings. "Right, then, you must be the bloke who's been sending all the postcards!"

I heard his amused laughter retreat into the flat, and in a blink he was back with a slim stack of picture postcards, fingers flipping through the bright, sunlight images of Indonesia and Hollywood. "Looks like you had quite a trip, mate." He nodded. "Sorry they missed your bird; quite a looker, that one."

The stranger slid the postcards into my numb hands. Around me, I heard traffic growing louder, voices from the streets amplifying, blending together in a blathering mix of inchoate tones and sharp, meaningless syllables.

"Do you know—"

He picked up my line before I even finished. "Took the flat back in the spring, only chatted a bit, really. She might be in London still, but I wouldn't know whereabouts."

And then from behind him, I heard a woman's voice call out, "Lionel? Who is it?"

"Milena?" I shouted, reaching my head around the well-dressed stranger blocking the passage.

I saw anger cross his smooth features. "Look mate, I already told you, your bird inn't here!"

I was about to bust past him when a black woman with short, close-cropped hair and a nose ring came to the door frame, fresh from the shower, rubbing a towel against her head. She stared skeptically at me. "Can we help you?"

Lionel nodded his head coolly. "This here's the one sending all those postcards from India."

"Indonesia," I murmured.

The woman tossed the towel over her shoulder. "Well, your girlfriend's not here anymore. Don't know her 'tall; we just took the flat."

"Did she say—"

"Sorry love, she didn't say anything, just handed over the keys." She turned to her man, voice insistent. "C'mon, Lionel, we're already late." She disappeared inside the flat.

"Sorry mate," Lionel said with a shrug.

As I stood motionless on the flat's threshold, staring down at the memory-soaked carpet, I heard the dapper stranger turn sympathetic. "Look, if she comes back, I'll tell her you were by. What's the name?"

In the flat, his girlfriend flipped on the radio, and I heard dance hall music pour through the door, adding its heavy pulse to the nocturnal urban mix. I looked up at the stranger and spoke, my eyes empty, my voice tones dead.

"Just tell her Neil was here," I heard myself say.

A final breeze of memories rippled my mind, and then I turned, slowly descending the red brick steps. The people-thick streets swallowed me up, and I lost myself, dazed, in the babbling flux, feeling my *happle* and the brightly colored postcards fall from my fingers, one by one, beneath the rushing feet all around.

Somehow, I found the Green Fellow, a desolate, joyless pub far from the bright crowds of Camden Town, deep in the darkness of London, on an unknown, cracked concrete corner. It was a dingy, joyless hole, perfect for drifting young Americans with broken teeth and failed manifestos, whose Italian dream women had just disappeared.

Three or four old geezers sat propped up on worn stools, while a struggling fire sputtered in an ash-stained hearth, and a hazy pall of cigarette smoke hung over it all like a funeral shroud. Two guys were leaned against the bar nearby, a Japanese dude about my age, wearing a simple blue sweater and easily smoking on a hand-rolled cigarette, and a Brit who looked to be a bit older, wrapped in dark sunglasses, dirty-blond hair pulled back tight in a pony tail. Pressing out his cigarette, I felt him staring at me through the impenetrable shield of his sunglasses, and the other looking at me strangely, leaning toward his friend and muttering something low.

"What'll it be then?" The bartender was an aging, played dandy; silk ascot around his neck, a tired look of acceptance on his puffed, sagging mask of a face.

"McCool," I answered, ordering the heavy, dark Irish brew. "And a whiskey, too."

I shot down my tonic and tried not to think about Milena. Tried not to think who she was . . .

"Another. Whiskey and a McCool."

In my mouth, I felt my tongue work through the

shattered pieces of teeth, up and down along the rough, fractured row as my thoughts tumbled. I had left Milena to go back to *Dusted*, only to have my world of words atomized before my eyes . . . Flash luring me back across the ocean with an asinine song and some pleading promises, then dashing into TV stardom, leaving me with a closet piled high with back issues.

"Whiskey and a McCool."

And now Milena was gone. Potential vanished somewhere in a swirling stream of indifferent citizens in this dreary, imperial city. And as I sat at the bar, tongue working madly, dark beer hammering away the visions of Milena, I realized I had nothing. There was no future now in this country of cold rain, no *Neil Before God*, no work, no woman . . . I was nothing but a broken mouth wandering lost in the stone streets, loveless and homeless.

"Whiskey and a McCool."

I had no home behind me, nothing but my parents' nightmare wedlock . . . the shouting matches my brother had stoned himself from hearing . . . Mom a wild-eyed harpy, screaming at Dad, silent Dad, ashen, seething Dad . . .

"Whiskey and a McCool."

Milena was gone.

I felt my tongue snake over the jagged fault line inside me, caressing the wreckage of my mouth, and I felt my head rocking slightly back and forth, moving with the motion.

Milena was gone . . .

My head tilted back, my mouth opened wider, my jaw cracked with a sharp snap in the dead, sullen pub, and I felt my tongue, near maniacal, stretching down after the single, infuriating speck, lodged deep in the savaged socket beneath my mind . . .

And then there was a tug, followed by a sharp bite of pain. A long, jagged piece of hardness rolled over my tongue and then, as if in a dream, tumbled out from between my numbly parted lips, falling with a clunk to the bar.

All vision went black around me as I stared at the half a tooth, lying wet and glistening and somewhat yellowed on the stained, thick wood before me, a touch of red blood on the very end. My tongue instinctively ran back to the socket, blood flowing freely from the fresh hole, where the anchored half of the back molar still remained, feeling rough and strange on its own, like some kind of newly discovered architectural ruin inside my head. I stared at the desperate survivor, finally uprooted and freed from the prison of my mouth, and imagined that this was the moment I was supposed to go insane.

"Neil?"

The English voice was hesitant, and slowly, in shock, I turned from my tooth and looked up at the long-hair nearby.

"*Dusted* Neil?" he continued, leaning farther forward.

His Japanese friend answered for me. "Yeah, it's him. I told you," he concluded with a laugh.

"I'm Sleek," the Brit said, excited, moving his stool closer and extending a hand encased in a worn leather knuckle glove. "And this is Tadashi . . . Tosh for short. We're the biggest *Dusted* fans in London! This is absolutely *mental* that you're here! We need a celebratory libation; what can I buy you?"

"Thanks," I stammered, "I'm cool."

"Another McCool? Absolutely, right away!"

As Sleek motioned for the bartender, Tosh put out his cigarette and started talking to me, his English halting but clear. "I thought it was you when you came and sat down. Yeah. You don't look so different now from your picture in the magazine. But I wasn't sure. But then your tooth fell out and I knew."

"Of course," I said, fingering the jagged tooth under the pall of yellow light.

"How are they?" he asked.

"What?" My mind, which had been reeling in interior loops ever since I stumbled from Milena's, was troubled to pull into conversational mode.

"Your teeth."

"Seems like they've had enough," I answered, gazing at the bloody shard I held in the palm of my hand.

"See this?" Tosh leaned closer and pulled back his top lip, revealing a greyish front tooth, cracked nearly in half. "I got kicked in the face at a show. It used to hurt a lot. Now it's just ugly. Yeah." He took a drag from his cigarette, studying my face. "They don't look so bad."

"What?"

"Your teeth. They look OK."

"Yeah, well, it's all on the inside," I said, wedging the chunk of tooth in my back pocket.

Tosh exhaled a stream of silver smoke. "I used to like it when you wrote about your teeth. Yeah. Sleek did, too. He thinks you're his favorite writer."

Sleek turned then, a grin on his face, sliding a round of foamy pints our way. "To *Dusted* Neil!" he proclaimed, raising his glass.

"Yeah, to *Dusted* Neil," Tosh saluted.

At a loss for what to celebrate, I just managed a smile and raised my glass along with theirs. As Tosh and Sleek pounded down deep, solid gulps from their lagers, I pushed my tongue into the open gap of my back tooth socket, carefully plugging the space before taking a hesitant sip. Directing the cold flow of alcohol to the other side of my mouth, I avoided the raw hole in the back row of my teeth, which was still leaking. A dark, tainted mixture of blood and beer trickled down inside me.

Sleek grinned wildly, showcasing a crooked, blackened British smile. "We've been reading *Dusted* ever since it came out! A mate of mine in the States has been sending us copies for years!"

Tosh nodded his head. "You're famous in the squats in Hackney. Everybody reads *Dusted*."

"Hackney?" I said, dazed.

"Yeah, Neil. You're in Hackney now," Tosh answered. "What are you doing here?"

"I don't know," I answered, unable to recall the blurred trail I had traced from Milena's in Camden Town. "I guess I just ended up here . . ."

"Are you here on assignment?"

"What?"

"You know, another *Neil Before God* installment?"

I looked strangely at both of them. "*Dusted* is over."

Sleek leaned back against the bar, mouth open, stroking at his goatee. "And I thought it was just Derrick, slacking off with the post."

"Nah, we went under last winter."

"That's too bad," Tosh said.

Sleek nodded his head. "A shame. Really thought you were on to something with *Neil Before God*."

"Hey, did you ever get the five quid we sent you?" Tosh asked.

I felt a smile on my face. "For *Teef Relief?* That was you guys?"

Tosh began to laugh. "We took up a collection in the squats. It's all we had. But there was a few sleeping pills, too."

"Right, I remember," I said. "Thanks."

Sleek wiped a trace of foam off his face with the back of his leather knuckle glove. "Well, not only have you found your way to Hackney, but you've stumbled upon the Green Fellow, our revolutionary headquarters. And you've found us at a very interesting moment, as well."

I took a sip of beer, feeling my tongue fishing in the gaping hole in my mouth, tasting the salty blood seeping up from the fresh wound.

Tosh lit up another cigarette. "Yeah, we're getting ready for the Chockapolacka riots."

A spray of bitter brew erupted from my mouth. *"WHAT?!"*

"Your big American 'punk' festival," Sleek said with a scoff. "Surely you know about it. The whole slew of alternative bands are coming to London for one final, filthy lucrative show."

"And we're going to have a riot," Tosh said. "To show them what punk really is."

The heat of excitement revved Sleek's words. "We've been watching them on the telly all summer, and seeing their interviews in the magazines—Rage Against the Chili Pepper and the whole lot of them—talking punk this, punk that, how underground they are and all that. It's all such raging bullocks!"

"Yeah. Punk started in London, not Hollywood. Me and Sleek are punk. Post Everything is punk."

"Post Everything?" I repeated.

"That's our band."

Sleek swigged the last of his lager, setting the glass down with a sharp smack on the bar. "We're going to set up outside the concert stadium, with all the squatters we can gather, and stage a right proper riot, real mayhem, like the Poll Tax riots . . . something big and juicy we can all sink our teeth into." He grinned. "If you can excuse the pun."

"It's going to be good, Neil," Tosh said. "You should come."

Sleek nodded his head quickly. "Right, Neil, this **has** to be destiny! I know *Dusted* used to interview the lot of those bands, but that was before it all got so bloody exploited. And you were always different . . . I mean, *Neil Before God* was something entirely on its own. And punk as all hell!"

"Do you have a place to stay in London?" I heard Tosh ask.

"No . . . no, I don't," I stuttered. One hand, I realized, was gripping the bar-stool, as the dark Hackney pub swirled around me. The faces of Sleek and Tosh hung expectantly before me, and I felt my fingers from the other hand prying into my back pocket, pulling out my uprooted tooth and running over the jagged edges.

It felt so tiny, out in the open.

12. hackney

"So why do they call you Sleek?" I asked as the skinny Brit messed with a coil of keys dangling from his metal-studded belt.

I had checked out of the Alfred early in the morning, skipping my toast and instant-coffee breakfast to catch a bus to Hackney. My heavy backpack weighing down my shoulders, I had walked the cracked, glass-strewn sidewalks of East London with my new friend, stopping before a paint-peeled wooden door beside a dark, dusty secondhand electronics shop.

"They call me Sleek," he answered, still ringing through his keys, "because in all my years of instigating, I have yet to spend even a single night in the nick."

"So the Chockapolacka riot won't be the first?"

"Good God, no. This upcoming riot is only the latest in a long, distinguished career of social disturbances. Protests, raves, riots . . . General mayhem, that's what we specialize here in Hackney. And I've always been sleek enough to dodge the law.''

He rattled the key and turned the knob, pushing up against the warped wooden door a few times with his shoulder, until the bottom begrudgingly gave way and it swung open with a shimmying rattle.

"Here we are,'' Sleek said with a blackened, crooked grin. "Flat sweet flat.''

The foyer was cramped, with a hissing old radiator set against one wall and an accumulated layer of back newspapers and unopened mail spilled over the dirty floor. Sleek bent down and picked up the latest batch of letters, shifting the envelopes in his leather-gloved hands.

"Bills, bills, bills . . . It's good to know you're loved.''

He gave a rueful laugh and tossed the letters over his shoulder into the swamp of unread mail, then turned a corner. Entering the shadowed flat behind my host, I looked around and took in my new home.

Shades were drawn down over the two windows, casting the squarish front room in a hazy, yellow pall. As my eyes acclimated to the darkness of the cluttered space, I saw that the entire room was covered in blankets. Pea green, mustard yellow, and other dull shades, they lay piled and draped across every item in the room, rising into muted peaks and drooping down to sagging valleys as they traversed items of furniture, obscuring every edge and corner into one thick, insulated blanketscape. Half burned out candles, their hardened wax overflowing from old wine bottles, formed congealed lakes about the blanketscape.

"Such a god-awful mess, I just decided to cover it

all up." Sleek laughed. I followed his heavy, clomping boots into the kitchen.

The sink wedged in the corner of the dank box was loaded with dirty dishes and old soup cans, and a pile of stained pots and pans lay strewn on the crumb-covered counter. A mildewed shower stood boxed in alongside the dirty window, trickling water into a greenish drain.

"Could use a bit of a swab," Sleek ventured.

"Won't take much," I assured. "Reminds me of home."

"Brilliant, brilliant."

With a thunk, I slid my pack down to the floor, and Sleek smacked his forehead.

"Bloody hell! You've been toting that massive thing around the world and here I am, touring the château!" He lugged my pack up onto his skinny shoulders and walked up a narrow, spindly stairway that lead to the next floor.

"What, you bring your television set along?" Sleek said, panting, as he dropped the heavy pack down onto the dirty carpet.

I joined him in the compact space, which featured a cracked window above a sunken bed, a cheap, plastic stereo and a chair.

"As you can see, this is a fairly limited living situation," Sleek explained. "I keep all my valuables at my mate's flat. I haven't paid my taxes in well over three years, and the London police are notorious for their dawn raids, where anything of value is confiscated to make up the loss."

"Is that yours?" I asked, gazing down at the floor

near the stereo, where a fist of shattered glass broke up from a grey slab of cracked plaster.

"My last sculpture." Sleek nodded, appraising it once again.

"You don't work anymore?"

"Ah, well, you know; art school. Got a scholarship, came to London, despised the teachers. Dropped out." He scratched at his beard and gave a yawn. "Now it's a time thing really. Everything's up in the air right now, what with Post Everything and my girlfriend and the Chockapolacka riot . . ."

He led me into the next room, which was well lit and open, a drafting table dominating the floor. Pieces of paper with half-finished drawings and etchings were strewn about, along with various drafting tools and pens and pencils. Shelves lined the walls, loaded with paperback science fiction and art-theory texts, and pinned up on a board between the windows, magazine cutouts of landscapes, tripped-out computer graphics, concert stills, and other visual triggers were layered one atop the other.

"Recognize this one?" Sleek said, stepping round the desk and tapping a cutout.

I looked closer and registered with strange shock the first excerpt from *Neil Before God,* clipped from the magazine along with Terrance's abstract designs along the margins.

" 'Life is for the daring, darling,' " Sleek said with a grin, quoting an imaginary character I had conjured up in the dead of a New York City night. "Truer words were never scribed."

I avoided his eyes and blushed; I still didn't know how to take a compliment. Perusing the other pictures,

I came across one of Sleek on a stage, covered with body paint, screaming into a microphone. Tosh was just visible off to the left, sweat pouring down his face as he thrashed his electric guitar with a mighty downstroke.

"What's this?" I asked.

"Post Everything in our finest hour; last New Year's Eve show at the Freezer."

"That's your band?"

"You could call it that. Although we prefer the classification *sonic assault technicians*." He looked over at the picture and shook his head. "Mental. Absolutely mental, that show. I scored enough acid for the band and the entire audience. Tripping like cripples down an escalator; the whole lot of us." He shook his head again. "Mental."

Sleek finished his cigarette and flicked open his lighter, immediately igniting another smoke. After a slow, contemplative drag, he spoke again. "Say, here's an idea. Why don't you join up with Post Everything for the riot?"

"How do you mean? I can't sing."

"Who said anything about singing? All I do is scream."

My tongue played along the broken rows inside my head. "I'm no good onstage, really."

I heard the excitement rise in his voice as Sleek took to his own idea, leaning forward in his chair. "You're an American! A pop-soaked Yank who's defected from the whole stinking sea to join the true punks in Hackney! Scales would love it!"

"Scales?"

"Post Everything's manager, among other things.

He's seeing the riot as prime promotion for our act;
behind it all the way. He's even talking about bringing some lads down from up North. Real heavies he
used to run with—football gangs and all that—to get
things moving. The bigger the mess, the better." Sleek
gazed up at my *Neil Before God* excerpt and sighed.
"Too bad *Dusted* isn't around; be a perfect piece for
your manifesto."

"Yeah," I mouthed, thinking of the empty notebook
I had left behind in Indonesia. The warm, lazy island
seemed like a dream now: the rattling buses, the tiny
*losmen*s, Ehrlina's calm home, and the sighing oceans
blurring together into one formless blob of lost time.

Turning to look closer at the pinup board, my eyes
lingered over my old words from *Dusted*, staring me
in the face again so many years later in London. I realized with a twist of angst that this would all be another
Neil Before God chapter if my manifesto were still alive:
Milena's disappearance, the run-in with Sleek, my
newly lost tooth . . .

Sleek's voice brought me back. "So what happened
to the lot of them?"

"Who?"

"The *Dusted* gang. Where'd they end up once the
floor fell through?"

I sat down on the edge of a stacked pile of crates.
"Terrance went back to the skateboard companies. Stu
got married and works at *Buddha Smoke*—you know,
our old rival. And Flash . . ."

Sleek kicked back in a tilted chair behind his drafting
table. "A nutter, that one. We had debates back in the
day about who was the punkest of you two. You're
deep, Neil, but Flash had some right mental situations

227

staged in *Dusted*. Like that time he went on that talk show? Pretending he was a mute . . .'' Sleek laughed long and loud, shaking his head. "Whatever happened to our dear friend Flash?''

"Um, well . . .'' My voice trailed off, and I felt my tongue sliding back to the soupy hole in back of my molars, hiding in the salty brine, wanting to protect my old friend. But then I remembered his pleading, singsong calls from New York that had lured me away from London, from Milena, a year ago. Remembered his grinning face featured on a bank of editing-room TV screens, remembered his bright green hair descending past the velvet ropes into the Adder Club. Remembered his secret riches . . .

I pulled my tongue out from its rancid bunker and spoke. "You'll probably see him at Chockapolacka.''

Sleek's face lit up from behind his dark sunglasses. "Flash is coming, too? Christ, both Neil and Flash in London at once! What a riot this'll be! Wait till I tell the others.''

I cut him off quickly. "Flash got his own show on The Channel; he's covering Chockapolacka for them.''

The Brit's face fell, and his eyebrows bunched up behind his shades. "The bloody sellout,'' he said softly, with deep disgust.

"He didn't have to sell out,'' I said, feeling as if I were jabbing pins in a voodoo doll of my old friend. "Flash was born cash. He's a rich kid . . . a *really* rich kid.''

Sleek's lip curled in ugly rancor. "Why, the two-faced bastard. To have the *nerve* to even utter the word *punk* . . .''

I heard a soft pattering on the roof and turned from

the angry squatter to look out the dirty windows, where a dark rain had begun to fall on the cracked streets of Hackney.

"Oh, we'll show him," I heard Sleek say, low and menacing, somewhere behind me in the abandoned art studio. He started coughing then, and I turned around to see my new friend doubled up from smoke, holding a joint out to me. "Care for some?" Sleek said, regaining his voice.

"Sure," I said for some reason.

Hungover, even though it was only five in the afternoon, I washed my face in the dripping sink and headed out the warped wooden door to the cold streets of Hackney. My feet kicked through the glittered glass of broken bottles, and my tongue ran back and forth in my mouth, still adjusting to the jagged hole left by my uprooted tooth. The tooth was lucky, I mused, to be finally freed from the grim prison of my mouth; turning another dark corner, I half hoped a massive, skyborne tongue would swoop down and pull me out from my place.

I had been spent two weeks in a lager and hashish haze, shrouding myself into a benumbed fog as the excitement of Sleek and his Chockapolacka riot brewed around me. The skinny Brit had served as my ambassador to Hackney, and in the evenings, the rounds had been made to surrounding pubs and squats, where I was introduced to the gathered revolutionaries as *Dusted* Neil.

"Not to be confused with the turncoat Flash," Sleek

would quickly follow up when showing me off, explaining my old friend's pedigree. It was his launching pad for a tirade of everything Chockapolacka, and as the others gathered around him, I would invariably sink away, drinking the free pints bought to honor my minor celebrity, or taking in the smoke passed my way to fade from the angry tirades.

It was what my brother, James, had done all those years while growing up, and I realized now his escape tactic had its merit. As I watched Sleek's face curse and spit through his nightly punk denouncements, I couldn't help but think of my mother and father, screaming at each other in the night, and how I had hid at the top of the stairs as a kid, my face pressed against the wooden poles of the banister, like some kind of ten-year-old inmate. James had always disappeared those days into his bedroom, locking the door on me, where I could hear him coughing as he strummed out hippie songs on his guitar. I had always hated the heavy smell of smoke that came from behind his door, but in the dim nights of East London, so many years later, I was finally acquiring a taste for it.

I looked down again at the scribbled address Sleek had left for me the night before and turned down another empty side street. This London of boarded-up, abandoned buildings, crumbling warehouses, and uneven sidewalks was light years away from the silken world of Milena I had dreamed of, but I found that it didn't really matter to me. Nothing mattered anymore, not my lost tooth, not Milena, not even the crazed coincidence of running into a platoon of English *Dusted* groupies. I felt as if my entire body had been root-canaled, the nerves sucked clean out through a hole drilled in my center, leaving behind nothing but a hard, emptied husk.

Passing a few warehouses, a score of empty row houses, an old, boarded-up church, and an Ethiopian coffee shop, I turned left onto a dead-end street, read the number again on my paper, and descended the cement stairs to a small, metal doorway at the bottom.

I pushed my way inside, finding myself in a near empty cement room, where a thirtyish rocker sat at a massive wooden desk, beating out drum rudiments with a mismatched pair of drumsticks. Atop the desk sat an old black telephone, a banged-up metal box full of cash, and leaning indifferently against the crumbling masonry wall, a chunky, bleached-platinum blond girl in a tilted bowler hat. As I crossed the mildewed room, she glanced quickly at me, calculating my potential in the blink of a jaded eye before returning, unimpressed, to the television in the corner.

"I'm looking for Post Everything."

The rocker stopped his drumming and looked at me, frowning. "Who?"

"My friend's band. We've got a rehearsal here tonight. They're called Post Everything."

"Sorry, mate, don't know the names of any of these outfits. I just rent out the studios."

The woman in the bowler hat scratched at a rip in her fishnet stocking, not looking away from the flickering screen as she spoke. "You know, hon. That's the outfit that paid in meth last week; Japanese fellow and the character in those sunglasses."

"Oh, right. Trying to get us interested in some riot or other."

"At Chockapolacka," I said.

The rocker laughed, a derision steeped slash. "Didn't take their demo tapes, so now they're going to riot." He shook his head. "Bloody Christ."

Before I could ask what he meant, the woman in the bowler hat read from a sheet of paper and nodded down a corridor. "Post Everything: room nine, end of the hall."

Her man grunted as I walked away. "Bloody idiots. They'll get tossed in the nick before they even strike a chord."

I left the couple and walked down the dimly lit studio hallway. Passing each warped door of the practice rooms, electrified shrieks of rage, frustration, and impending Armageddon pushed heavy against my ears, roiling over the muffled tides of ill-tuned instruments.

Pushing open a cracked studio door with my shoulder, I was swallowed in a seamy pool of trapped body heat, cheap-cigarette smoke, spilled lager, and blasting, screaming noise. I couldn't help but think of how far I was from Flash and his air-conditioned, leather-lined editing complex back in Hollywood. Tosh stood in a corner of electronic devices, his feet working back and forth between duct-taped effects pedals as the programmed drum rhythm carried him through the song.

Lined up at microphones next to Sleek were the two other members of Post Everything, a woman and a man, attempting to harmonize amidst the crushing din. The woman was short, dark-haired, and wearing torn jeans, her left arm covered elbow to wrist in heavy, metal bracelets. The man looked to be the oldest of the group, his hairline receding, and veins throbbing beneath the skin of his temples, like furious little worms about to burst through to the surface as he sang.

Finally, I heard something like a crescendo, and the song ground to a halt, leaving my ears ringing in the silence.

Sleek looked my way and grinned broadly, showcasing the dental disaster of his mouth. "May I introduce to you . . . *Dusted* Neil!" he said to his bandmates, gesturing with a grandiose sweep of his arms, then taking a pull from a can of lager.

"Right. I'm Desmond, and this is Lucy," the older man said, wiping the sweat off his brow with the frayed sleeve of his shapeless, coal-colored sweater.

Lucy nodded and gave a little wave, then sipped her lager and cleared her throat. "Sleek says you're joining the band?"

"Uh, yeah, I mean, I guess."

She tapped a cigarette out on the floor. "Brilliant. Play any instruments?"

"Nah," I said, voicing my one regret in life.

Desmond frowned. "What's this, Sleek? We've already got three of us singing to one guitar."

"But he's a fantastic writer. A famous writer. He'll scribble up some brilliant lyrics for us, right, Neil?"

"Sure. I mean, I don't know if it'll be down with what you're doing . . ."

"Of *course* it will be." Sleek turned to his bandmates. "*Dusted* Neil is going to be a key element for our entire enterprise: underground American writer, defecting from his own pop culture to join us in the battle against Chockapolacka. What could be better?" He took another pull from his lager and raised it before him. "In fact, I'd like to take this moment to officially appoint Mr. *Dusted* Neil as the official Post Everything minister of propaganda. Any official objections?"

SHHERHHRIIEEEEEK!!

Desmond winced tightly and screamed over the screeching guitar feedback that suddenly filled the room, "TOSH COULD YOU **PLEASE** GET THAT UNDER CONTROL!"

The Japanese guitarist tapped one of the foot pedals, which didn't do much to kill the sound, and then began to kick at it, which only upped the amplitude.

SHHHHHEKEKEKENNENERRTTTTZZZZZT!

Screaming words no one could hear, Desmond stormed over to the effects pedals and started stomping on them in turn, until the barrage of noise finally cut off with an abrupt electric fizzle.

"Sorry," Tosh said. "I thought I fixed that one."

"Evidently not!" the lead singer spat, running a hand through his thinning hair as he returned, cursing, to his microphone, a long piece of duct tape stuck to his shoe. Flipping through his lyric sheets, he turned toward me.

"Why don't you just listen for a while, see if you can pick up what we're doing?"

"Come now, Desmond," Sleek said with a bemused grin as he lit another cigarette. "We're not exactly the *belle* tones here."

Desmond lashed out. "Look Sleek! You might just be interested in torching a few police vans, but I'm a musician!"

"And what does that make me?" Sleek shot back, dark anger lining his words.

"Easy now, boys," Lucy said, taking Desmond's arm.

Desmond shook his head in disgust. "Well, I can't imagine us as much of a threat to Chockapolacka like

234

this. If we're the last bastions of bloody punk rock, we'd do better just digging the bloody grave."

"Come on, Des, punk's not dead!" Tosh said cheerily. "It's just been taking a wee bit of a nap."

And then the Japanese guitarist crouched low to the ground and punched in a series of commands on the drum machine at his feet, and a heavy-edged rhythm pounded through the sweaty, smoky practice space. A programmed bass line synced in a few measures later, his guitar began to wail, and then Post Everything leaned as one into the microphones, and everybody started to scream.

Sleek and I left the studio together. Catching a red double-decker bus, we walked down the empty aisle to the seats in the back. It was just as I had done when riding the bus in school days as a stoned fifth-grader. Sitting in the last seats, I was as far as possible from the captain of the craft, my back was covered, and lined up neatly before me sat a range of hapless targets, mine to peg at will with boogers, nasty names, and other random projectiles. Some things didn't change, I guessed, as Sleek and I sat ourselves down in the last row of the rumbling London bus. Backseat stoners rode for life.

"Important meeting tonight at William's squat," Sleek explained to me as we rumbled on into the night.

"Chockapolacka plans?"

"Right you are. Not much longer to get it together, either. Just about a week."

My tongue made a sweep again for the ragged hole in the back of my broken teeth, still adjusting to the

235

space. We passed by an old, boarded-up church, and I cleared my throat. "Say, back in the studio, the guy at the desk mentioned something about demo tapes to Chockapolacka. What was he talking about?"

Sleek reached for his sunglasses, adjusting them on the bridge of his nose, then coughed quickly into his hand. "Ah, yeah, that. I guess the, um, concert promoters took out an advert in the city papers soliciting demo tapes from the London punk outfits."

"To play at the show?"

"Right, opening acts or something. But it's all dodgy to me; just some massive exploitation scam, I'm sure. Can't trust the likes of them."

We rolled on in silence, farther into Hackney as a thin drizzle began to patter down against the bus windows.

"Did you send in a tape?" I asked.

"Don't know." Sleek shrugged, turning to gaze out at the dreary, drifting cityscape. He stroked his bearded face, reflected in the cold, rattling pane of rain drop-beaded glass. "Lucy might have."

The bus stopped and Sleek bounded up the aisle, and I followed. Down a few side streets we walked, until we reached an old wooden building, boarded up and abandoned looking. Sleek knocked on the door, and I stood with him for a moment in the drizzling cold, until the old door creaked open.

A tall, sleepy guy with long, greasy hair and a heavy, drooping sweater stood framed before us. "Hey Sleek. And *Dusted* Neil. C'mon in."

I followed Sleek into the squat, a run-down, dim space illuminated only by what grey light managed to find its way in through the unwashed windows. A street-salvaged furniture collection of slanted old sofas, crooked, overstuffed chairs, and three-legged coffee tables loomed like shadows around the room. As my eyes adjusted to the general gloom, I eventually made out the forms of people slumped about, quietly smoking cigarettes.

Sleek gave a round of greetings and found a seat on a sofa. "Now that I've arrived with *Dusted* Neil, shall we call our meeting to disorder?" He gave a laugh as he cleared a space for me on the sunken cushions beside him. "We *are* anarchists after all, wouldn't do right calling anything to order."

William sank into a chair, and down the creaking stairs came another squatter, tall and sallow skinned, who sat on the worn, thinning carpet nearby.

"Neil, I think I speak for everyone when I say we're honored to have you in on the action," Sleek started off.

"Right . . . yeah . . . cheers . . ." A low round of mumbles came in concert from the surrounding gloom.

"And we definitely want you to be involved in the riot. But after thinking over the strategy, we've concluded that you'd be of much more value inside," William told me.

"How do you mean?" I asked.

"A force of disturbance, like, backstage," a sullen voice said from across the room.

A pale hand flicked a lighter near the window, and I watched the flash of flame illuminate a frowning, unshaven face. "Yeah. You know Flash; he can get you backstage. And once you're inside, you can havoc it all to hell." The flame abruptly cut off, leaving only the glowing red ember of a cigarette hanging in space.

I shifted uncomfortably in the mushy cushions of the couch. "That sounds kind of, um, serious."

"T'is. We're thinking LSD in the water. . . . Sleek, you can secure the 'cid, correct?"

Sleek grinned. "Already placed the order with Scales."

Another squatter mumbled out from the dim pall, "William here knows a thing or two about electronics. Won't take much to sabotage the sound system. A cord here and there, tweak a knob or two . . . maybe a bit of fire."

"And there's a mate of mine who knows all about chemical reactions," a different dull voice cast in. "We'll fashion up some kind of sulfur bomb to smell up the place. Like really stinky and all. Make it miserable as all hell back there."

Sleek passed a soggy-ended joint my way, and I took it between my fingers, drawing down the hashish-tobacco mix as I listened to his excited words.

"You'll be our agent of chaos on the inside, while Post Everything's sonic assault brews up a nice, proper riot outside the gates. Already got the blokes from up North confirmed, and everyone from the squats. It's working out to be a true melee, but having you dosing the superstars backstage would make it a true punk protest, inside and out. What do you say?"

Although I could barely make out anything but the dimmest forms in the light of the squat, I felt the expectant eyes of the squatters pinned on me. I shifted in the sofa. "Well, uh . . ."

"You know, our very way of life is being threatened here," the tall, skinny one who had answered the door said to me. "It starts with some bloody American commercial fiesta like Chockapolacka calling itself punk, and then next thing you know, there's a hair salon in Hackney, and then a cinema showing some Hollywood bullocks, and we're tossed from the squats to make way for cappuccino boutiques."

"He's right, you know," a woman's voice added. "We've got to draw the line somewhere."

"We've read all your articles, like; we know you're on our side. Wouldn't be here with us if you weren't."

Sleek nodded his head. "He's right, Neil. You belong in Hackney. You're one of us."

I looked around me at the dark, run-down room, at the dirty windows, cracked walls, plaster-peeled ceiling, and sinking shadows. The assembled crew of slouched squatters slowly nodded in agreement as Sleek took another puff of the spliff.

"So what do you say, *Dusted* Neil? You with us or what?"

I shifted my weight awkwardly, feeling stoned now that I was trying to move, and for a panicked moment I imagined the soft pit of a couch was sucking me into its mushy depths. "W-well . . . ," I stammered.

Sleek rose to his feet beside me. "Course he is. We'll work out the details in the week, before the riot."

He reached a knuckle-gloved hand out for me, pulling me up out of the sofa, and I started with him toward the door.

"You *will* be our agent on the inside, right?" a squatter asked.

"Uh, yeah, sure," I said, nodding my head, glad that no one could see the hesitance in my hash-clouded eyes.

And as Sleek pulled open the groaning door of the

squat, I heard a slack, empty voice come from the darkness behind me. " 'For the daring, darling,' " it said, almost seeming to taunt me. "Like you said, Neil, 'life is for the daring . . .' "

With a shiver, I rushed away from my quoted prose, into the shadows of the Hackney night.

13. the taste

The taste woke me up.

It was a dark, familiar flavor, but it had been several long years since it had last saturated my mouth. As I stared up at the flaking ceiling above me, my tongue eased back to the chasm at the back of my bite line, which was now a deep pool of bitter, sour brew. Raising myself from Sleek's grimy mattress, I walked to the dusty mirror nailed to the wall, then opened wide, peering in at the hole in my mouth, neglected now for weeks.

The surrounding gums were pink and angry, puffed up like enemy bunkers around a crater of fractured enamel. I slowly moved my finger between my parted, chapped lips, pressing down on the sore, infected gums, wincing as the odious taste ran sick over my tongue. It was the morning before the Chockapolacka riot, but as I stood before the mirror, my mind flew back through the years, to when the taste had first flooded my mouth.

In the excruciating months after my ill-fated window escape, my jaw had been so badly contused that it was stuck shut, and the family dentist could do nothing but watch as the injured teeth died away, one by one. And with each tooth that went, infection had set in, eating through the nerves, the roots, then into the cavities below.

"Lucky for you, son, your teeth are cracked in half," I remembered the old, liver-spotted dentist saying to me as I sat bound in pain before him. *"If they weren't, I'd have to break your jaw open for a few root canals."*

As "luck" would have it, my jaw remained clamped shut, the deep cracks in my teeth serving as floodgates for the bitter taste of infection to pour through. It was an awful, acrid taste, black and putrid, and with my face clenched in a cold mask of agony, I had grimly swallowed it for months, until everything had died and there was nothing more for the infection to feed on. But now in London, so many years later, another piece had fallen from the battered history of my mouth, setting the place for a greedy infection to feast, once again.

I closed my mouth and took in my unshaven reflection in the dusty mirror. Tentatively, I pushed my tongue against the dark well inside me: fluid oozed forth, the taste spreading slow and sickening over the span of my tongue. I swirled the rancid rinse slowly around my mouth, almost savoring it, and stared into the gaze of my own blank eyes. And then from deep inside my soul, I felt a raging wave of fury building up, blacker and more vile than the taste in my mouth. My teeth . . . My teeth . . .

"My goddamn teeth!"

I screamed in the empty flat, then lashed out with

my fist, smashing my hand against the hard plaster wall before me. A sharp pain railed up the nerves of my arm, and it felt good. Suddenly, I despised the sight of my unshaven face staring back at me. Without even thinking, my head smashed forward, cracking into the cheap mirror, which I felt bending before me, shards mashing up against the cardboard backing behind it.

Breathing fast, heart hammering, I pulled back and stared at the fragmented glass. Slices of my image echoed back at me, abstracted and violently askew, and I felt my fingers reaching to my head, which was warm with tingling energy. There was no blood, only a grim pulsing beneath the skin, and I stood feeling it for some time, gazing at my distorted reflection until I made my way downstairs.

Sleek's kitchen was cluttered thick with the collected items of mayhem waiting in store for Chockapolacka. Furious, I pushed my way past a group of ragged amplifiers and rust-speckled microphone stands, an old pile of army flares and a spray-painted banner, heading toward the smudged cabinets in the back. Surrounded by the stale smell of old breakfasts, I slammed open the cabinets in turn, peering deep into their darkness.

A few minutes later I found a dented metal salt shaker, probably stolen on a drunken night from the chips counter. There was no soap to wash the single dirty glass I found, so I trudged back upstairs and returned with last night's beer can. Filling the small, greasy kettle from the broken stove, I placed it on the hot plate, then flicked the switch. I stood in silence as the water began to heat up with a low, hissing sound, and when the steam came, I took the kettle off the plate and poured the hot water into my beer can. Unscrewing the salt-shaker top, I added in a long stream of salt, stirred, then sipped the saline rinse and began swishing it slowly in my mouth.

If I had learned anything at all about dental damage control, it was of the mighty powers of a regular saline rinse. But ever since my tooth had tumbled through my lips, I had faded myself into a hazy reality of bitters and hash, and the Tooth Fates had cashed in on my denial with malevolent glee, serving me up a nice, juicy infection . . . and in England, too. Shaking my head as I kicked through the riot equipment, I realized I'd probably end up with an overbite and a harelip just going in for a checkup.

Passing through the blanketed main room, I saw that Sleek had left a note for me last night before leaving for his girlfriend's. In his left-leaned, stretched script I read: *The Green Fellow,* with the words *half eight* scrawled beneath it, along with <u>*Call Flash!!*</u> I groaned as I stuffed the message in my dirty jeans, remembering Sleek's bounding excitement as Post Everything had moved their equipment into the kitchen the previous evening:

Chockapolacka is just the latest in complete corporate culture exploitation of the human soul!

"Go to hell, Sleek," I heard myself spit. The angry hole in the back of my mouth had suddenly sucked up any spare concern I had for the cause of punk. Gingerly, I reached my tongue backward, sensing that the flow of goo had been quelled somewhat by the saline rinse. Absently, I wondered if Sleek knew any squatting pharmacists I could cop some antibiotics off. Then I pulled on my bomber jacket and tumbled down the steps, out into Hackney, having no idea where I was heading.

The cracked sidewalk moved under my feet, and I realized that I was too far gone even to raise the fury anymore. I was just so achingly, miserably tired of it all. The teeth falling out, the money running out, the stupid, furious family back home, the pathetic memories of Milena I had held like a kid with his blanket . . . Wandering the world, wondering where my next paycheck was coming from, wondering when my next tooth would fall out . . . I had no home, no money, no love, no power, and for some reason, someone, somewhere, was entertaining Himself by scripting out a twisted dental farce to play itself out in my mouth indefinitely.

"Go to hell, you bastard," I muttered toward the grey sky.

I laughed. For the first time in years, I realized that I wasn't going to play my part in the Tooth Show. Every one of the miserable little chompers could die if it wanted to. To hell with them all. Savoring the taste of rebellion, mixed with the bitter brew of my infected tooth, I stopped into a store and grabbed a tall can of cheap bitters, pushing my way through the raincoat-covered old ladies, picking their way through malnourished vegetables. Who cared if it was lunchtime? Who cared if I was going broke? If the world did what it wanted to me, then I would do what I wanted. And I wanted to get drunk. Drunk, dour and bitter, just like dear old Dad.

I laughed out loud as I scuttled down the steps to the underground. Somewhere in the heavens, the sadistic spinner of the Tooth Show was getting a curveball in

His demented narrative. Neil, suffering Neil, his trusty cosmic punching bag, was walking.

"I quit, you bastard," I said, hard and forceful under my breath, sucking down a thick, black strand of the taste.

The train screeched to a stop before me, and I got on, laughing to myself, picturing myself as I would have acted in the past: looking for a phone, frantically trying to reach the *Dusted* boys, or *Bop Cheese*, panicked and scrapping for work to fix my teeth. The thought of it made me shudder. To hell with them all.

My hand pulled the crumpled piece of paper from my pocket, and I saw the words again:

Call Flash!!

Flash. Goddamn Flash. Flash and his smile. Flash and his luck. Flash in town with his glamour girlfriend and Channel crews, while I rumbled drunken under the London streets, my mouth a fetid pool of harsh infection. Flash, whose life was one long, brilliantly edited, perfectly lit music video by the Great Director, while my existence was one long, gruesome root canal at the hands of the Cosmic Dentist.

Call Flash!!

To hell with calling Flash. I couldn't even look at Flash now. Couldn't see his gleaming, laughing blue eyes without wanting to smash his jaw. Ever since that meal with Mandy, I had felt nauseated every time the thought of the rising video star crossed my mind. After all the years we had racked up together, the overtime hours of deadline madness, the *Dusted* road trips, the late-night New York rap sessions that went on till dawn . . . all those days and nights together, and I had never known who the pranking, haranguing, green-haired, singsong kid really was.

And what made me feel even more sick inside, as the London underground rumbled on, was that Flash *really* knew who I was. In all those hours we had spent together, talking, laughing, contemplating, philosophizing, I had exposed the whole picture for him. There was a gaping chasm between the Neil that dazzled in *Dusted* and the Neil that dragged his ass day through day. Flash was the only one who knew the depth of that chasm. He knew all about my mom's church trip, my dad's college grudge, their endless screaming, my brother's dealing, and every little tripped-out weirdness that had formed the swirl of my soul.

And Flash knew about the now, too. The crazy depressions that swooped down on me, the ridiculous relationships I tangled myself up in, the dark days of drinking, the holes I punched through the walls and then covered up with pictures from martial arts magazines . . . Over the years, one by one, every card that I usually kept hidden, clutched close to my chest, had slowly been laid out before Flash.

And my friend had sympathized, he had understood. He had listened, he had shook his head slowly, he had laughed me out of dark corners and poured me the last beer. He had spoken softly in the quiet nights, laying out a few hands of his own, adding to the stakes. Flash had been there with me, right across the table, but it was only long after he had left the game that I found out he had been palming his ace card all the while.

Call Flash!!

The train groaned to a stop and I got off, finishing

my bitters as I emerged into the sullen sheen that passed for daylight in London. A laughing gang of children in school uniform rushed past, and as the rain fell, I realized I really *did* want to call Flash. I wanted to look into his bright blue, trust-fund, Channel-superstar eyes and call him on the game he had been playing all along.

My feet began moving. They took me down the sidewalk, past a post office, and stopped in front of a red phone booth. I walked inside and shut the door behind me as the cold, spattering rain picked up, spitting against the glass. Picking up the receiver, I looked around me in the booth. Phone-sex cards and stickers pasted the glass around me at eye level, and directly above the phone, a cartoon-fantasy brunette with gleaming, globe-like breasts smiled wickedly.

"I'll do ANYTHING!" she whispered at me, in italicized script across her thighs.

I gazed at another ink-sketched naked lady and thought of Milena. Thought of those nights . . .

I shook the vanished love from my mind, and my fingers worked the dial, punching numbers I had memorized long ago in the *Dusted* days. Time passed with a few rings, and then a familiar voice spoke into my ear.

"Buddha Smoke."

"Stu?"

The operator's voice stopped me from talking any further. *"You have an overseas collect call from Neil. Will you accept the charges?"*

"Say yes, Stu," I intoned.

His voice was faint. "Hmmm, Neil who?"

"C'mon, Stu, don't be a—"

The operator cut me off. "Caller, identify yourself further please."

"NEIL THE BEST GODDAMN WRITER IN THE WORLD!"

I heard her voice again. *"A collect overseas call from Neil the best goddamn writer in the world. Will you accept the charges?"*

"Well, if it's him, I guess I should."

"Thank you for using Globe Phone." Her voice vanished.

"Neil?" His voice was faint.

"Yo."

"Sorry, didn't mean to irk you. Just messing around. You OK?"

"Fine. Just a little stressed," I said, too hard.

It was silent for a moment, until Stu found an angle. "So when did you become the best goddamn writer in the world?"

I slumped against the glass, wishing I hadn't shouted, glad that he was joking. "I won the Ultimate Writer steel-cage match in Jakarta. Didn't you catch it on pay-per-view?"

There was a pause while my joke made its way across the ocean to my old editor. "Must have missed it. Where are you?"

"London."

"Did you finish your manifesto?"

I scraped at the corner of a *Lusty Lithuanian Lesbians* sticker. "Yeah, I've got a draft done. Needs some rewrites."

"What about the mysterious Italian woman? Did you two reunite in a cloud of bliss?"

"Mad bliss."

"How are your teeth?" he continued, asking the regulation question.

"Fine," I lied outright, sucking down a thin thread of infectious seep. "And how's *Buddha Smoke*?" I asked, turning the tables. I had personally heard Stu announce he would rather be a scab in a Chinatown trashman strike than ever work for our rival mag.

I heard him yawn. "Temp gig, I'm just helping the boys out for a while. Axle broke his arm in a drunken Jet Ski wreck; tried to jump an oil tanker wake with the New Guy on the back. They asked me to edit a few issues until Axle runs out of painkillers and can form a complete sentence."

"And the New Guy?"

"He was in a coma for a week, but ever since he got out, they stopped calling him the New Guy, so he's happy."

"Give him my congrats." An ugly little old lady in mildewed rain gear walked up to the phone booth and glared at me, then looked down at her watch and frowned. "Look, besides calling to say hello, I need some help."

"Yeah, well, I'm pretty broke from the honeymoon . . ."

I scowled. "I don't need your money, I need to find Flash. Do you have any idea how to reach him?"

"Actually, I do. *Smoke* just did an interview with him about the movie talk."

"*What?*"

"Yeah, The Channel has that whole movie branch. They saw his first few shows and they're talking about doing a feature with him."

"Jesus Christ," I muttered. The little old lady outside

the booth frowned at me even harder. The rain picked up and she held up a withered old arm to show me her tarnished watch. I turned my back on her.

"Hey, have you been called a 'bloody fool' yet?" Stu asked.

"No, but I'm working on it." Rain pattered against the cold glass, and I stared vacantly at an old brick church across the way.

"I got called a 'bloody fool' three times while I was in London. Wait, let me find Flash's number; he's staying in some poshed-out hotel."

I peeled a Transsexual Nursing School phone card from the glass and wrote down Flash's London number as my old editor recited it. As my pen moved across the sticky paper, I suddenly felt as if I hadn't gone anywhere. Despite my desperate, death-defying attempt to escape the Chockapolacka Universe, there I was connected to Hollywood again, trying to track down Flash, feeling a part of some eternal *Dusted* assignment that would never deadline.

"OK, Samurai," Stu concluded. "Someone's going to sweat me about this bill. But everything's cool in the olde country?"

"Peaches."

"Have fun, then. And don't go joining the IRA or anything."

"Too late," I said dully.

"Blow up something for me then, will you?" my old editor quipped. "I'll talk to you when you come back cross the pond."

There was a momentary pause. The pug-faced old lady outside finally gave up on waiting, shouting some garbled curses before waddling off. Stu's voice spoke again, faintly, and I realized I had been straining to hear him over the London traffic the whole time.

"Is there anything else?" he asked somewhat hesitantly.

There was a lot else. There was a showdown with Flash and a hideous mouthful of taste. There were no more *happles* ever again, no more *Neil Before God*, no more money, and hardly even a reason to keep moving. I had lost a tooth and was close to losing my mind in a drug-dabbling, techno-anarchist outfit in Hackney.

"I guess not," I heard myself mouth. "Except goodbye."

There was a slight delay as my words made their way across the ocean, and then I heard a soft, distant response. "So long, Neil."

Halos of light surrounded the streetlamps of Hackney, capturing the precipitation as it poured from the black night in cinematic, windblown waves. I pulled my hood tighter and tagged after Sleek through the downpour, following the skinny squatter through the shadowed side streets.

"So you're certain that you'll see Flash?" he asked yet again.

"I left a message at the hotel desk, said it was urgent, and I needed to see him."

"What time?" Sleek asked, checking his watch.

"Nine, at the pub next door. But he's crazy busy with Chockapolacka, so I don't know if he'll show."

"Well, he'd better make time for his old mate Neil, if he knows what's good for him," the squatter growled.

Back at the Green Fellow, where we had met up an

hour earlier, Sleek had been a portrait of postevery-thing cool. A broad, blackened grin on his bearded face, lazy streams of smoke trailing from the spliff between his fingers, and a tall pint of bitters before him, the squatter had radiated a glimmering, malevolent energy. I had sat sipping lager, working the cool liquid around the infected hole in my head, as Sleek held court for a scraggly crew of anarchists, art students, and dropouts. Everyone in Hackney, it seemed, knew him, and they all seemed roused and ready to riot.

Sleek turned another dark corner, talking fast and excited as he splashed through a murky puddle. "Talked to Tosh earlier; all the equipment's right sorted. All that's left now is some substance, for your backstage work." He shot me a grin in the dark as we cut through the cold rain. "Time to get back at your old friend Flash, eh?"

I nodded my head absently, trying to ignore the high, singing note of pain that was calling out from the ooz-ing hole in my teeth. We walked on in silence through the walls of cold wetness, farther into the depths of Hackney.

"Not to scare you or anything, but we've got to watch our step around here. This is about as dodgy as it gets in London," Sleek said quietly over his shoulder as we crossed another deserted street.

I had been through my share of shady urban glades, but there was something especially sinister about the dark cement I found myself navigating now. I was edgy, I guessed, because of my tooth, and my regula-tory stoned paranoia. But another factor had been fad-ing in and out for days and was rising up strong tonight.

A few days back, Sleek and I and another squatter had passed a travel agency with a sign reading *Explore Ireland!*

"Doubt that," the squatter had scoffed. "It's full 'a bloody filthy Irish." He had laughed ruefully and Sleek joined in, and I had stepped along behind them, in an empty kind of shock.

I had been beaten down for a wide array of cultural offenses while I was growing up in the States, catching wreck for everything from the way I dressed to the words I wrote, but never before had I been pegged for just being Irish. I knew how to defend myself against most attacks, but the Irish gibe had caught me off guard, bruising me hard, as there was no precedent to ease the blow. I had pictured myself as being down with Sleek and his crew: squatting with them, smoking out, screaming in their band . . . But that offhand comment had driven an invisible wedge between the Brit squatters and me.

From that day on, my ears pricked up in the pubs, and I heard more Irish rubs, each one pounding the wedge deeper. I didn't say anything, as these same people were buying me beers and opening what passed as their home to me, but I began to feel more uneasy as the Chockapolacka riot approached.

It's full 'a bloody filthy Irish.

My uncle Barney's Thanksgiving stories ran through my mind in ever-increasing loops, and I began to think about the thick-brogued, walleyed old man. In my buzzing hash paranoia, it seemed I could almost see my uncle Barney's floating eye hanging before me in the gloomy streets of the imperial city. What would he think of me now, passing spliffs with this ragtag bunch of our ancient oppressors?

"Here we are," Sleek announced softly, cutting us through a back alley, entering a council-house lot. I followed as he bounded up an exterior staircase to a second-floor balcony, overlooking the sunken parking lot below. Dim lights flickered overhead as Sleek pressed a bell halfway down the line, at a door leaking muffled techno music into the pouring night. Moments later, I heard the sounds of heavy footsteps, and then a thick, suspicious-sounding cockney voice.

"Yeah? Who's it?"

"Hey, Scales, it's Sleek."

The door slowly opened, and a massive chest filled the frame.

"Sleek, how's things?" Scales turned, and I watched his brow furrow as he took me in; a faint scar running from his tightly cropped blond hair to the blunt end of his chin curved slightly as he frowned.

Sleek quickly explained my presence: "Hope you don't mind, I brought a mate of mine, *Dusted* Neil. He's sound."

Scales sized me up, taking in aspects of my appearance before deciding for himself. After a tense moment, his frown lifted, and the dealer extended his giant's grip to me: "Good to meet you, Neil, come on in."

I shook his hand and then followed through the door, past a small kitchen into a square living room. A low glass table centered the room, records and CDs lined the walls, and a tall, spiky green plant rested near a deep red velvet chair near the door. Sleek and I hung our dripping jackets on the hooks near the window and took our place on the long couch Scales pointed us to.

"Post Everything up and ready for the riot?" the huge man asked, settling into the red velvet throne.

"Indeed." Sleek rubbed his hands briskly together, water seeping from the dark leather of his knuckle gloves.

"Hope so. Got the lads from up North coming down, wouldn't want to vex 'em."

"Should be a smashing show," Sleek said.

"Brilliant." Scales leaned down and pulled a wooden box out from under his seat and placed it on the glass tabletop before him. Opening the lid, he revealed a neatly parceled stash of white powder, green buds, and stacks of multicolored pills. He began spooning white powder into a smaller bag, held over a tray posited to catch the debris. Then taking it in hand, he moved to a set of scales hanging from a thin chain by the mantel. They were old-fashioned pans, beautifully crafted, and I watched as Scales took a series of small weights from atop the mantel, placing a pair on one pan, against the bag of white powder in the other.

Sleek turned to me. "Scales runs the cleanest pans in London."

"These are me favorite ones. Antiques, really, worth a few quid at that. And right on the nose they are." The massive, cockney dealer eyed the balance keenly, striking a final balance amidst the pans. Taking the small bag of white narcotic powder, he licked the top of the plastic, sealed it, and tossed it down on the glass table.

"Brilliant crank. What else you need?" He wiped his

hands over the tray on the table and, folding up his larger stash, placed it in the box.

"Could use about a quarter more of that hashish, and, uh, that acid I was asking for." Sleek grinned nervously. "Can't be overturning police vans on an empty mind."

A question crossed Scales' rough features. "Now what were you needing all this blotter for? Quite a pop I'm handing over."

"Neil here is an American, and friends—or should I say—formerly acquainted with some of the Chockapolacka stars. He'll be strolling backstage to dose everyone there clear out of their capitalist minds."

"And what's wrong with being a capitalist?" Scales demanded.

My friend laughed nervously. "Nothing! Nothing at all . . . just as long as you call yourself a capitalist and don't go around parading yourself off as some punk rock—"

Scales got to his feet, cutting off the rising rant. "Ah, what's in a name, Sleek? It's all about the cash now, inn't it?" The big, blocky man shot me a wink. "Or *bucks*, like you Yanks call 'em, right, Neil?"

I gave a smile and nodded my head in agreement, gazing at the packed box of illegal drugs before me, half-hallucinating tight waves of paranoia emanating from its narcotic hold. My uncle Barney's eye floated before me again, and I saw a quick preview of *Neil's London Bust*: bobbies bashing through the door, a screaming mangle of cuffs and chains, the blur of a trial in a foreign system; the gavel hammering down, the cell door slamming shut, and my life locked away forever in the cold horror of a British prison . . .

Next to me, I heard the flick of a lighter and smelled the scent of hashish as Sleek lit up again.

Scales cleared his throat. "Don't bother with that, Sleek. Got me a *très* I still haven't torched."

I sensed the squatter's eyes light up from behind his dark sunglasses. "Fantastic!"

Scales edged forward in his chair, tapping his thick finger on a black tray lying on the table before him. "I do all my business over this tray here," he explained to me. "Careful about me work, but everybody spills a bit now and again. Every few months, there's enough to roll yourself quite a spliff. *Très* serious, as me mates from gay Paris like to say." He smiled as he tilted the drug-sprinkled surface; white dust, green leaves, and brownish twigs all sliding together into the corner.

"Before that *très*, how 'bout a line of this meth?" Sleek offered.

Scales waved him off. "Nah. Me bird's coming over . . . wouldn't want to be all up and jittered."

From somewhere deep inside me, far away from the numb, stoned shell I had built up for almost a month, I felt a voice calling out. *Milena, where are you? I don't want to smoke a* très, *I want to eat happles . . .* Images cut before me: I saw Flash, flirting with Gertie in his plush hotel, saw Stu curled up with his wife on that pea green sofa in West Hollywood, saw a long-lost London I had shared with Milena . . .

"Neil?" When I looked up, I saw Scales staring at me, with a strange, peering expression. I felt an overwhelming rush of paranoia, and for a moment I imagined I was a narc so deep undercover that even *I* didn't know.

"What happened to your face there?" he asked,

touching his scarred cheek. "Got a warm Hackney welcome, did you?"

Relieved, I touched my cheek, wincing at the pain as I sucked down another trail of the bitter infection. "Just a little tooth problem. Nothing much."

"Teeth. There's a bloody bother. Got me the only sensible solution." Scales set his face, made a clicking noise in his throat, sucked in his cheeks, then opened his mouth and extended a set of false teeth on his tongue for a flash second. Just as quickly, he pulled them back in, slipping them back in place with another clicking noise, then bellowed with laugher.

"Had 'em knocked out me face five years back and never had a problem since," the looming dealer proclaimed proudly, and with a flashing flick of his silver army lighter, lit up the *très*. A strange chemical scent filled the room, and a moment later, Scales exhaled a massive cloud of blue smoke in a racking cough, laughing as tears burned his eyes.

"*BLOODY CHRIST!*" he shouted. "There's a hit!"

He passed on the *très* to Sleek and when his coughing died down, spoke again. "If you need yourself some dental work, just let me know. Got plenty of mates who'd offer their services, with pleasure."

Sleek laughed, the *très* smoldering between his fingers. "Right, maybe you could even get one of the lads to perform some custom dental work for us: Neil's got a score to settle with an old friend who'll be at the show." The anarchist drew the narcotic blend to his lips and inhaled, the joint snapping and crackling as if mini land mines were loaded along its length.

Scales laughed again, louder. "Shall we have him kiss the curb for us, Sleeky?"

"Kiss the curb?" I asked as Sleek erupted in violent coughing, handing the *très* off to me.

Scales nodded his thick, scarred head. "A trick the lads use up North. Corner a bloke on the street, like someone you've got a vex about, and you tell 'em t' kiss the curb or you'll break his face. So the bloke gets down on his knees and puckers up. And that's when you boot down on the back of his head, like, split his jaw right in half. Seen it done: teeth all over the place." He shook his head slowly. "Nasty, nasty . . ."

Looking down to find the *très* in my fingers, I brought it up and inhaled, feeling the smoke, harsh and toxic, searing the soft pink passageway of my throat, then expanding like a fire in my lungs. For a moment I held it, then like a chemical explosion, it erupted out of me, scorching my brain in a fury of coughs. My ears started to pound, the sounds from the room faded, my head rushed, a thunder of heat roared through my body, and a buzzing grew in my head, louder and louder, until it filled the room.

A vision from youth flew into my head: some teenage summer night when I was happily drunk and hiding in the bushes, the sweet, bitter taste of underage beer on my lips as police flashlights roved through the forest, searching for us no-good-kids.

I never got caught, they never caught me, I never got caught . . .

I repeated the words over and over in my mind, remembering again the open window I had flown through . . . how I had soared into the lush spring darkness, a panicked party detonating in my wake . . . the crunch . . . the cops . . . and how I had escaped through the thick tangle of bushes, untouchable even with a mouth full of broken teeth . . . Escaping that party, that town, my parents . . .

But now it's for real. This is really for real Neil.

In a tilting universe, *Neil's London Bust* raced through my mind again, and I wondered if I would make it even to the door before the bobbies kicked it in. Then I wondered for a fleeting instant if I could really, honestly be scared of something called a "bobby." Bobby? *Très?* Lads up North? Kiss the curb? Flash . . .

"Neil! Mate!" Scales' cockney bark cut through the edge of consciousness. *"Come on back!"*

I regained my balance on the couch and the room came back to me, along with the sounds of Sleek and Scales' English laughter. I pulled my tongue out from my infected hole, where it had instinctively gone to hide, and felt the sweat trickle down my forehead as I sat, skin tingling all over my trembling, shaking body.

"That's just a little taste for the road, why don't you two take it with you," Scales said, snuffing out the *très* and passing it over to Sleek.

"Much obliged," Sleek said with a blackened grin, getting to his feet and pocketing the spliff. "Neil? We best be on the move if you want to make your rendezvous."

As I got to my feet, I saw Sleek stop short, staring at me hard. "Christ," he murmured, "that cheek of yours really is all puffed out. Don't suppose you have any tooth pills in there, do you Scales?" he asked, nodding toward the wooden box.

"I just might."

"It's nothing," I shot back, slurping down a thick trickle of taste before the dealer could answer.

"Nah, take these," Scales said, placing a few pink

pills in my hand. "Can't quite remember what they are, but they should set you straight."

"Thanks," I said, slipping them into my pocket.

"Right then, I'll see you two at the riot," the dealer said, leading us to the door. He slapped me hard on the back and gave me a big grin with his false teeth. "And be sure to point out your chum, Neil. We'll get him sorted."

I nodded my thanks and wrapping up against the fury of pouring rain, stepped out into the darkness.

Jittered from the *très* at Scales', fuzzed further from the mixture of hash and bitters I had used to bring myself down, I found myself a seat in the chatty, fire-warmed pub where Flash and I were to meet. Shaking off Sleek had been some hassle, but I had convinced him that I needed to see Flash alone, and then agreed to meet up at Tosh's squat afterward. The riot ringleader assumed I was securing my backstage passes, but my concerns for the Chockapolacka sabotage had slowly sunken in the dark pool of my infected tooth. This long-overdue meeting with Flash was about something far more personal.

I sat back down into the faded cushions of the booth, and my mind traveled back, seeing Flash in a million different moments from our past . . .

Flash in the New York club where we had first met, jumping up on the tables and tap-dancing, kicking over a bodybuilder's beer. Flash taking me up to the Hollywood Hills, crashing some young movie star's party before he knew them all, pretending we were German porno stars who hardly spoke English. Flash stage-diving at a folk concert on a rainy New York Sunday afternoon, then running down the block over the tops of parked cars in Alphabet City, car alarms wailing in his wake. Flash pretending we didn't have money at a restaurant in Seattle, convincing them to let us wash dishes for the whole night, then creating chaos in the kitchen until they kicked us out. Flash snapping pictures of scary strangers in the city streets, getting us chased across town at least once a week . . .

Flash just being Flash, as if the world were his playground and recess were going on forever. And me just being me, with my broken teeth and my dental bills, envious of Flash's reckless glee, staying tight and hoping some might rub off. But hard as I tried, I could never capture his style of wrecking through reality without a spit of care for Fate's fury. Somewhere in my mind, or maybe in my mouth, as I dashed along through mayhem scenarios with my speed-driving, stage-diving, laughing wild friend, I always held on to a trembling twinge of fear for the bill.

And Flash, of course, never seemed to care. Maybe it was something you learned on a skateboard, I used to think, something you picked up after the first big half-pipe wreck. It was punk, pure and simple, and I didn't have it, not like Flash did, and I always felt the lesser of him for it. But now, in the softly hued London pub, after what Mandy had told me in Hollywood, I figured that my friend had always had a million good reasons to be as punk as he wanted to.

The door swung open, and I saw Flash walk in the door with Gertie. As they approached, I watched my old friend brushing the blond hair from around his famous girlfriend's ear, cooing something that caused her to giggle. His bright eyes turned then, scanning the pub, and in an instant, he met mine in the dim, back corner.

"Neil!" Flash shouted. The green-haired video host came bounding through the crowded pub toward me. "Why it's Neil, young American! Wandering bard! Come here, you old son of a son!"

He leapt toward me with open arms, and I noticed that he was wearing the same old stupid beat-up sneakers and cheap pants, accentuated now with a cheesy *London!* tourist sweatshirt. But just as he came near, Flash stopped, concern crossing his face.

"Your mouth . . . what's wrong?"

"What?" Inside I cursed.

"Your cheek: it's puffy, and kind of red, too," he said, leaning forward and squinting a bit as he examined me. "Is everything OK?"

"No, well, maybe. I think I got a chunk of bangers or mash stuck; maybe it's a little infected. No big deal."

"You should probably get it looked at."

"I've got something set up for tomorrow," I lied, just to end it.

Flash turned to his girl. "Gertie, you remember Neil. He was at Chockapolacka. We used to work together at *Dusted.*"

She smiled at me. "Oh yeah. Hi."

"Hi."

"What're we drinking?" Flash asked, stroking his chin as he searched for a concoction. "Maybe a, um . . . Jolly Old Bloody Brilliant?"

"No, I'm good."

He became British. "No worries, mate, it's on The Channel. I'll put you on the bloody expense account as my crumpets consultant." And before I could answer, he slapped me on the back and dashed from the table toward the bar.

I watched him move easily through the plush surroundings of the pub, then looked furtively at Gertie, wondering if Flash had ever detailed our old rivalry over her image.

"So, all ready for the big rock and roll show?" I finally asked.

"Yeah, I guess. But we're leaving for Paris when Chocka's done. That'll be better. Paris is a dream."

A question I didn't know was in me suddenly leapt from my mouth. "Do you miss Nile?"

"What?" she said with a strange laugh, looking up at me.

"Do you miss Nile Rivers? I mean, since he died."

"Well . . . yeah. I do. He was really sweet. I haven't really thought about it that much, though. It was a while ago." She took out a pack of cigarettes, sliding a thin, brown smoke into her hand.

"It wasn't that long ago."

"OK . . . ," she said, raising her eyebrows. "I guess it *wasn't* that long ago, then."

There was a silence between us, the sounds of pub conversation hanging low in the surrounding air. For a second, I remembered her as a little girl in pigtails, with the big-eyed baby dinosaur, the CIA chasing them across that movie screen I had gazed up at as a child. My big brother beside me in the dark, Saturday-matinee theater, both of us cheering Gertie on, so many years ago . . .

"Why didn't you guys do anything?" I asked her.

She laughed. "What are you talking about?"

265

"Nile Rivers. Why didn't you do anything to help him?"

"Nile was a smack head. A really sweet, really talented, really messed-up smack head. Do you know how many there are in Hollywood?"

"Yeah, but he was Nile Rivers."

"What was I supposed to do?" Gertie asked, frowning. I could tell she was getting annoyed.

"I don't know. Something."

Fury rippled through her photogenic eyes as they bored into mine. "Look: a junkie is a junkie is a junkie. They're either going to die or kick, and there's nothing you can do about it except make sure they don't puke on your carpet or OD in your bathroom!"

A tense silence set in.

"Gertie."

"What?"

"I really loved you in *Tooky*."

Flash suddenly zipped back into the picture, setting a tall, dark drink before me and sliding into the booth next to Gertie. "There you are, good fellow," he said in a fake Brit accent, then wrapped his arm around his girlfriend, giving her a series of little kisses on her cheek.

Gertie pulled away. "I'll meet you at the club."

"No, stay," he coaxed, holding on to her arm as she stood up. "Neil is going to regale us with tales!"

Gertie was already sliding into her leather jacket. "Bye," she said to me with a little wave.

"Bye," I said to the movie star.

"You're OK?" Flash said to her, concerned.

"I just think you guys should be alone. After all, it *is* urgent." She smiled at her boyfriend, then squeezed between a few tables toward the exit, leaving us with our Jolly Old Bloody Brilliants.

"OH MAN! It's Neil! He's back from Java!" Flash suddenly shouted. "Tell me about it! I want to know everything! I see you now, landing in Java, getting off the plane: traveling Neil, his pack of troubles slung over his shoulder, moving through the . . ."

His voice faded away from me, but I watched his face. His sparkling blue eyes, his green hair, his straight, white smile as he transformed my travails into an ironic music video. And then Scales came to mind with his barking laughter, Sleek and his stink bombs, the lads up North who would make my old friend kiss the curb . . .

"Are you sure your teeth are all right?" I heard Flash ask, and I was brought back. "You really don't look that great. Is everything OK? You said it was urgent."

I muttered something offhand and casual and took a sip from my dark beer, the sickening taste of infection mixing in as it flowed down my throat. Something was twisting inside of me and I couldn't put words to it. I was scared to put words to it. First I had come here wanting to throw everything in my friend's face, but now here he was across from me, just being Flash. Millionaire or not, he was fun kid, good guy, pal-around Flash. How could I be mad at him? But he cheated me, right? He never told me who he was. He left *Dusted* and *Dusted* died. Wasn't I supposed to do something back?

"I can't believe we hit London at the same time. Hey, what about *Neil Before God!* I wanna see it!"

Dusted had died when Flash left. Flash left 'cause it never really mattered to him anyway. His life never depended on it, it was all just a game, all just a silly little song: a cheap little date he could ditch when The Channel winked from across the room. And I was just a used-up sidekick: some quirked-up, irked-out character study he met while slumming it downtown.

"How about your Italian woman? Where is she?"

He was a rich kid, playing it broke. He did it well; he duped me. I was a broke kid, playing it rich, but I couldn't cut it; I didn't know how to act around movie stars. And now it felt like an accident that I had ever met someone like Flash. We came from different places, Flash had the world handed to him, I had the world shoved on top of me. He strolled, I struggled.

"Do you want tickets for the show tomorrow? I can get you backstage."

It was all just a foolish, stupid joke; the whole exotic world-wandering trip, as I tried to fashion myself into some dashing expatriate literary styler . . . I was just a dumb kid from the suburbs with a broken mouth, and I was ridiculous thinking I was anything more. The *Dusted* joyride was over and the players were turning back into what they were. Flash a rich kid, getting richer. Me a broken kid, breaking further.

Getting nervous across the table, Flash beat out an awkward drumbeat on the tabletop:

> "Neil from Java,
> Hot as lava,
> on the run,
> in Lon-don . . . ?"

". . . . with a rich-kid friend and his fat trust fund."

It went quiet. And then I watched Flash's bright,

white smile crumble, and his expression fall slowly, dejected, until his whole head dropped, staring blankly down at the carpeted floor. I felt a thin, nauseating trail of infection slip down my throat and masked it with a smile.

Instantly, I knew I had done it all wrong.

"What's up Neil?" my old friend said, voice cool.

But it was too late to hold back the accusations that had been churning in me all the way round the world. "Mandy told me all about your trust fund," I spit at him.

"Yeah, so what are you talking about?"

I leaned in over the table, hearing my cold words cut through the pub's gentle warmth: "How was it playing punk? Was it real, Flash? Did you almost forget how rich you were?"

My friend looked at me blankly for a moment, then dropped his head. When he spoke, I could hardly hear his voice.

"I should go."

He was halfway across the pub before I could even catch my spinning, buzzing balance and chase after him.

"No! Flash! Wait!"

I ran out of the pub after him, into the dark, raining London street. Flash was walking across the sidewalk, fast, and I grabbed him, spinning him round to face me.

For the first time, I saw anger on my friend's face, and I was thrilled. Thrilled to see that gross, repulsive anger that I had never seen mar his bright features, now contorting them before me.

"Is that what's so urgent, Neil? Five thousand things

I need to do before tomorrow's show, and I rush over here to meet you, so you can pick a fight?!"

"Flash, I just . . . Why didn't you tell me!"

"What was I supposed to do, hand you my bank statements every month? So my parents have money! Does that mean I'm not real? Does that mean I'm not *down*, Neil? Does that mean I'm not as punk as you? What should I do, break my teeth?!"

Knocked back by Flash's sudden venom, my words didn't sound half as hard as I needed them to. "All . . . all that time together, when you were just pretending to be broke, I really was broke! It wasn't a game to me! I didn't know how I was going to make it!"

"And that's my fault?"

"You used me!"

He let out a bizarre laugh in the night air. "What the *hell* is your problem!?! I am not your enemy, Neil! *I am your friend!*"

"You faded me so hard in Hollywood! You and your show! Your stupid, asinine show!"

Flash's face was ugly and hard. "Why don't you wake up? *Dusted* is over. It's DONE!! Would you do something with your talent? You are so sharp, *so good!* You could do whatever you want! But you're just so full of yourself and your teeth, and your pain, judging and hating everything that—"

A burning fury surged through me. "Maybe I don't have a chance 'cause I'm busy chasing after the **money** to fix my mouth! Do you know what that's like, FLASH? NO, YOU DON'T! You'll NEVER, EVER know what that's like!"

We stared hard at each other, face-to-face in the pouring night.

"Why didn't you help me, Flash?"

"Why didn't you ask, Neil?"

"Why didn't you save *Dusted?*"

" 'CAUSE I WAS SICK OF BEING DUSTED!''

With a scowl, he spun away, but it was only a few steps before he turned back, shouting. "So it doesn't mean anything?!? We were never friends because I was born into something I DIDN'T EVEN ASK FOR!!!"

Like a dying gasp of heat, my anger suddenly left me, and I was left looking at my friend, feeling sorrowful strains blanching through my body. "Flash . . . wait, it came out wrong. I'm just really—"

He backed away, yelling at me in the night. *"DO YOU REALIZE, OH RIGHTEOUS ALL-KNOWING NEIL, THAT I DIDN'T EVEN ASK FOR IT?!?!?"*

"Wait—"

"DO YOU EVEN KNOW WHEN'S THE LAST TIME I TALKED TO MY PARENTS!?!"

"Flash—"

Bitter, furious tears streamed down his face. "It's been a year! A GODDAMN YEAR! I have my own stupid show on The Channel, and they haven't even called just because I'm—OH FORGET IT!!!"

He turned and started away from me, walking fast down the sidewalk in his *London!* tourist sweatshirt.

"Flash! Come back!"

My old friend spun to face me, pointing at me with a trembling hand as he continued backing away. "TO HELL WITH YOU, NEIL!! TO HELL WITH YOU AND YOUR MOUTH! I'M SICK OF TRYING TO MAKE YOU CHEER UP!! TRYING TO MAKE YOU LAUGH!!"

"I don't want you to make me laugh, I just want to—"

"YOU AND YOUR PAIN!! YOUR MISERABLE PAIN!! I'M THROUGH WITH IT!! JUST STAY AWAY FROM ME!! JUST GO AND FIX YOUR TEETH!!"

I started after him, my pace speeding up as I called after him. *"Flash! Wait!"*

He turned, arms wrapped tight around his body, moving back and forth in tight weaves down the shadowed London street.

"BE CAREFUL TOMORROW!!" I yelled as loud as I could in the night. My voice strained in my throat as I ran forward, tripping into a bag of metal cans, which skittered wildly across the pavement. Sent sprawling to the sidewalk, I cursed and staggered to my feet, stumble-running as I screamed after my old friend:

"FLASH!!"

But it was only a few lurching steps before I saw that Flash was gone, his bright green hair lost in the gloomy darkness. I slowed to a stop, chest heaving, face burning in the cold night as I gazed down the deserted London street that had swallowed my old friend.

14. dawn

"**A**h, there's our undercover agent!"

I shut the creaking door of Tosh's squat slowly behind me and looked into the dingy bedroom where Sleek's voice had come from.

"Backstage arrangements settled?" he asked, excited.

I looked at him blankly, and then around the room. A single, dim yellow lamp lit the crooked space, where a thinning grey carpet covered the warped wooden floor, and a sparse collection of thirdhand furniture leaned about. Sleek stood poised before a peeling, smudged white dresser, a rolled pound note in his hand. Looking closer, I noticed a small mirror before him, lined with flaky, white rows of chopped speed. A fat girl with limp brown hair, wearing dirty white stretch pants and an argyle sweater, stood expectantly near the window, gazing in turn at me and the narcotics awaiting on the mirror.

I saw Sleek's eyebrows jump in concern. "Tell me it all went right . . . ?"

The raging fury I had woken up with that morning had been lost in a furious buzz of paranoia at Scales, and that paranoia had been doused by a heavy, ponderous wave of depression after leaving Flash. And now standing before Sleek in the dingy squat, soaking wet, fazed from a sizzling flux of drugs and a fresh infection chewing at the back of my mouth, I knew another exhausting swing of circumstance would erupt if I spoke the truth. So as a black ooze of taste trickled down my throat, I felt my head begin to nod, and then heard the words the tattered revolutionary needed to hear fall through my lips.

"Yeah Sleek, we're in."

"Brilliant! Now we've *really* got something to celebrate!"

The blackened grin returned to his face as he extended the rolled pound note to the fat girl. "Would we care for a nozzleful?"

"We would!"

As she gleefully crossed the room, I stood uncertain on the center of the carpet, wondering if I would make it through the night. The cocktail of chemicals from Scales' were tracing through my brain, touching reality with a quavering sheen. Looking around me, I imagined I could see every particle of dust and dirt hanging about the walls and floor, every single split in the fibers from the sagging couch, every hairline crack in the paint peeled wall.

"Ooooch!" the big girl shouted, jumping back from the speed-lined mirror as she blinked furiously and rubbed at her nose.

"Strong enough for you?" Sleek asked with pride.

"Almost bloody blinded me!" She laughed, sending

a thin rope of speed-thick mucus flying from her red-dened nose.

"Scales is a proud purveyor of only the finest in nar-cotic substance." Sleek turned to me, holding out a rolled-up pound note. "Neil?"

The painkilling effects of the *très* we had smoked was wearing off, and I had felt the hurt slowly easing its way back into my mouth ever since leaving Flash. Thinking anything might help, I reached out and took the bill from Sleek, sliding it up my nose as I moved before the white-lined mirror atop the bureau. Staring momentarily at the reflection of my red, bloodshot eyes, I pushed the foreign currency quickly along the glass, sucking the bitter dust up into my head.

"God *damn!*" A white hot chain-saw blade rammed into my brain, and a wave of burning tears welled up instantaneously in my eyes, then began streaming down my face. The delicate insides of my nose scorched ablaze as Sleek and the girl began laughing loudly.

"If you sniff a bit of water up your nose, it usually helps," the skinny dealer suggested.

"No luck there," the big girl said, wincing and rub-bing her nose. "Ned and Tosh are still fiddling with the pipes."

"Well, you could maybe use a touch of cider, at least it's wet," Sleek offered, picking his bottle off the floor. "Neil?"

The inside of my head a howling blaze, I held out a shaky hand, half wondering if some chemical reaction of speed and cider would blow the nose right off my face. Desperately, I snuffled up the meager pool of alco-hol from my palm.

"How'd we do?" the big girl asked.

"Lovely." I mumbled, sucking and swallowing the residue of raw stimulant in my throat as my mind, singing and burning, began to rev up in my skull.

Sleek was bent over the mirror now, taking in a line of his own. I watched his head whip back, heard his cry of pain, heard the big girl start to laugh. Then through the thin walls, I heard another wave of dull laughter, coming from the next room. The big girl cocked her head for a moment and turned quickly to look at an old, cracked wall clock.

"Oh! Mr. Pea!" she shouted, clapping her hands and dashing out of her dim bedroom.

"New program this week, isn't it?" Sleek asked, excited and pleased, following her out the warped bedroom door. I tagged along, shaking my head and blinking my burning eyes, swallowing the bitter, thick narcotics clotted in my tightening throat.

"Find a seat," Sleek suggested as I entered the flickering room. "We're just in time for Mr. Pea."

I groped through the darkness and found a folding chair on the far side of the room. My eyes widened to the gloom, and I made out five or six squatters, their faces glowing white in the flicker of TV light. The floor was a rising and falling landscape of refuse and layabout: bottles, clothes, old pieces of music equipment, and trash all bound in a flickering web of television light. A tweed-jacketed twit I guessed to be Mr. Pea pratfalled his way into a case of mistaken identity on the television, and tomorrow's revolutionaries laughed.

I watched TV for a moment, surrounded by hanging half-smiles in the darkness, feeling jumpy and needing to talk. Then with a wicked, unexpected rush, I was suddenly flashed back to my parents' home. The constant bath of TV images seeping into my parents' minds, their eyes glassy after a day's work, smoke from their cigarettes curling into the air about their heads, tinkling ice cubes in glasses of Scotch . . .

"Ready for the riot tomorrow?" I suddenly said, my voice almost a shout.

A murmur of something like affirmative response came from a few squatters, and then a Mr. Pea antic had them all laughing.

My mind flipped back to my parents again, and I remembered how I used to sneak around to the back of their house on dark, winter nights when I came home early. Standing before the big picture window of the TV room, hidden from their view by the glare of the window, I would stand and watch them watch TV. As my parents sat transfixed by the programming, I could examine their faces for long, enduring moments, and half afraid, half in awe, I would inevitably zero in on my father. Potato chips at his side, newspaper before him, he seemed in his brooding silence like a lion guarding his den, set to tear into pieces anyone who dared threaten that lair, kill any who challenged that bag of chips. Dad. Dear old angry Dad. Why did we have to be enemies? Jesus, we could have been friends. We could have had a good time together. . . .

"So, everyone ready for Chockapolacka tomorrow!" I suddenly burst out.

The muttering telly gazers didn't seem like much of a revolutionary army, and I was suddenly struck with the thought that this riot was all in Sleek's head. I brushed it away and got up from my chair, fumbling my way through the darkness. Squatters leaned to the left and right, craning their necks around me to see the TV high jinx; heart hammering, brain whirring, I escaped the room, my mind still looping around my father.

Dad. Dad and Mom. Angry Dad and whacko Mom. Dad drank 'cause Mom was whacked, or Mom was whacked 'cause Dad drank. Who knew? Who even cared anymore? No one did. Not them. Not my pot-smoking brother. Nobody cared about that mess in our house except me. Nobody even *saw* it except me, and they all just treated me like a little idiot. A messed-up writer kid with a stupid broken mouth who didn't have a real job like the rest of the world. Why was I thinking of them? I didn't want to be thinking of them anymore . . .

I found my bottle of scrumpy in the big girl's room and took a long, cold, thirsty sip. As I looked around at the dimly lit space, I remembered the one depressing visit I had made to my brother in San Francisco. In my mind, I saw James in his creaky old Victorian house, exhaling his eighty-eighth bong hit of the day, strumming some old classic rock hit with a cute little hippie girl from the Haight curled up at his side. And around him, of course, the gathered crew of old stoners from home, a flannel-shirted, scruffy bearded bunch who had followed James to California like a gang of pothead apostles; each nodding his head along on a foggy San Francisco afternoon, the wasted time oozing like melted rubber through the floorboards all around them.

And little brother Neil was now in London, a hand mirror on the bureau, dusty white narcotics flaked across its surface. Not quite a hippie, but about as punk as punk could be: chilling out on riot's eve with a bunch of squatting speed freaks. Gazing around at the chipped walls in the rugged urban wreck of Hackney, I grimly congratulated myself on reaching the Big Time.

The front door creaked open, and a second later, Tosh poked his head in the room.

"Hey. *Dusted* Neil."

"Yo. How's it going?"

"It took a long time to get all the sound together. Yeah. But it's going to be really loud tomorrow." He laid down a handful of wires and cords near the stairs. "So, you like my house?"

"It's punk."

"Come on, I'll show you my room."

His body disappeared from the door frame, and I followed, through the small hallway, past the TV shadows to the door at the end of the hall. Tosh turned the knob, pushed it open with his shoulder, and flipped the light.

It was the neatest room in the squat. The bed was made in the far corner, a wooden desk sat lined with books, a small amp and a guitar leaned near an empty fireplace, and a string of cassettes, guitar wire, and records were grouped together in a corner.

Tosh stopped before he sat down, peering at me with a frown and then touching his face. "Your cheek is really big. And red. Does it hurt?"

"Nah," I lied, touching the puffed area with my finger. "It just tastes bad."

He laughed a little. "It looks kind of funny."

Tosh nodded his head and took off his coat, laying it down on the back of his chair near his desk. Then he sat cross-legged on the floor and pulled his electric guitar onto his lap.

279

"I hope we don't get beat up too bad tomorrow. Or I hope we get to play for a while before they turn off the system," I heard him say as I drank down some more scrumpy. The hole in my mouth was starting to feel as big as my face.

"Tosh, can I ask you a question?"

"Sure." He picked at his guitar.

"Do you like it here?"

Tosh nodded his head and smiled, as if surprised. "Yeah, I do. It's funny, you know, for me to be here. From Japan, and then the farm in Burma, to be living in a squat in Hackney, and playing in a band at a riot, it's really a funny thing."

"You grew up on a farm?"

"Yeah."

"My grandfather was a farmer in Ireland," I said, as if realizing it for the first time. "What was it like?"

"Um, well, it's a lot of work. But it's good work. And my pig was there, who I grew up with." He laughed in recollection. "A pet pig, yeah. It's really a great thing to have if you're a kid." He pulled his sweater tighter around him in the chilly room. "But then he blew up."

"*What?*"

"There was mines left over from all the guerrilla fighting, yeah, and my pig stepped on one. He blew up."

I started laughing, then cut it back. "Sorry . . ."

"No, it's really weird, isn't it?" Tosh said with a strange smile. "I laughed, too, when it happened. Yeah, I was sad, but you know, it was funny. And I left then. Time to go when your pig blows up."

"I guess it is." I thought of a little-kid Tosh, playing around with a pig somewhere long ago.

Tosh tapped out a smoke from his pack of cigarettes. "Some people in London, they don't treat me well because of my English, which isn't so good. And because I'm Japanese. But Sleek and his friends, they're really cool to be around. Yeah, I like it here in Hackney."

"That's good then," I said, suddenly sadder, wishing I liked it somewhere, too.

The door opened with a creak and Sleek entered. "Hey there, Tosh. All set up with the sound and what not?" he asked, tossing his army lighter across the room to the Japanese squatter.

Tosh grabbed it from the air and flicked back the top, striking a flame and catching his cigarette. "Everything should be OK. Yeah."

"Brilliant, brilliant. And with Neil headed backstage, that means everything's right sorted." Sleek paced the room slowly as he stroked his beard, then slowly closed the door behind him and lowered his voice. "So Neil, have you got those tooth pills?"

"Ah, dental dope," Tosh said. "That's the best."

Sleek walked over in his heavy boots and extended his hand; I reached into my pocket and dropped the six pink pills into the creased black leather of his knuckle gloves.

"Scales handed them over tonight as we left," he explained to Tosh. "Said they'd set Neil straight with his dental problems."

"What are they?" the guitarist asked.

"Couldn't say. Bound to be something fairly mental, though, knowing Scales." Sleek reached into his pocket and pulled out the snubbed narco cigarette the cockney dealer had rolled for us. "I figure with these and the *très* . . ."

Tosh's face lit in wonder. "Wow, a *très?* From Scales?"

"That's right. And I figure as we don't have anything to do tonight except bide our time, we could take a little experiment and find out what these little beauties are." Sleek gazed at the pink pills, lying docile in his palm.

Tadashi picked at his electric guitar, running down some Post Everything riffs sans ear-crushing amplification, his face pulled in thought. A moment later he concluded, "It's up to Neil. Yeah. They're his teeth."

My mind looped as Sleek turned his expectant gaze to me. I was already feeling shaky from the speed, woozy from the scrumpy, hazy from the hashish, and who knows what from the *très.* The few molecules of reason functioning within the chemical dump site of my head activated, and I heard myself speaking up.

"I don't know man, I'm kinda faded already."

"*Dusted* Neil! I'm disappointed in you. Why settle for merely 'kinda faded' when you could be *utterly* faded."

I thought of the flickering TV room, and how without the net of conversation I had collapsed into a past of dark memory. "I guess if we do them, we'll be up all night together?"

Sleek grinned, showcasing his car wreck of a mouth. "Absolutely! It'll be good for you, too; looks as if you're drifting away."

I felt the bitter pain in the back of my mouth pulling at me, threatening to drag me down into its black, solitary hole, and realized with a mounting panic that I couldn't be alone in my mouth tonight, not for a single instant.

"All right," I agreed.

"Brilliant!" Sleek moved toward me, a grin on his face, a bottle of scrumpy dangling at his side. "There's six here; I figure we do two each, as one of anything usually isn't good for much." Passing Tosh, he dropped two pills in his hand, then came over to me. I watched his spindly fingers as they picked up the two pink points and held them before me. I hesitated.

"Come now, *Dusted* Neil, open up. Dentist's orders."

I opened my hand, and Sleek dropped the pills, one after the other, into my palm under the harsh light of the angled desk lamp. He took his own two then and held them up before his grinning face.

"Here's to Neil's teeth!"

"Yeah," Tosh said. "And to the riot."

"Absolutely!" Sleek affirmed. "To a smashing, mental riot!"

"Cheers," I said quietly, placing the drugs on my tongue and swallowing them down smoothly. Tosh ate his one at a time, chewing them up and spreading them around in his mouth. Sleek popped his pills past his crooked teeth and chased them down with a few huge gulps of cider.

"And off we go," the dealer said from the center of the room, flicking his lighter and igniting the ashen end of the *très.* "To who knows where."

I noticed it first when I breathed. The air came down like liquid, pooling in my lungs, as if I were drinking a cool and delicious cocktail deep into my being. Into my nose, down to my lungs, seeping into my blood, pumping through my heart . . . Suddenly, breathing seemed the best thing in the world, and I couldn't imagine anything better. Then, in a shimmering realization, I suddenly understood why my parents smoked.

"*Goddamn*, I'd love a cigarette," I said aloud.

Sleek heard me. "Here." He held out his pack.

"No thanks, I don't smoke." I watched his face quiz up, and then I laughed, turning to Tosh, who had been strumming the same space riff for what seemed like an eternity. "What kind of effects do you have on your guitar?"

"Hmm, I don't know." Tosh looked down at his hands as they played his guitar, then followed the lines of the instrument to the amplifier. He started to laugh.

"What's so funny?" I asked.

"It's not even plugged in."

"Oh my, we're in for it tonight," Sleek said slowly.

And then we all three fell headlong into laughter together, and I closed my eyes, my reality collapsing into blackness. The only sound in the universe was our laughter, and it echoed around me, bounding through my mind, until mine became Tosh's and his became Sleek's and there was nobody anymore, just a single wave of hilarious nonsense reverberating through everything. And then Tosh's room cut off from the rest of the house and silently speeded out into the night sky, rushing quietly and furiously out of the earth's orbit, blurring past every known planet and whirling white galaxy until it suddenly stopped, hanging and bobbing in some weird corner of deepest space, a thin line of drugged reality our only mooring to the crumbling squat on the spinning planet, somewhere far and long away.

*   *   *

"We're going to show them tomorrow," Sleek said darkly.

Time had passed. The laughter had died at some point, and in the silence I had sunken deep down into the cluttered corridors of my mind. My thoughts were opaque and I couldn't think them, only stroll through them, gazing at the obtuse, clouded shapes, like patterns of frost on frozen morning windows. Sleek's words brought me back into the room, and I struggled to find my voice.

"Yeah, when Post Everything plays, people will probably forget the Chocka poseurs for the real thing. You know, your music," I agreed.

Sleek snarled, "To hell with the music, I'm talking about some nice, cracking violence. I want to see flames tomorrow. I want to see smashed windows and battered police. I want to see the lads up North stomping your sellout friend Flash."

"Yeah, but our sound system should be good," Tosh added, his voice slow and deliberate.

Sleek leaned in, conspiratorial. "The government, they have the most massive sound system around. But they don't use it all at once, see. Just a bit here or there: in the lift or on the telly or in the department stores. It's always somewhere, and no one really notices. But it's on, washing everyone's mind every minute of the day. But tomorrow . . ."

"Tomorrow we Post Everything them," Tosh picked up.

I looked at Sleek and saw the angry energy radiating from his face in greasy, hallucinated spirals that wavered and bent whenever he moved. "That's right! Our music's going to get the people on their bloody feet! We need to start people breaking things in London! There's not enough being smashed these days . . . we need to crush everything in this corporate Chockapolacka nightmare until it's all shattered completely to pieces!!"

I felt a question forming inside me. I didn't know exactly what it was, but I knew it was a question, and I felt it rising like an awkward bubble up through the jumble of filmy thoughts scattered in the echoing halls of my mind. I waited as it rose, growing curious as shape came to it, but I didn't know what I wanted to ask until I heard it come out of my mouth and enter the run-down room.

"Sleek, can I see your eyes?"

I saw an incredulous curve wrap around his lips. *"What?"*

"I've been living in your house for a month now, and spending just about every day with you, but I still haven't seen your eyes."

"Oh come on now, don't get like this, Neil," he grumbled.

"Like what?"

"Insistent, like. Badgering, even. They're just eyes. Your average visual-input jacks. Ask Tosh."

I turned to Tosh, to find the Japanese guitarist stroking his chin and frowning in thought. "I don't think I've ever seen your eyes either, Sleek."

Sleek let out a sharp laugh. "That's absurd! We've been playing in the same sonic assault outfit for two years now! You must have seen my eyes somewhere along the line."

Tosh slowly shook his head. "No, I haven't."

We both stared at Sleek, sitting behind his sunglasses across the room. He broke into nervous laughter.

"You've got me all bothered about them now."

"C'mon Sleek. Just show us your eyes."

He laughed again nervously, then stopped when we didn't join in. Then he exhaled and muttered something under his breath, and as we watched, Sleek reached up and took hold of the thick, black, impenetrable shades and pulled them slowly from his face.

They were small, dark eyes, moving back and forth between Tosh and me in hard defiance, but they couldn't conceal that they wanted to hide. And with the revolution talk gone, with the shields finally down, the eyes made him suddenly seem skinnier, smaller, and less the threat he seemed before. More than anything, the eyes looked scared.

The dealer swallowed loudly, pulling his lips tight and maintaining his gaze, as he slid behind his sunglasses once again. "There you are, *Dusted* Neil. Me bloody eyes."

I felt a cold vacuum in the room as Sleek pulled his energy back into himself. He withdrew, back into the dark world behind his sunglasses: a fantasy world of riots and screaming and shrieking electric music. A world of breaking glass and breaking jaws, blazing police vans and smoking skies. I saw Sleek's grin spread slowly over his face, and I realized he was really looking forward to breaking something tomorrow. Breaking and screaming, shattering and burning, tearing it all to pieces or being battered down in the whole horrible process.

It was quiet in the room for a long, long time.

"Tosh?"

I needed to talk. But Tosh didn't answer, and as I

got ready to speak again, swallowing to clear my constricting throat, I took down a gushing flow of bitter infection.

The taste. I had forgotten all about it in the bizarre whirl of drugs, but suddenly it was back, bitter and slimy and acrid and foul. I swallowed and felt nausea rise in my stomach.

"Tosh?"

"Whmmn?"

As I looked to see him lying on the carpet, I felt a surging rush of paranoia: the drugs were peaking out, harder and higher and suddenly very, very darkly.

No! I don't want to be tripping. I don't want to be on drugs anymore . . .

And with that thought, my head slowly caved in, falling back on itself, my mind leaking into the pool of infection at the end of my teeth. In a panic, I swallowed the vile fluid, which I knew for certain was now feeding on my brain. It had eaten up all my teeth, and now it was eating my mind: I was swallowing bitter pieces of my burned-out psyche. The panic grew louder.

No, Neil, you're tripping. Tripping out of your mind. Sleek's still here. He's used to this kind of thing. Sleek can help.

"Sleek?"

Nothing from the dealer across the room.

I called out again. "Sleek?"

"What?"

"Need to ask a favor."

"Neil?"

"Yeah?"

He laughed. "Brilliant pills."

"I think something might be wrong with my head."

"Oh. You, too?" He shifted in his sitting, but still didn't pull his hands away from the side of his head. Still didn't look up at me. I saw a dark grin spread on his face. "What's it?"

"I think . . . um, I think . . . this is going to sound weird. But I think my head is caving into the hole in my teeth."

"Oh, dear."

"Yeah." I swallowed and felt another piece of my brain, bitter and gooey, slide down my throat. "I was wondering, do you think you could look at me and tell me if it is for sure?"

Sleek was silent, and entirely motionless. "Well, Neil, I'd love to help you, but I'm afraid I can't at the moment. I'm stuck, really."

"Stuck?"

"My hands here have fused into the side of my skull. I'd love to look at your head, but I just can't pull it off. Not now."

"Oh."

"You could give Tosh a try."

"Tried."

The room went heavy and shadowed, the darkest it had been all night. I breathed for a while in the dull heaviness of the Hackney squat, then I heard Sleek's voice:

"There's a mirror downstairs in the loo, if you fancy you can make it."

My body brought me to my feet before he finished his sentence. To the door before he even noticed I was up. My hand turned the knob and I heard Sleek speak as I stepped through into the hall.

"Careful down there, Neil. Mirror can be a tricky item at this stage in the game."

Through the dark squat, I walked to the stairway and stood at the top, looking down the doomed flight to the single lightbulb glowing weak and yellow in the shadows at the bottom. I took a deep breath and stepped on the first stair. The weakened wood groaned as I descended into the gloom, leaving trailing images of my body motion in the space behind me, like a confused cubist study scrawled through the dank basement air.

A single warped door, paint peeling and stuck shut, waited for me at the bottom of the squat. I pulled on the handle. The door creaked open, and I walked inside.

It was a small space, dim and black. I slid my hand along the wall, feeling for a switch, and coming up short, waved my other hand slowly through the air, hoping to find a dangling string that would lead to a light. A few moments later, I closed around a metal-beaded cord, and with a sigh of relieved tension, I closed the door behind me and pulled down. There was a click, then a weak light from the dangling bulb instantly coated the room. I found myself standing directly before the mirror, staring at my face.

A hideous, phantasmic vision from some far-flung ring of a demented dental inferno blazed before me. My turgid cheek bulged from my grim frown, pulsing like some inborn demon waiting to burst ripping through the side of my head. My lips had entirely disappeared, leaving only ragged strings of black taste clinging to my teeth, and as my eyes widened in terror from their sunken, shadowed pits, I watched my wretched, desiccated mouth turn slowly in its battered socket and, with the tiny, wet bites of a teething baby, begin to slowly chew into my own head.

My mouth was eating me alive.

I felt a raging scream forming somewhere far away, senseless and scrambling, but before it could take over, my legs went weak, and I collapsed down to the floor, landing before the old corroded toilet. My skin burning, sweat soaking my body, I moaned, and the bathroom groaned around me. Then suddenly, with no warning, what felt like my entire digestive system roared from inside me and came hurtling up my throat. A spewing flood of bitters and bangers and mash and speed spattered into the browned pool of water before me. My body coiled and tightened, spasms ripped through me, and a name for my new manifesto blithely strolled by, from a humorless corner of my mind.

Neil Before Toilet.

The food went fast, but the vomit didn't stop. My jaws locked and pain seized my insides; what felt like the lining of my stomach began ripping through my broken teeth, splashing in stringy, dangling threads into the toilet.

I'm Nile Rivers. Every drug in the world boiling through my brain. But I'm not going to fade out on Sunset Boulevard like a Hollywood legend. I'm going to die in a squat in Hackney like a doomed, failed writer boy.

Frozen like some ghastly sculpture, my broken mouth locked open, I began to throw up everything that was churning in my mind. Visions of a screeching mother, of an old home, cold and chilling, visions of *Dusted* days, New York nights, rivers of recorded interviews, clustered pages of words and stories, Ehrlina's eyes, Milena's kisses, Flash's trust fund, Dad's Scotch, passports and airports, dealers and dentists, drunks and drugs; it all came out in a bitter, fuming flood that sprayed through my aching, broken mouth, on and on for what seemed forever until my body disappeared and I was nothing but a gush of noxious vomit, puking myself up into a stinking pool of me.

When it finally stopped, I collapsed back onto the floor. Weakened, my clothes soaked with sweat, I took in air, slowly and carefully, as if afraid I might throw up my breath itself. And when I could speak, I looked up, exhausted, and addressed the general direction of the heavens, which seemed very, very far away.

"Where the hell *am* I?"

No one answered me.

"Come on," I continued, straightening myself up against the wall. "I'm asking You: Where am I?"

Nothing.

"Answer me." I felt anger rush through me as I glared hard at the crumbling ceiling overhead. "I said answer me, you bastard! I'm your goddamn lost little lamb!"

But of course, there was nothing but silence. And I sat in the silence for a long time, until finally, I pulled myself, shaking and unsteady, to my feet.

"I just want to know where I am," I muttered softly, to no one, as I moved to the toilet and pulled the handle down.

The bowl shook for a moment, then flushed down, and a moaning of pipes surrounded me from the walls of the bathroom. Creaking and clanking, screeching and banging, the ancient, neglected plumbing threatened to burst, and I suddenly feared for my life. But just as a crescendo of metallic din was reached, and I was certain the ceiling would cave in with a rush of freezing, filthy water, the sounds subsided and settled back into silence.

From the corner of my eye, I caught motion in the white tub. And turning to look, I watched in disgust as a thick, black bile rose up from the depths of the squat, oozing its way through the metal screen of the drain and filling the basin in a silent, odious flow of dark liquid.

I heard a gurgling from the sink and turned to see the same black substance rising from the drain, filling up in the white porcelain, filthy and vile. Transfixed in disgust, I stood watching as the viscous black fluid slowly seeped its way across the length of the bathtub and covered the white basin of the sink.

"Jesus, where am I?" I muttered ruefully. And then a lost voice from the past came back to me:

Every part of the world is a part of you, bro . . .

"Oh my God," I whispered. My tongue slowly slid back to the dark infection in my mouth, seeping through my teeth, and I stumbled back against the wall, struck dumb by revelation.

There was a knock on the door.

"Neil?" Sleek's voice came through the warped wood. "Neil, are you all right? You've been down here some time. Everything's OK?"

Slowly, I pushed open the door and found Sleek standing in the frame, his sunglasses firmly in place.

"Sleek?"

"Neil?"

I grabbed him by the shoulders. *"I know where I am!"*

"I'm thrilled for you."

I squeezed hard. *"I'm in my mouth!"*

He frowned, confused, and another revelation took me over. My jaw dropped open, and I stared at the skinny, unshaven figure slumped before me. I let go of Sleek, and my arms lowered slowly to my side.

"What is it?" he asked.

"If this is my mouth, and you're in here, then that means . . ." The words stopped in my throat. I felt my eyes widen as my hand slowly came up to my cheek.

"What?"

"You're . . . MY TOOTH!"

"Have you gone absolutely bonkers?" Sleek laughed ruefully. He turned away into the dark hallway.

I followed quickly behind, illuminated and ecstatic. "You're my tooth! And this house, this place, it's my mouth! I've been wandering around the whole world, running away from it for years, but I've finally ended up back in my mouth! It all makes so much sense!"

"Oh dear, can see you did a bit much tonight." The dealer began to clump up the stairs and I followed, thrumming with excitement. We passed a hole in the wall, the paper blackened and mildewed around it.

"Don't you see," I said. "Nile Rivers said that every part of the world is a part of *you*, and that means this place is my mouth! I've been sitting here, tripping out in it all night. Tripping out with my *teeth!*"

We entered Tosh's room, and Sleek stopped, turning to face me.

"Neil, I like you, and I know that you've consumed an absolutely extraordinary amount of drugs this evening. But I might have to leave if you insist on referring to me as your tooth. It's unsettling."

My tooth slumped back down in his corner of my mouth and lit another cigarette. "Why don't you go pick on that tooth over there?" he muttered, nodding his head toward Tosh. "He's a bit crooked as well."

"What are you talking about?"

I turned to Tosh. Tosh my tooth. I started laughing. He was a great tooth.

He was confused. "What's going on?"

"This is my mouth. You are my tooth. I'm finally taking on the Great Work. I'm going to fix you up."

"Uh-oh," I heard him mutter. "Still tripping."

I walked to the window, feeling filled with a charged energy. The dark world beyond the dirty pane seemed to be expanding, and a strong, cool confidence suffused my limbs. I felt my chest growing wider, opening up to the future, and I suddenly realized with a flash of inner light what I was in the scheme of things.

"And I must be my tongue. My wonderful, smooth, soft tongue."

Sleek spoke up. "Well maybe you should stop talking for a while, Tongue. Take a bit of a breather. We teeth have got a big day tomorrow. A historic riot to bite into."

I shook my head. "We have to forget the Chockapolacka riot tomorrow. You guys are just going to get bashed up some more."

"Well, that's kind of the point."

I smiled gently. "You're a crooked tooth, Sleek. You need to be straightened up. Bonded, bridged, cared for, strengthened."

I saw a menacing look cross over the unshaved face of my tooth. "If you weren't my favorite writer, and I didn't personally know how many drugs you had

295

consumed this evening, I might have to take offense at that."

I looked out through the window again, into the darkness of Hackney, which was now becoming grey, a dim light dawning somewhere far away. "The problem isn't out there; it's right here, in my mouth. We're living in it, I mean, look at this place."

"You have a problem with our home?" my tooth growled, gesturing about at the run-down mouth.

"No, I mean, it's the best we could do up to now. But we have to forget about the fighting for a while. It's not helping in here any, and that's what we have to concentrate on."

"Well maybe the reason 'in here' is so offensive to your sensibilities is because of what's going on *out there*," my angry, riotous tooth spat, standing up and jabbing his finger toward the window.

For the first time in years, it was all so clear. Patiently, I explained, "Yeah, but the first thing is our mouth. Nothing in the whole world is gonna seem right until we fix it."

His voice was loud and angry from the corner. "No one's fixing anything! There's a riot tomorrow, and you're still tripping out of your skull!" He blew out a thin, tense trail of cigarette smoke. "Remind me, Tosh, to never do drugs with a bloody utopian tongue again."

I turned and looked at my tooth, smoldering in the corner of my mouth behind his sunglasses. Then I walked over to him slowly and put my hand on his skinny, tense shoulder. "Look, for whatever this is worth, I'm sorry. I know you're really angry, and you have a good reason to be. I should have fixed you up a long time ago."

Sleek shook off my hand with a furious yank of his arm and pushed himself right into my face. "WILL YOU SHUT UP WITH THESE INSANE DENTAL DE-LUSIONS, YOU BLOODY FOOL! **I AM NOT YOUR TOOTH!**"

Tosh came quickly between us. "Maybe we should go for a walk, Neil."

I gripped his arm with my hands and stared into his eyes, almost shouting myself. "No! I can't run away from you guys again!"

There was a shuffling sound in the hallway, and the door opened. Two sleepy teeth wandered in, scratching at their greasy hair.

"What the hell is going in here?" one spoke with a frown. "You woke up the bleedin' house."

I looked around me at my teeth. They were all here now. A ragtag bunch. Angry, tired, confused, scared, and suspicious. I looked at Sleek glaring at me in fury and wondered if there was enough of him left to be saved. Then in the doorway, two more bleary-eyed teeth. One sunken chested, his worn pajamas baggy around skinny hips, his eyes black and heavy, face un-shaven; he needed an inlay, possibly a crown. The other was an overweight, tousled tooth, face puffy and eyes slits of drug-reddened excess. She needed some serious bonding. And Tosh in the middle of it all, a tooth with such potential, trapped in the broken wreck-age of my mouth; the strong one who would have to be the anchor for the bridge. I hoped with a pang that the dentist wouldn't have to file him down too much.

A tear came down my cheek, and then another and

another. "I'm sorry," I said through a cracking voice. "Jesus, I'm so sorry."

"Come now, you don't have to cry, we can go back to bed," someone muttered.

The tears came down my face harder, and I began sobbing, heaving. "I should . . . I should have done. Something. Sooner." I dropped my face in my hands and the racking wave of tears took me over. *"I should have fixed my teeth!"*

There was a strained, pained silence in the crumbling squat as I cried in the middle of the room. No one said anything, and no one made a motion to stop me as I sank to the creaking floor. It felt as if a frozen glacier were melting inside me, gushing out of my eyes, and I thought it might never stop as I fought the weeping, violently sucking and gasping for air, my face red and vision bleary.

And for a long time, I cried.

At some point, I felt the tears begin to ebb, the frozen pain sinking slowly down again, deep inside my chest. And when I looked up, the room was quiet and empty again. I didn't see Sleek at first, but then in my second pass over the room, I made out his curled form on the carpet next to the bed, his back to me. The squatters had gone back to bed, and Tosh was sitting quietly on his desk, smoking a cigarette and looking at me.

Without a word, he came to me, nodding his head toward the door and leading me down the hallway, to the empty front room. A thin sheen of morning light came through the dirty windows, and the grey-painted floorboards creaked under our feet, the sounds big and echoed in the unfurnished space. Tosh sat down on the radiator near the window, looking at me for a long moment before he spoke.

"Do you still think I'm your tooth?"

I looked at him, confused, wondering what he was asking, then remembered that just a short while ago I was convinced I was my tongue.

"No . . . I . . . how long was I crying?"

Tosh shrugged. "A long time. Everybody left. I figured I'd just let you go, you know. Get it out. Yeah." He took a drag on his cigarette.

A while passed, and then Tosh laughed a little. "There was a hairbrush on my desk, and I hid it. I thought you were going to try to start brushing us." He looked closely at me in the dim dawn light. "You know, your cheek doesn't look so bad anymore. Yeah."

I touched softly at my face, surprised to find the pain was almost gone. And then rolling my tongue through my teeth, I discovered the taste had vanished, too.

"I think it's OK," I said slowly. Then I suddenly remembered Sleek's angry face, shouting at me. "Oh no. What did I say to Sleek? I got him mad, didn't I?"

"Yeah. You did. But it was nothing too bad. I don't think he'll be too mad. Those things happen to Sleek all the time. Someone's always freaking out on drugs around him. He's got crazy stories."

"I guess he's got another one, then."

I saw my black bomber jacket, the one I had bought to look good for Milena, hanging near the door. I walked to it and was relieved to find it dry and slipped into its warmth. I turned back to Tosh, wiping at my eyes once more.

"I have to go."

"OK. I'll see you later at the show."

"No, I mean, really go. I have to fix my teeth."

"Oh." Tosh cleared his throat and, after a while, spoke. "Well, I guess Hackney isn't the best place to do that."

"No, I don't think so."

"Hmm." He looked down at the floor for a while. "Well, I'm glad I met you, even if you did think I was your tooth for a while."

"Me too. And sorry about all that."

Tosh gave a little laugh. *"Dusted* Neil."

"Just Neil," I said.

We smiled for a while, looking at each other in the empty room. And then I turned and walked through the dim hallway, dull grey now in the dawning light, and passed through the creaking door, out onto the street.

I walked on in silence for a long time, over cracked sidewalks sprinkled with the glitter of shattered glass, not knowing where I was going, not caring. After a while, I reached a row of hedges near the sidewalk, which stopped and became a low brick wall. Farther down the wall I spotted a crooked, black metal gate hanging open and headed toward it.

I turned through the gate and followed a pathway through green, poorly tended grass. The city fell behind me as I moved farther down the path, into a roughly kept park. A footbridge came up beneath me, and I walked over a silent, still, brown stream, continuing on toward another row of scraggly hedges, which opened up like a doorway. I walked through, leaving the path behind.

"Wow," I said softly.

A massive expanse of green opened before me, the grass glistening with silver drops of dew, a low fog hanging over the grounds. For almost as far as I could see, the fields were covered with white, rusty soccer goals, their nets long since ripped away, the lines marking their boundaries lost in the soggy, wet ground. Goal after abandoned goal cluttered the field, placed side by side, wedged back to back, and crowded in at abstract angles to maximize the precious urban space. Gazing on, I lost reference to the fields of play they represented, until I beheld nothing more than a mass of staples punched randomly into the wet, marshy earth by some forgotten race of giants.

I walked onto the damp grass, water oozing up around my boots as I cut a trail through the silver dew and entered the fog-shrouded field of forsaken goals. Overhead, more sky than I had seen in months was steeped in clouds, the sun a silver disc somewhere far away. A honking flock of geese flew overhead, and the sun crept up a bit higher in the chill morning sky. More light came to the day, and the glistening grass around me became a deeper, stronger green. A smile came from my soul, finding its way to my face.

"Ireland," I heard myself say.

There was a clang from across the field, and I turned to see an old man in checkered pants on the far end of the foggy green, a golf club in his hand and a playful beagle bounding at his side. A handful of golf balls lay scattered in the grass beside him, and I heard him whistling as he chipped them, one by one, toward a goalpost. There was another soft clang as the old man hit the goalpost again, and I heard him cheer to himself as his dog bounded excitedly off through the green.

"Ireland," I confirmed.

I moved silently across the wet grass of the gaming fields, through the scattered goals, making my way toward the other side. And as I neared a row of trees, standing not far from a street becoming busy with morning traffic, I spied a single phone box standing alone, as if it had been waiting for me all night.

I walked to it and made the call.

Home

15. roots

"**G**ot to say, Neil. In all my years, I never had an appointment set up from overseas. And I fancied myself a pretty cosmopolitan mouth man, too."

I was reclined back in the old, familiar chair, with the angled work light shining down on me, warm and comforting. Dr. Deal's shining tools were laid out in neat rows on a tray nearby, and the sharp, clean smell of disinfectant cut the air of the bright, white examination room.

"But how come it took you so long to get here?" my dentist continued, rolling closer on his wheelie stool. "It was back a month ago that you called from London."

"I had to go to Ireland. Maxed out my credit card, but it was worth it. You know, the whole roots trip."

"Oh yeah?" His foot hit a switch, and the chair hummed softly as it lowered me down. "Well, I hope your roots in Ireland are better than the ones in your mouth."

"They are," I said as Dr. Deal adjusted the light. "I saw my grandfather's house, chilled in his old village, and I met eight guys named Neil who all looked like me. Cool as hell, too."

"Hope they had better kissers. Although Europe ain't exactly the dental promised land, is it?"

"Tell me about it. If you ever want to do some relief work, England could use a mercy mission."

He smiled, shaking his head. "That must have been what did it, huh? Getting that nasty infection, and seeing nothing but a bunch of British smiles around. It sent you running back home, begging for the Great Work."

"Yup, pretty much."

"Well, I'm glad, Neil. It's been a long time coming."

"Yeah, it has."

Dr. Deal leaned closer, his calm, bearded face looking down at me. In his steady hands, the gleaming metal instruments hovered, waiting for entry. I felt my tongue slowly working over the shattered molars, feeling them softly, lingering as if to remember the ruin for the last time.

"Shall we?" he asked.

I opened my mouth slowly, as much as I could without hearing the crack.

"Good man," Dr. Deal said.

Another lite hit began on the stereo, and my dentist started the work.

acknowledgments

Scholastic Inc., Dick Robinson, Lewis Lapham and *Harpers*, John Kennedy, Jann Wenner, Bob Love, and *Rolling Stone* magazine. The Master Cluster: Mark Lewman, Spike Jonze, and Andy Jenkins. Helen Breitwieser, William Clark, Debra Goldstein, and everyone at William Morris Agency for the years of help and humor. Joe Frank, Liza Richardson, KCRW Santa Monica, Will Ackerman and Gang of Seven Records. *Way Cool* Jon May and Suzanne Bolch. Martin Epstein, Angela Jenklow-Harrington, Doug Rushkoff, National Public Radio, Comedy Central, Douglas Coupland, John Batelle, *Wired*, and most expecially, *Dirt*.

To Nino Sacetti, Jon Galkin, Jordan Rubin, Paul (D.J. Spooky) Miller, Ryuhei Shindo, Michelle Costas, Stu Miller, Jason Schulamn, Aaron Rose, Dave Aron, Harmony Korine, Thomas Campbell, Susanna Howe, Mike Mills, and all from the Ludlow Street/Alleged days. Shayla Jackson and every proud member of the Hugh Brown Shü Nation. Beth Coleman, Howard (MC Verb) Goldkran, the Soundlab, Akin Adams, S.A.M., Vinnie and the Antenna crew, and every far-flung head from the Molecular dyaspora. To The Jammers, Chris Fahey, Peggy Jameson, Art Club 2000, Carol Greene, Julian

acknowledgments

LaVerdiere and Vince Mazeau in the Big Room. Lots of love to Anne Leiner, for caring so much, and thanks to Karen Hopenwasser as well as Ernesto and da boys. The California Garrity Clan (especially Bronwyn), Noelle Tan, Cristina (wherever you are), Aunt Sarah (keepin' it real in Donegal), and the family: Mom, Dad, Mike, Sheila, and Aileen.

To Emily Bestler and my publisher, Simon and Schuster, for their patience, Tom Miller for opening the door, Jeanne Lee for the beautiful cover, and extra special thanks to my editor, Greer Kessel, for her invaluable attention and patience as I learned to spell "its."

My loving gratitude to Claudia Cohl, a true patron of the arts, for believing in me from the very first, and helping so much along the way.

And of course, thanks to all who took the time to read.

teeth

HUGH GALLAGHER

ABOUT THIS GUIDE

The suggested questions are intended to help your
reading group find new and interesting angles and
topics for discussion for Hugh Gallagher's *Teeth*.
We hope that these ideas will enrich your
discussion and increase your enjoyment of the book.

Many fine books from Washington Square Press
include Reading Group Guides. For a complete
listing, or to read the Guides on-line, visit
http://www.simonsays.com/reading/guides

DISCUSSION QUESTIONS

1. What are the initial conflicts that trigger Neil's decision to leave New York City and embark on a journey? Are those conflicts resolved? How?

2. Dental work is the central metaphor in *Teeth*. How do Neil's teeth break? What is his parents' response? How does the high cost of their repair effect Neil's decisions? Ultimately, what do his bad teeth symbolize?

3. Pop culture is prevalent throughout *Teeth*. The narrator embraces some of these icons, yet rejects others. What are his criteria for this dichotomy? The author disguises the names of various pop culture figures and establishments. Why do you think he does this? Does it work?

4. In Hollywood, Neil becomes deeply disillusioned by his friends, particularly Flash. What is the source of disappointment? Is he right to confront Flash?

5. On his trip to Java, the narrator abandons the manifesto "Neil Before God" at the steps of a Buddhist temple. Is the location important? How is it significant to the subsequent scuba diving scene?

6. Neil's mother once says to him, "Just wait and see. You'll end up behind a desk like everyone else." What is the source of the antagonism between Neil and his family? What does he want from his family?

7. Milena, the Italian love of his life, is not in London when he arrives. What does he find instead?

8. When Neil finds himself with real punks in London squats, how does he respond? How is this significant in terms of his former rejection of MTV pop culture in L.A.?

9. What inspires Neil to visit Ireland?

10. In this coming-of-age novel, how does the main character change? What impression of him are you left with?